BUYING HIS BRIDE OF CONVENIENCE

BY
MICHELLE SMART

MILLS
BOON

First Published in Great Britain 2017
By Mills & Boon, an imprint of HarperCollins*Publishers*
1 London Bridge Street, London, SE1 9GF

© 2017 Michelle Smart

ISBN: 978-0-263-92475-6

Printed and bound in Spain
by CPI, Barcelona

'If you agree to marry me, this money—all one million dollars of it—will be handed to the Blue Train Aid Agency tomorrow morning. And that is only the start.'

'The start?' Eva asked faintly, looking back at all that lovely money.

'Agree to marry me and this money goes directly to your charity. On the day of our marriage I will transfer another two million into their account, and a further three million dollars for every year of our marriage.'

Eva's head spun. Had she slipped into some kind of vortex that distorted reality?

She shook her head and took a breath. 'You want to *pay* me to be your wife?'

'Yes.'

'Why would you want to marry me?'

'It's nothing to do with want. It's to do with need. I need a wife.'

'You've already said that. But why would you choose *me* for the role when there are hundreds of women out there who would take the job without having to be bribed into it? Why marry someone who doesn't even *like* you?'

There was no point in pretending. She didn't like him and he damn well knew it.

'That is the exact reason why I want you to take the role.'

'You've lost me.'

A tight smile played on Daniele's lips. 'I don't want to marry someone who's going to fall in love with me.'

Bound to a Billionaire

Claimed by the most powerful of men!

Felipe Lorenzi, Matteo Manaserro
and Daniele Pellegrini.

Three powerful billionaires who want for nothing—
in business *or* in bed. But nothing and
no one can touch their closely guarded hearts.

That is until Francesca, Natasha and Eva are each
bound to a billionaire…and prove to be a challenge
these delicious alpha males can't resist!

Don't miss **Michelle Smart**'s stunning trilogy

Read Felipe and Francesca's story in

Protecting His Defiant Innocent

Matteo and Natasha's story in

Claiming His One-Night Baby

&

Daniele and Eva's story in

Buying His Bride of Convenience

All available now!

Michelle Smart's love affair with books started when she was a baby, and she would cuddle them in her cot. A voracious reader of all genres, she found her love of romance established when she stumbled across her first Mills & Boon book at the age of twelve. She's been reading them—and writing them—ever since. Michelle lives in Northamptonshire, England, with her husband and two young Smarties.

To the always amazing Nic Caws.

Thanks for everything you do—
your encouragement and enthusiasm
never fail to lift my spirits. xxx

CHAPTER ONE

'WILL YOU KEEP STILL?' Eva Bergen told the man sitting on the stool before her. She'd staunched the bleeding from the wound on the bridge of his nose and had the tiny sterilised strips ready to close it up. What should be a relatively simple procedure was being hampered by his right foot tapping away and jerking the rest of his body.

He glared at her through narrowed eyes, the right one of which was swollen and turning purple. 'Just get it done.'

'Do you want me to close this up or not? I'm not a nurse and I need to concentrate, so keep still.'

He took a long breath, clenched his jaw together and fixed his gaze at the distance over her shoulder. She guessed he must have clenched all the muscles in his legs too as his foot finally stopped tapping.

Taking her own deep breath, Eva leaned forward on her stool, which she'd had to raise so she could match his height, then hesitated. 'Are you sure you don't want one of the medics to look at it? I'm sure it's broken.'

'Just get it done,' he repeated tersely.

Breathing through her mouth so she didn't inhale his scent and taking great care not to touch him anywhere apart from his nose, she put the first strip on the wound.

It was amazing that even with a busted nose Daniele Pellegrini still managed to look impeccably suave. The quiff of his thick, dark brown hair was still perfectly placed, his hand-tailored suit perfectly pressed. He could still look in a mirror and wink at his reflection.

He was a handsome man. She didn't think there was a female aid worker at the refugee camp who hadn't done a double-take when he'd made his first appearance there a month ago. This was only his second visit. He'd called her thirty minutes ago asking, without a word of greeting, if she was still at the camp. If he'd bothered to know anything about her he would've known she, like all the other staff based there, had their own quarters at the camp. He'd then said he was on his way and to meet him in the medical tent. He'd disconnected the call before she could ask what he wanted. She'd learned the answer to that herself when she'd made the short walk from the ramshackle administrative building she worked from to the main medical facility.

When Hurricane Ivor had first hit the Caribbean island of Caballeros, the Blue Train Aid Agency, which already had a large presence in the crime-ridden country, had been the first aid charity to set up a proper camp there. Now, two months after the biggest natural disaster the country had ever known and the loss of twenty thousand of its people, the camp had become home to an estimated thirty thousand people, with canvas tents, modular plastic shelters and makeshift shacks all tightly knit together. Other aid agencies had since set up at different sites and had similar numbers of displaced people living in their camps. It was a disaster on every level imaginable.

Daniele was the brother of the great philanthropist and humanitarian, Pieta Pellegrini. Pieta had seen the news about the hurricane and how the devastation had been amplified by the destruction of a large number of the island's hospitals. He'd immediately decided that his foundation would build a new, disaster-proof, multi-functional hospital in the island's capital, San Pedro. A week later he'd been killed in a helicopter crash.

Eva had been saddened by this loss. She'd only met

Pieta a few times but he'd been greatly respected by everyone in the aid community.

She and the other staff at the Blue Train Aid Agency had been overjoyed to learn his family wished to proceed with the hospital. The people of the island badly needed more medical facilities. They and the other charities and agencies did the best they could but it wasn't enough. It could never be enough.

Pieta's sister, Francesca, had become the new driving force for the project. Eva had liked her very much and admired the younger woman's determination and focus. She'd expected to like and admire his brother too. Like Pieta, Daniele was a world-famous name, but his reputation had been built through his architecture and construction company, which had won more design awards than any other in the past five years.

She'd found nothing to like or admire about him. Although famed for his good humour and searing intellect, she'd found him arrogant and entitled. She'd seen the wrinkle of distaste on his strong—now busted—nose when he'd come to the camp to collect her for their one evening out together, a date she'd only agreed to because he'd assured her it *wasn't* a date and that he'd just wanted to get her input on the kind of hospital he should be building as she was something of an expert on the country and its people. He'd flown her to his exclusive seven-star hotel on the neighbouring paradise island of Aguadilla, spent five minutes asking her pertinent questions, then the rest of the evening drinking heavily, asking impertinent questions and shamelessly flirting with her.

She would go as far as to say his only redeeming features were his looks and physique and the size of his bank account. Seeing as she was immune to men and cared nothing for money, those redeeming features were wasted on her.

The look on his face when she'd coldly turned down his offer of a trip to his suite for a 'nightcap' had been priceless. She had a feeling Daniele Pellegrini was not used to the word 'no' being uttered to him by members of the opposite sex.

He'd had his driver take her back to the airfield without a word of goodbye. That was the last she'd seen of him until she'd walked into the medical tent ten minutes ago and found him already there, waiting for her. It was immediately obvious that someone had punched him in the face. She wondered who it was and if it was possible to track them down and buy them a drink.

'I'm not a nurse,' she'd said when he'd told her he needed her to fix it.

He'd shrugged his broad shoulders but without the ready smile she remembered from their 'date'. 'I only need you to stop the bleeding. I'm sure you've seen it done enough times that you have a basic idea of what needs to be done.'

She had more than a basic idea. Principally employed as a co-ordinator and translator, she, like most of the other non-medical staff, had often stepped in to help the medical team when needed. That didn't mean she felt confident in patching up a broken nose, especially when the nose belonged to an arrogant billionaire whose suit likely cost more than the average annual salary of the Caballerons lucky enough to have a job.

'I'll get one of the nurses or—'

'No, they're busy,' he'd cut in. 'Stem the bleeding and I'll be out of here.'

She'd been about to argue that she was busy too but there had been something in his demeanour that had made her pause. Now, as she gently placed the second strip on his nose, she thought him like a tightly coiled spring. She pitied whoever would be on the receiving end of the explosion that was sure to come when the coil sprang free.

Taking the third and last strip, she couldn't help but notice how glossy his dark hair was. If she didn't know it was a genetic blessing, having the same shine as the rest of the family members she'd met, she'd think he took a personal hairdresser with him everywhere he travelled. And a personal dresser.

If she was feeling charitable she could understand his distaste for the camp. Daniele lived in luxury. Here there was only dirt and squalor that everyone's best efforts at cleaning barely made a dent in. Being in front of him like this made her acutely aware of the grubbiness of her jeans and T-shirt and the messy ponytail she'd thrown her hair back into.

Who cared about her appearance? she asked herself grimly. This was a refugee camp. All the staff were prepared to turn their hand to anything that needed doing. Dressing for a fashion shoot was not only wholly inappropriate but wholly impractical.

It was only this hateful man who made her feel grubby and inferior.

'Keep still,' she reminded him when his foot started its agitated tapping again. 'Almost done. I'm just going to clean you up and you can go. You'll need to keep the strips on for around a week and remember to keep them dry.'

Reaching for the antiseptic wipes, she gently dabbed at the tiny drops of blood that had leaked out since she'd first cleaned his nose and cheeks.

Suddenly a wave of his scent enveloped her. She'd forgotten to hold her breath.

It was perhaps the most mouthwatering scent she'd ever known, making her think of thick forests and hanging fruit, a reaction and thoughts she would have laughed at if anyone had suggested such romantic notions to her.

How could such a hateful, arrogant man be so blessed?

He had more talent in his little finger than she could spend a lifetime hoping for.

And he had the most beautiful eyes, an indecipherable browny-green, his surroundings dominating the colour of them at any particular moment. Eyes that were suddenly focussed on her. Staring intently into hers.

She stared back, trapped in his stare before she forced herself to blink, push her stool back and jump down.

'I'll get an ice pack for your eye,' she murmured, flustered but determined not to show it.

'No need,' he dismissed. 'Don't waste your resources on me.' He dug into his inside suit jacket pocket and pulled out his wallet. From it he took some notes and thrust them into her hand. 'That's to replace the medical supplies you used.'

Then he strolled out of the medical tent without a word of thanks or goodbye.

Only when Eva opened the hand that tingled where his skin had brushed it did she see he'd given her ten one-hundred-dollar bills.

'There has got to be an alternative,' Daniele said firmly, pouring himself another glass of red wine, his grip on the bottle tight enough to whiten his knuckles. '*You* can have the estate.'

His sister Francesca, who he'd directed this at, shook her head. 'I can't. You know that. I'm the wrong gender.'

'And I can't marry.' Marriage was anathema to him. He didn't want it. He didn't need it. He'd spent his adult life avoiding it, avoiding any form of commitment.

'Either you marry and take control of the estate or Matteo gets it.'

At the mention of his traitorous cousin's name, the last of his control deserted him and he flung his glass at the wall.

Francesca held out a hand to stop Felipe, her fiancé, an ex-Special Forces hard man, who'd braced himself to step in. Her voice remained steady as she said to Daniele, 'He's the next male heir after you. You know that's a fact. If you don't marry and accept the inheritance, then Matteo gets it.'

He breathed deeply, trying to regain control of his temper. The red liquid trickled down the white wall. Looking at it from the right angle, it was as dark as the blood that had poured from his nose when anger had taken possession of him and he'd flown at Matteo, the pair exchanging blows that would have been a lot worse if Felipe hadn't stepped in and put a halt to it. Since that exchange he'd felt the anger inside him like a living being, a snake coiled in his guts ready to spring at the slightest provocation.

Matteo had betrayed them all.

'There has got to be a legal avenue we can take to override the trust,' he said as the wine, splattered over the wall, obeyed the laws of gravity and trickled to the floor. He'd have to get it repainted before he got new tenants in, he thought absently. He owned the apartment in Pisa but his sister had lived in it for six years. Now she was marrying Felipe and moving to Rome, and unless he thought of an alternative he would be forced to marry too. 'It's archaic.'

'Yes,' she agreed. 'We all know that. Pieta was working with the trustees to get it overturned but it isn't as easy as we hoped it would be. The trust is cast-iron. It'll take months, maybe years, to get that clause overturned and while we're waiting, Matteo can marry Natasha and take the inheritance.'

The bloody inheritance. The family estate, which included a six-hundred-year-old *castello* and thousands of acres of vineyards, had belonged to the Pellegrini family and its descendants since the first stone had been laid by Principe Charles Philibert I, the original bad-boy Prince of the family. The family had renounced their titles decades ago but the *castello* remained their shining jewel. To keep the estate intact, primogeniture ruled and thus the eldest male descendant always inherited. This ruling hadn't been enough to satisfy Principe Emmanuel II, a particularly cruel and mad prince from the nineteenth century, who had suspected his eldest son of being a homosexual and so had drawn up a ruling, still enforced to this day, that the eldest male descendant could only inherit if he was married. Principe Emmanuel must have had some insight to how social mores would evolve in the future because the marriage clause had specifically stated the spouse had to be female.

This archaic marriage clause had never been an issue. After all, *everyone* married eventually. It was what people did, especially those of the aristocracy. But times, along with social mores, changed.

Daniele had been a toddler when his grandfather had died and his own father had inherited the estate. Being the second son, Daniele had always known Pieta would inherit when their father died. He was comfortable with that. He didn't want it. He hated the draughty old *castello* that leaked money as quickly as it leaked water, and he especially hated the idea of marriage. It had given him perverse satisfaction throughout his adult life to remain single, to be the antithesis of the dutiful, serious Pieta.

But now Pieta was dead.

For two months Daniele had clung to the hope that Pieta's wife Natasha might be pregnant—if she was and the child was a boy, the child would inherit the estate and Daniele would be free to continue living his life as he'd always enjoyed.

It transpired that Natasha was indeed pregnant. Unfortunately, Pieta wasn't the father. Before her husband was even cold in the ground, she had embarked on an affair with their cousin Matteo, the cousin who had lived with them as a sibling from the age of thirteen. The disloyal bastard himself had told Daniele that she was pregnant with his child.

Now there were two routes that could be taken. Daniele either found himself a wife and gave up all his cherished freedoms to inherit an estate he didn't want, or their disloyal cousin inherited everything his father and brother had held dear.

He clenched his jaw and rolled his neck, thinking of his mother and her own love and pride in the family and the estate she had married into as a nineteen-year-old girl.

When it came down to it, there was only one route.

'I have to marry.'

'Yes.'

'And soon.'

'Yes. Do you have anyone in mind?' Francesca asked quietly. She knew how much he loathed the idea of marriage. She had an even sharper legal mind than Pieta had done. If she couldn't think of a way to overturn the clause without Matteo taking everything, then it couldn't be done.

One day it would, he vowed. The next generation of Pellegrinis would never be forced into a deed they didn't want, a deed that came with such a heavy price.

Daniele's mind flickered through all the women he'd dated throughout the years. He estimated that of those who were still unmarried, approximately one hundred per cent of them would high-tail it to a wedding dress shop before he'd even finished proposing.

And then he thought of his last date. The only date he'd been on that hadn't ended in the bedroom.

Unthinkingly, he touched his bruised nose. The steri-strips Eva had so carefully put on him were still there, the wound healing nicely. He remembered the distaste that flashed in her crystal-clear blue eyes whenever she looked at him.

She'd acted as a translator for him on his first trip to

Caballeros a month ago. On an island surrounded by so much destruction, the prevalent colour brown with all the churned-up mud, she'd shone like a beacon in the gloom. Or her scarlet hair had, which she wore in a girlish pony-tail. It was a shade of red that could only have come from a bottle and contrasted with her alabaster skin—she must lather herself in factor fifty sun cream on an hourly basis to keep it so colour free—so beautifully he couldn't see how any other colour, not even that which nature had given her, could suit her so well.

Despite dressing only in scruffy jeans and an official Blue Train Aid Agency T-shirt, Eva Bergen was possibly the most beautiful and definitely the sexiest woman he'd met in his entire thirty-three years. And she hated his guts.

Daniele looked at his sister's worried face and gave a half-smile. 'Yes,' he said with a nod. 'I know the perfect woman to marry.'

When he left the apartment an hour later, he reflected that whatever else happened, at least his mother would finally be happy with a choice he'd made.

Eva queued patiently at the staff shower block, playing a game on her phone to pass the time. There was limited fresh water at the camp and the staff rationed their own use zealously. She'd become an expert at showering in sixty seconds of tepid water every three days. Like the rest of the staff, she experienced both guilt and relief when she took her leave, which was every third weekend, and she had the luxury of flying over to Aguadilla and checking into a basic hotel. There, at her own expense, she would laze for hours in sweet-smelling, bubbly, limitless water, dye her hair, do her nails and cleanse her skin, all the while trying to smother the guilt at all the displaced people at the camp who couldn't take a few days off to pamper themselves.

One thing that wasn't in short supply at the camp was

mobile phones. It seemed that everyone had one, even the tiny kids who barely had a change of clothes to their name. The current craze was for a free game that involved blasting multiplying colourful balls. A technology whizz had linked all the camp players together, refugees and staff alike, to compete against each other directly. Eva had become as addicted to it as everyone else and right then was on track to beat her high score and crack the top one hundred players. At that moment, playing as she waited for her turn in the skinny showers, she had three teenagers at her side, pretending to be cool while they watched her avidly.

When her phone vibrated in her hand she ignored it.

'You should answer that,' Odney, the oldest of the teenagers, said with a wicked grin. Odney was currently ranked ninety-ninth in the camp league for the game.

'They'll call back,' Eva dismissed, mock-scowling at him.

With an even wickeder grin, Odney snatched the phone from her hand, pressed the answer button and put it to his ear. 'This is Eva's phone,' he said. 'How may I direct your call?'

His friends cackled loudly, Eva found herself smothering her own laughter.

'English?' Odney suggested to the caller, who clearly didn't speak Spanish. 'I speak little. You want Eva?'

Eva held her hand out and fixed him with a stare.

Glee alight on his face, Odney gave her the phone back. 'Your game didn't save,' he said smugly to more cackles of laughter.

Merriment in her voice—how she adored the camp's children, toddlers and teenagers alike—Eva finally spoke to her caller. 'Hello?'

'Eva? Is that you?'

All the jollity of the moment dived out of her.

'Yes. Who is this?'

She knew who it was. The deep, rich tones and heavy accent of Daniele Pellegrini were unmistakable.

'It's Daniele Pellegrini. I need to see you.'

'Speak to my secretary and arrange an appointment.' She didn't have a secretary and he knew it.

'It's important.'

'I don't care. I don't want to see you.'

'You will when you know *why* I need to see you.'

'No, I won't. You're a—'

'A man with a proposal that will benefit your refugee camp,' he cut in.

'What do you mean?' she asked suspiciously.

'Meet me and find out for yourself. I promise it will be worth your and your camp's while.'

'My next weekend off is—'

'I'm on my way to Aguadilla. I'll have you brought to me.'

'When?'

'Tonight. I'll have someone with you in two hours.'

And then he hung up.

CHAPTER TWO

EVA'S HEART SANK at the sight of the plush hotel at the end of the long driveway Daniele's driver was taking her down. It was the same hotel Daniele had tricked her into dining with him in at on their 'date'. She supposed anywhere else would be beneath him. The Eden Hotel was the most luxurious hotel in Aguadilla and catered to the filthy rich. She was wearing her only pair of clean jeans and a black shirt she'd been unable to iron thanks to a power cut at the camp. She couldn't justify using the power that came from the emergency generators to iron clothing when it was needed to feed thousands of people.

When Daniele had driven her—he'd actually deigned to get behind the wheel himself then—into the hotel's grounds the first time her hackles had immediately risen. She'd turned sharply to him. 'You said this was an informal discussion about the hospital.' She'd thought they would dine in one of the numerous beachside restaurants Aguadilla was famed for that served cheap, excellent food, upbeat music and had an atmosphere where anyone and everyone was welcomed.

'And so it is,' he'd replied smoothly, which had only served to raise her hackles further. They'd walked past guests dressed to the nines in their finest, most expensive wear. She'd been as out of place as a lemming in a pigpen.

Dining in the restaurant had been a humiliating experience the first time around but this time she at least had that experience to fall back on, and it served to steel her spine as she walked into the hotel's atrium with her head held high. She wouldn't allow herself to feel inferior even if she did look like a ragamuffin, despite her sixty-second shower.

A hotel employee headed straight for her. At close sight she saw the title of 'General Manager' under his name on the gold pin worn on his lapel.

'Ms Bergen?' he enquired politely, too well trained to even wrinkle his nose at her.

She nodded. She guessed she'd been easy to describe. Just look for the scarlet-haired woman who doesn't fit in.

'Come with me, please.'

Like a docile sheep, she followed him past an enormous waterfall, past the restaurant she'd dined in a month ago, past boutiques and further restaurants and into an elevator that came complete with its own bellboy. It was only when the manager pressed the button for the top floor that warning bells sounded.

'Where are you taking me?'

'To Mr Pellegrini's suite.'

They'd arrived at the designated floor before he finished answering. The bellboy opened the door.

Eva hesitated.

Dining in a private hotel suite had very different connotations to dining in public. Under no sane marker could it be considered sensible to go into a rich man's suite alone.

The manager looked at her, waiting for her to leave the safety of the elevator and be led into the lion's den.

All she had to do was say no. That would be the sensible thing. Say no. If Daniele Pellegrini needed to see her so badly that he'd flown to the Caribbean for the sole purpose of talking to her, then he could dine with her in public. She could demand that and he would have no choice but to comply.

But, for all his numerous faults, including being a sex-mad scoundrel with no scruples over who he bedded, her gut told her Daniele was not the sort of man to force a woman into anything she didn't want. She wasn't being led into the lion's den to be served as dinner.

She stepped out of the elevator and followed the manager up the wide corridor to a door on which he rapped sharply.

It was opened immediately by a neat, dapper man dressed in the formal wear of a butler.

'Good evening, Ms Bergen,' he said in precise English. 'Mr Pellegrini is waiting for you on the balcony. Can I get you a drink?'

'A glass of water, please,' she said, trying very hard not to be overawed by the splendour of the suite, which was the size of a large apartment.

Having a butler there relieved her a little. It was good to know she would have a chaperone, although she couldn't fathom why she felt she needed one.

The manager bade her a good evening and left, and Eva was taken through a door into a light and airy room, then led out onto a huge balcony that had the most spectacular view of the Caribbean Sea, dark now, the stars twinkling down and illuminating it. To the left was a private oval swimming pool, to the right a table that could comfortably seat a dozen people but was currently set for two. One of those seats was taken by the tall, dynamic figure of Daniele Pellegrini.

He got to his feet and strolled to her, his hand outstretched.

'Eva, it is great to see you,' he said, a wide grin on his face that was in complete contrast to the set fury that had been on it three days ago when he'd demanded she fix his nose.

Not having much choice, she reached her own hand out to accept his. Rather than the brisk handshake she expected, he wrapped his fingers around hers and pulled her to him, then kissed her on both cheeks.

Her belly did a little swoop at the sensation of his lips on her skin, diving again to inhale his fresh scent, which her senses so absurdly danced to.

As much as she hated herself for the vanity of it, she was thankful she'd so recently showered. Daniele looked and smelled too good, his easy, stomach-melting smile back in its place. And he was clean, his dark grey trousers and white shirt immaculately pressed. Everything here in this hotel, including the guests, was spotless. Standing before this beautifully smelling, impossibly handsome man made her feel, again, like a ragged urchin. No matter how hard she tried to keep herself presentable, living in a refugee camp where dust and mud were prevalent made it an impossible task.

She was even more thankful when he let her go, and had to stop herself wiping her hand on her jeans in an attempt to banish the tingles from where his fingers had wrapped around hers.

'Your nose looks like it's healing well,' she said, for want of something to say to break the fluttering beneath her ribs. The swelling had gone down substantially and her vanity flickered again to see the butterfly stitches she'd applied were still perfectly in place. There was slight bruising around his left eye but that was the only other indication he'd been in a fight. Her curiosity still itched to know who his opponent had been. One of Caballeros's corrupt officials? A jealous boyfriend?

'You did a good job.'

She managed the smallest of smiles. 'Did you see a doctor?'

He made a dismissive noise in his throat. 'No need.'

The butler, who she hadn't noticed leave the terrace, returned with a tray containing two tall glasses and two bottles of water.

'I didn't know if you'd prefer still or sparkling so I

brought you both,' he said, laying them on the table. 'Can I get you anything else before I serve dinner?'

'Not for me, thank you,' she said.

'Another Scotch for me,' Daniele requested. 'Bring the bottle in.'

'As you wish.'

Alone again, Daniele indicated the table. 'Take a seat. To save time, I've ordered for both of us. If you don't like it, the chef will cook you something else.'

Eva bristled. She wasn't a fussy eater—with her job she couldn't be—but his presumption was another black mark against him. 'What have you ordered?'

'Broccoli and Stilton soup, followed by beef Wellington.' He flashed his smile again as he took his seat. 'I thought you'd be homesick for English food.'

Bemused, she took the place laid out opposite him. 'Homesick for English food? But I'm from the Netherlands.'

'You're *Dutch*?'

His surprise almost made her smile with the whole of her mouth but not out of humour, out of irony. They'd spent a whole evening together in which he'd flirted shamelessly with her but not once had he cared to ask anything of substance about her. She'd just been a woman he was attracted to, whom he'd been determined to bed. He'd assumed she'd be so honoured to be singled out by him that she would accompany him to his suite—this suite?—like some kind of fawning groupie and climb into bed with him. 'Born and raised in Rotterdam.'

A groove appeared in his forehead. 'I thought you were English.'

'Many people do.'

'You have no accent.'

'English people notice it but you're Italian so it's not obvious to your ear.'

The butler brought Daniele's bottle of Scotch and asked if Eva wanted anything stronger to go with her meal.

She shook her head and fixed her eyes on Daniele. 'I think it's best I keep a clear head this evening.'

Daniele smiled grudgingly. He should keep a clear head himself but after the last few days he liked the idea of numbing everything inside him. The Scotch would also help him get through the forthcoming conversation.

'What other languages do you speak?' Eva spoke English so precisely and fluently it hadn't occurred to him that she was any nationality but that. When he'd first met her she'd acted as a translator for him and his now despised cousin Matteo. He had only a rudimentary comprehension of Spanish but her translations between them and the Caballeron officials had sounded faultless.

'I speak English, Spanish and French with full fluency and passable Italian.'

'Prove it,' he said, switching to his own language.

'Why?' she retorted, also in Italian. 'Are you trying to catch me out?'

He shook his head and laughed. 'You call that passable?' It had been rapid and delivered with near-perfect inflection.

'Until I can watch a movie in the host's tongue without missing any cadence, I don't consider myself fully fluent,' she said, switching back to English. 'I have a long way to go before I reach that with Italian.'

'Then let us speak Italian now,' he said. 'It will help you.'

Her ponytail swished as she shook her head. 'You said you had important things to discuss with me. Your English is as good as mine and I would prefer to understand everything and not have anything lost in translation that will give you the advantage.'

'You don't trust me?'

'Not in the slightest.'

'I admire your honesty.' It was a rare thing in his world. His family were faultlessly honest with him but since he'd really stamped his authority in the architecture world and made his first billion—canny investments alongside his day job had helped with that—he hadn't met a single outside person who openly disagreed with a word he said or ever said no to him.

The butler returned to the terrace with their first course. He set the bowls out on their placemats and placed a basket of bread rolls between them.

Eva dipped her head to inhale the aroma and nodded approvingly. 'It smells delicious.'

The butler beamed. 'The rolls are freshly baked but we have some gluten-free ones if you would prefer.'

'I'm not gluten-intolerant,' she said with a smile. 'But I thank you for the offer.'

Eva was the only woman Daniele had been on a date with in at least three years who hadn't been gluten-intolerant or on a particular fad diet. It had been refreshing, yet another difference between herself and the other women he'd dated. It showed on her physically. She had curves for a start and heavy breasts that just begged to have a head rested upon them. Eva Bergen was one sexy lady and he couldn't wait to see what she looked like when wearing feminine clothes. No clothes at all would be even better.

When they were alone again, she helped herself to a bread roll and broke it open with her fingers. 'What is it you wished to discuss?'

'Let's eat first and then talk.'

She put the roll down. 'No, let's talk while we eat or I'll think you've brought me here under false pretences again.'

'There were no false pretences on our last date,' he countered smoothly.

'I was very specific that it wasn't to be a date. You made

it one. The questions you asked me about the hospital could have been dealt with over a five-minute coffee.'

'Where would the fun have been with that?'

'My work isn't fun, Mr Pellegrini—'

'Daniele.' He must have told her a dozen times not to address him so formally during their date that, according to Eva, wasn't a date. It hadn't occurred to him that she would be anything but delighted with his attention. His family name and looks had always been a magnet for the ladies. Once the architectural accolades and money had started rolling in he couldn't think of a single woman who hadn't looked at him with fluttering eyelashes, not until he'd met Eva. There had been a spark of interest there, though, a moment when their eyes had locked together for the first time and a zing of electricity had passed between them.

It had been the first real hit of desire he'd experienced since his brother had died. In the two months since Pieta's death, Daniele had lost all interest in women. The opposite sex had flown so far off his radar that the electricity between him and Eva had been a welcome reminder that he was alive.

After that initial zing her manner had been nothing but calm and professional towards him, which he'd assumed had been a product of the environment they'd been in. He'd also assumed that getting her out of the pit of hell that was Caballeros and into the more picturesque setting of Aguadilla would remove the straitjacket she'd put around herself. He'd certainly got that wrong.

Despite the zings of electricity that had flown between them that evening, she'd remained cool and poker-faced, his usually winning attempts at flattery being met with stony silence. She'd outright rejected his offer of a nightcap. Not only that, but there had been contempt in her rejection too.

There had been no denying it—Eva Bergen had been looking down her pretty little nose at him. At *him*.

No one had ever looked at him like that before. It had felt bitter and ugly in his guts and he'd dismissed her without a second thought. Rejection he could deal with but contempt?

It had been too much like the expression he'd seen on his father's face when the media reported on one or another of Daniele's dalliances with the opposite sex. His parents had been desperate for him to marry. Pieta had found a woman to settle down with—even though it had taken him six years to actually exchange vows with her—which meant it had been time for Daniele to settle down too.

Daniele had had no intention of ever settling down. His life was fun. He pleased himself, not answerable to anyone. If he wanted a weekend in Vegas, all he had to do was jump on his jet and off he would go, collecting some friends on the way to share the fun with. His perfect brother had never behaved anything but…perfectly, and he'd been held up as the shining beacon for Daniele to emulate. He'd been held up as the shining beacon before Daniele had even been out of nappies.

Well, Daniele had had the last laugh. He'd earned himself a fortune worth more than Pieta's personal wealth and the estate Pieta would inherit combined.

And then the last laugh had stopped being funny. Pieta had died in a helicopter crash and the man he'd loved and loathed in equal measure, his brother, his rival, was no longer there. He was dead. Gone. Passed. All the terms used to convey a person's death but none with the true weight of how the loss felt in Daniele's heart.

'I take my job very seriously, *Mr Pellegrini*. I'm not here to have fun.' Eva said it as if it were a dirty concept. 'Your flirting was inappropriate and your offer of a nightcap doubly so.'

No doubt his sister would call him a masochist for choosing to marry a woman who openly despised him. Francesca wouldn't understand how refreshing it was to be with a woman without artifice. She wouldn't understand the challenge Eva posed, like an experienced mountaineer peering up from the base of Everest, the peak so high it was hidden in the clouds. To reach the top would be dangerous but the thrills would make every minute of danger worthwhile.

The only danger Eva posed was to his ego and he would be the first to admit that his ego could use some knocks. He despised thin-skinned men and looking back to his reaction when Eva had rejected his offer of a nightcap, he could see he'd been as thin-skinned as the worst of them.

'I would have thought an intimate meal for two in a Michelin-starred restaurant was the most appropriate place to flirt with a beautiful woman.'

The faintest trace of colour appeared on her cheeks. 'If you flirt with me again I'll leave.'

'Without hearing what I wish to discuss first?'

'That's up to you. If you can control your natural tendency to flirt and actually get to the point, it won't be an issue.' She put a spoonful of soup into her wide, full-lipped mouth.

Daniele took hold of his spoon. 'In that case I shall get straight to the point. I need a wife and want you to take the role.'

A groove appeared in her forehead, crystal-clear blue eyes flashing at him. 'That is not funny. What do you really want?'

He sipped at his soup. Eva was right. It was delicious. 'What I *want* is to get on my jet and fly away from here, but what I *need* is a wife, and you, *tesoro*, are the perfect woman for the job.'

There was a moment of stunned silence before she

pushed her chair back and rose to her feet. 'You are despicable, do you know that? You can keep your mind games to yourself. I don't want to play. And for the record, I am *not* your darling.'

Snatching her canvas bag from the foot of her chair, Eva turned to stalk away from the terrace, out of the suite, and far away from this arrogant man who she had no intention of ever seeing again.

She hadn't taken two paces when the sound of clicking echoed in the air and Daniele said, 'Before you leave, I have something to show you.'

'You have nothing I want to see.'

'Not even a million dollars in cash?'

Against her better judgement—again—Eva turned her head.

There on the table, beside his bowl of soup, lay an open briefcase.

She blinked. How had he moved so fast? What was he? Some kind of magician?

The briefcase was neatly crammed with wads of money.

She blinked again and met his eyes.

'Do I have your attention now?' he asked. All his previous good humour, which she had already suspected of being a façade, had been stripped away.

She nodded. Yes. He had her attention, but there was a part of her that thought she had to be dreaming. A briefcase stuffed with cash only existed in dreams or the movies. Not in real life.

Daniele Pellegrini didn't exist in real life either. He was a billionaire from an old and noble family. His life couldn't be more different from her reality than if he'd been beamed in from the moon.

'If you agree to marry me, this money, all one million dollars of it, will be handed to the Blue Train Aid Agency tomorrow morning. And this is only the start.'

'The start?' she asked faintly, looking back at all that lovely money.

'If you sit back down I will explain everything.'

Eva inched her way back to her seat, resting her bottom carefully while she kept her gaze fixed on Daniele so he couldn't pull another rabbit out of a hat that wasn't even there.

He downed his Scotch, poured another three fingers into the glass and pushed it to her.

She didn't hesitate, tipping the amber liquid down her throat in one swallow, not caring that his lips had pressed against the same surface just moments before. It was the smoothest Scotch she'd ever tasted and she had no doubt the bottle cost more than her weekly salary.

'Agree to marry me and this money goes directly to your charity. On the day of our marriage I will transfer another two million into their account and a further three million dollars for every year of our marriage. I will give you a personal allowance of a quarter of a million dollars a month to spend on whatever you wish—you can donate the whole lot for all I care, it won't matter as I will also give you an unlimited credit card to spend on travel and clothing and whatever else you require for the duration of our marriage.'

Eva's head spun. Had she slipped into some kind of vortex that distorted reality?

'Can I have some more of that Scotch?' she mumbled.

He took a drink himself then passed the glass back.

Drinking it didn't make his words any more comprehensible.

She shook her head and took a breath. 'You want to pay me to be your wife?'

'Yes.'

'Why would you want to marry me?'

'It's nothing to do with want. It's to do with need. I need a wife.'

'You've already said that, but why would you choose *me* for the role when there are hundreds of women out there who would take the job without having to be bribed into it? Why marry someone who doesn't even like you?' There was no point in pretending. She didn't like him and he damn well knew it.

'That is the exact reason why I want you to take the role.'

'You've lost me.'

A tight smile played on his lips. 'I don't want to marry someone who's going to fall in love with me.'

CHAPTER THREE

HE WAS MAD. He had to be. No sane person could make such a suggestion.

And then she looked into those green-brown eyes and thought them the eyes of a man who was perfectly sane and knew exactly what he was doing. Far from reassuring her, the expression in them frightened her, and Eva was not a woman who scared easily. She'd learned to hide it. She hid it now.

'There's no chance of *that*,' she said, hoping Daniele couldn't hear the beats of her hammering heart in her words.

He shrugged and took the glass back, pouring himself another hefty measure. 'Good. I don't want a wife with romantic dreams. I'm not marrying for love. I'm marrying to inherit my family estate.' He must have read her blank expression for he added, 'My brother died without children. I'm the spare son. I can only inherit if I'm married.'

'What do you need the estate for? You're worth a fortune as you are.'

'To keep it in the family.' He swirled his Scotch in his glass before drinking it. 'Duty has finally come calling for me.'

'You need a wife to inherit?'

'*Sì.* The estate is…' She could see him struggle to find the correct English. 'It is bound by an old trust that states only a married heir can inherit.'

'Is that legal?'

He nodded grimly. 'To unravel the trust and make it fit for the modern age will take years. I don't have years. I need to act now.'

'Then find someone else.'

'I don't want anyone else. Everyone else is too needy. You're tough.'

'You don't even know me,' she protested darkly. 'Twenty minutes ago you thought I was English.'

If she was tough it was because she'd had to be. To turn her back on her family when it had made her heart bleed, then to lose Johann and find that same heart torn apart had put a shell around her. It had been an organic process, not something she had consciously built, a shell she'd only become aware of four years ago, back when she'd been living and working in The Hague and a drunk colleague had accused her of being an unfeeling, ball-breaking bitch. She'd returned home to the small apartment she'd once shared with Johann and looked in the mirror and realised there was truth in what her colleague had said. Not the part about being a ball-breaking bitch. She wasn't those things, she knew that. But unfeeling…? Yes. That, she had been forced to accept when she'd looked in that mirror and realised she no longer felt anything at all. She was empty inside.

'I know all I need to know, *tesoro*,' he countered. 'I don't need to know anything else. I have no interest in your past. I don't want to exchange pillow talk and hear about your dreams. This will be a partnership, not a romance. I want someone practical and cool under pressure.'

And he thought that person was her?

She didn't know whether to laugh or cry. Had she become so cold that someone could think she would be agreeable to such an emotionless proposition?

Once she had been warm. She had felt the sun in her heart as well as on her skin.

And what did his proposal say about him? What had made him this way? she wondered. How could someone be so cynical about marriage?

'Marriage is not a game,' she said slowly, thinking hard, her eyes continually drawn between the wads of cash and Daniele's smouldering gaze. That money would make an incredible difference at the camp. The Blue Train Aid Agency was fully dependent on donations and there never seemed to be enough of it to go around all its different projects.

Those eyes…

She pulled her gaze away and stared into the distance at the sea, unable to believe she was even entertaining this ludicrous proposal.

'I'm not playing games,' he said, his words soaking through her. 'Marry me and we all win. Your charity gets a guaranteed income to spend as it sees fit, you get unlimited funds to spend on yourself, my family get the knowledge the family estate is secure for another generation and I get my inheritance. You're a practical person, Eva. You know what I'm suggesting makes excellent sense.'

She hadn't always been a practical person. She'd been a dreamer once. She'd had so many hopes but they'd all been flattened into the dust.

'I don't know…' She tightened her ponytail. 'You say it isn't a game but then you say everyone's going to be a winner out of it. Marriage is a commitment by two people who love each other, not two people who don't even like each other.'

He raised his hefty shoulders and leaned forward. 'My family's ancestry goes back as far as there are written records. The most successful marriages were arranged for practical reasons; to build alliances, not for love. I've never wished to commit my life to one particular person but I am prepared to commit myself to you. It won't be a marriage built on love and romance, but I can promise you a marriage built on respect.'

'How can you respect me if you're trying to buy me?'

'I won't be buying you, *tesoro*. Consider the cash an inducement.'

'I won't be your property.' She'd never be someone's property again. She'd run away from her family the moment she'd turned eighteen, the day she'd stopped belonging to her parents, no longer subject to their stringently enforced rules. She flexed her left hand and felt the phantom ache in the tendons of her fingers. The fingers had long since healed but the ache in them remained, a ghost of the past, a reminder of everything she had run from.

'If I wanted a woman I could own, I wouldn't choose you.'

Before she could think of a response to this, the butler came in to clear away their soup. Eva was surprised to find her bowl empty. She couldn't remember eating it.

She waited until their next course was brought in, a beef Wellington that was sliced and plated before them, before asking her next question.

'If I say yes, what's to stop me taking the cash you give me and running off with it?'

'You won't receive any money for yourself until we're legally married. Under Italian law, you won't be allowed to divorce me for three years but that wouldn't stop you leaving me. I have to trust that you wouldn't leave without discussing it with me first.'

He would have to trust her. But the question, she supposed, was whether she could trust him.

The beef Wellington really was superb. Having never eaten it before, Eva had always assumed it consisted of an old boot baked to within an inch of its life. Instead she cut into the pinkest beef wrapped in a mushroom pâté, parsley pancakes and delicate layers of puff pastry.

'If you don't want a traditional marriage, what kind of marriage do you have in mind for us?' she asked after she'd taken her second mouth-watering bite. She couldn't entertain a traditional marriage either, not with Daniele or anyone. But a marriage of convenience where pots of cash were given to the charity she held so close to her heart... that, she found to her surprise, she *could* entertain.

Daniele Pellegrini was an exceptionally handsome man. He had an innate sex appeal that poor Johann would have given both his skinny arms for. But that was all on the surface. Her body might respond to him but her heart would be safe. *She* would be safe. Daniele didn't want romance or pillow talk, the things that drew a couple together and forged intimacy and left a person vulnerable to heartbreak.

She would never put herself in a vulnerable position again. She couldn't. Her heart had been fractured so many times that the next blow to it could be permanent.

'The outside world will see us as a couple,' he replied. A slight breeze had lifted a lock of his thick dark hair on the top of his head so it stuck up and swayed. 'We will live together. We will visit family and friends as a couple and entertain as a couple.'

'We will be each other's primary escorts?'

He nodded. 'That's an excellent way of putting it. And one day we may be parents...'

Immediately her food stuck in her throat. Pounding on her chest, Eva coughed loudly then took a long drink straight from the bottle of water.

'Are you okay?' Daniele asked. He'd half risen from his seat, ready to go to her aid.

'No.' She laughed weakly and coughed again. 'I thought you said something about us being parents.'

'I did. If we're going to marry, then we're going to share a bed.'

'You didn't think to mention that?'

'I didn't think it needed spelling out. Married couples sleep together, *tesoro*, and I will sleep with you.' His eyes gleamed. 'Sharing a bed with you is the one plus point to us marrying.'

'I don't want to have sex with you.'

Instead of offending him, he laughed. 'That, I think, is the first lie you have told me. You cannot deny your attraction to me.'

'If I was attracted to you, I wouldn't have turned your offer of a nightcap down.'

'If you weren't attracted to me, you wouldn't have hesitated before turning it down. You think I don't know when a woman desires me? I can read body language well and you, my light, show all the signs of a woman fighting her desire. I understand why—it can't be an easy thing to admit that you desire a man you dislike so much.'

'Have you always been this egotistical?'

'It's taken years of practice but I got there in the end. And you still haven't denied that you're attracted to me.'

'I'm not attracted to you.'

'Two lies in two minutes? That's bad form for a woman who's going to be my wife.'

'I haven't agreed to anything.'

'Not yet. But you will. We both know you will.'

'Let me make this clear, if I agree to marry you, I will not have sex with you.'

'And let me make this clear, when we marry, we will share a room and a bed. Whether we have sex in that bed will be up to you.'

'You won't insist on your conjugal rights?'

'I won't need to insist. Deny it until your face goes blue but there is a chemistry between us and lying under the same bed sheets will only deepen it.'

'But will you try to force me?'

Distaste flickered over his handsome face. 'Never.

I can't promise that I won't try and seduce you—*Dio, tesoro*, you're a sexy woman… I'd have to be a saint not to try—but I respect the word no. The moment you say no, I will roll over and go to sleep.'

It was on the tip of her tongue to ask if he planned to take a mistress. It stood to reason that if she wouldn't have sex with him he would get it from someone else.

But that was a whole new quagmire that instinct told her to leave alone. She'd been celibate for six years and had never missed sex. She had missed the cuddles but never the sex, which deep in the heart of her she had always found underwhelming. Why people made such a big deal out of it she would never understand, but they did and to expect Daniele to be celibate was like expecting a lion not to eat the lame deer that limped in front of it.

'If I agree I will want to continue working.' If he could list his requirements, then she should too.

'You won't need to work.'

'Are you going to quit *your* job?'

He raised his eyebrows. They were very nice eyebrows, she noted absently.

'You don't need to work,' she pointed out. 'You could retire right now and never want for anything for the rest of your life.'

'You *want* to work?'

'I love my job.'

Now his brows knitted together in thought before he said slowly, 'You won't be able to work at the camp any more.'

Her heart sank. She loved working at the camp. Her job might be listed as administrative but it was so much more than that. She was useful there. She'd learned skills she would never have picked up anywhere else. In her own way, she'd made a difference to many of the people who'd lost so much.

'I can't just leave,' she whispered.

'Why not? The charity will be losing one employee but gaining three million dollars a year from it. Any loss of salary for you will be more than replaced by the allowance you'll get from me.'

'It's not about the money.'

'Then what is it about?'

She inhaled deeply. How could she explain that her job in the camp had given her a purpose? In the midst of all the deprivation she'd found hope when she'd been so sure there was no hope left inside her. And even if she could find the words to explain it, what would Daniele care? For him, money ruled everything. Marrying her meant he stood to inherit even more filthy lucre.

That made her mind up for her.

Fixing her eyes on him, she said, 'Five million a year. That's what you'll have to pay the charity for me to marry you. And I'll want it in writing. A legal document.'

His eyes didn't flicker. 'It will form part of our prenuptial agreement.'

'I will have my own lawyer approve it.'

'Naturally.'

'I need to give a month's notice and—'

'No.' His refutation was sharp. 'That is too long. There are many things that need to be arranged and it can't wait. I want us to be married in Italy as soon as possible and there is much to organise. You will hand your notice in tomorrow and tell your bosses you'll be leaving with immediate effect or this suitcase of cash stays with me and I find another wife.'

He must have noticed her mutinous expression at his non-subtle warning that he could easily find another woman to be his wife, and likely one who was a hundred times more malleable, for he added, 'I will arrange for someone suitable to take your place until the charity can find a permanent replacement for you.'

'And if you can't find a suitable replacement?'

'I will.' He looked so smugly confident in his assertion that she longed to smack him. 'But the second I hand over the cash tomorrow you are committed to marrying me. There will be no going back on your word.'

'Providing my lawyer agrees that the prenuptial agreement is unbreakable, I will not go back on my word.'

'Then do we have a deal? You will marry me? You will quit your job and come to Italy with me tomorrow?'

'Only if the agency agrees that your "suitable replacement" is suitable.'

'They will,' he said in that same smugly confident tone.

'I'll need to go home before I go to Italy.'

Now he drummed his fingers on the table with his impatience. 'What's your excuse for that?'

'You're an Italian national but I'll be considered an alien. I used to work at the Ministry of Foreign Affairs so I know what I'm talking about. I need to go to my home in The Hague to collect the papers your officials will require from me.'

'I'll send someone to get them.'

'I'm not having a stranger go through my possessions.'

He studied her for a moment before giving a sharp nod. 'Okay, I will take you to the Netherlands first. But that is it. I will agree to no further delays. Does this mean we have a deal? Do I instruct my lawyers to draft the prenuptial agreement?'

Her throat suddenly running dry, Eva cleared it, trying to ignore the chorus of rebuttals ringing in her head.

What did it matter if she was agreeing to a cold, emotionless marriage when her life had been cold and emotionless for six years? Marrying Daniele meant the Blue

Train Aid Agency would have the wonderful benefit of his money, which would be of far more value to it than she was as a lowly employee.

As Daniele himself had said only minutes ago, marrying him meant everyone was a winner.

But still the chorus in her head warned that for there to be a winner someone had to be the loser.

How could *she* be the loser in the deal? She wasn't giving Daniele her heart, only her physical presence. She wasn't giving him *anything* of herself so how could she be the loser?

So she ignored the chorus and met his gaze, her cold heart battering her ribs. 'Yes. We have a deal.'

'You will marry me?'

Closing her mind to the image of Johann that had fluttered to its forefront, she nodded.

'Say it,' Daniele commanded.

'Yes. I will marry you.'

His firm lips turned at the corners, more grimace than smile. 'Then I suggest we have a drink to drown our sorrows in.'

Daniele, looked at his watch and sighed. The money had been handed over to the astounded Blue Train Aid Agency bosses, his temporary replacement for Eva approved with only the most cursory of glances at the replacement's CV, and the prenuptial agreement was in the hands of his lawyers and expected to be completed by the time they landed in Europe. Her canvas backpack had been put in the boot of his car by his driver, all the paperwork for the termination of her employment done. They should be long gone from this godforsaken camp by now but Eva had disappeared, muttering something about needing to say some goodbyes. He'd imagined it would take only a few minutes but she'd been gone for almost an hour.

He accepted another sludge-like coffee from a female employee who turned the colour of beetroot every time he looked at her and forced a smile. All he wanted was to be gone and away from this place that made him hate himself for the privileges he'd been born to. Although he would never admit this to Eva, he would have donated the million dollars cash to the charity that morning even if she'd turned his proposal down.

Just as he drained the last of the disgusting liquid—he'd have to add a lifetime supply of decent coffee for all staff and refugees to his donation, he decided—Eva appeared in the dilapidated building he'd been hiding in.

'Ready to go?' he asked in a tone that left no room for doubt that she'd better be ready to go or he'd chuck her over his shoulder and carry her out.

She nodded. She'd hardly exchanged a word with him since his arrival at the camp mid-morning and hadn't met his eyes once.

'Come on then.'

It was only a short walk to his car. His driver spotted their approach and opened the passenger door.

'Eva!'

They both turned their heads to the sound and saw three teenage boys come flying over to them, jabbering and calling out in Spanish.

Eva's face lit up to see them.

She embraced them all tightly in turn and, much to their pretend disgust, kissed their cheeks and ruffled their hair. Only after she'd embraced them all for a second time did she get in the car.

Daniele hurried in behind her so she couldn't use another excuse to delay, and tapped the partition screen so his driver knew to get going.

The boys ran alongside the car as they left the camp,

waving, hollering, blowing kisses, which were all returned by Eva.

Only when they were on the open road with the camp far behind them did Daniele see the solitary tear trickle down her face.

CHAPTER FOUR

Eva stepped into the small one-bedroom apartment she'd shared with Johann with a weight sitting heavily in her chest.

As she walked slowly through the living room, dust dislodged and filtered through the air. She hadn't set foot in it for over a year. She hadn't lived in it properly in four years. Intellectually she knew she should sell it or at the very least rent it out, but she couldn't bring herself to.

All the old photos were where she'd left them. She picked up one on the windowsill, dislodging more dust. The picture was of her and Johann in the snow. Not even the thick winter clothing he'd been bundled up in could disguise Johann's skinny frame. They both looked so young. They'd *been* so young, only nineteen when the picture had been taken.

She kissed the cold glass and put the frame back where it had been, pushing the old memories clamouring in her head aside and ignoring the urge to get the duster and vacuum cleaner out. She'd promised Daniele she would only be ten minutes.

He hadn't been happy at her insistence he wait in the car. She didn't want him in her apartment. This was the place she and Johann had made into a home when they'd been little more than children playacting at being grown-ups, neither having any real idea of what it entailed, learning as they went along, right down to when she'd put a nail in the kitchen wall to hang a picture, not having any idea that electric cables were nestled behind it and that she'd drilled right into them until they started receiving electric shocks every time they touched the tap or fridge. The electrician they'd had to scrape all their loose change together to afford had sternly told them they'd had a lucky escape—if either of them had touched the nail they would have been electrocuted. Even today, she couldn't believe she'd been so lucky. What had been the odds that she could hang the picture without touching that live nail? At the time she'd considered it as evidence of their good luck; vindication that running away with him had been right.

But their luck had run out.

With a sigh, she pulled the suitcase down from the top of the wardrobe and quickly filled it with her meagre number of warm clothes. Snow was settling on the streets outside, the weather a complete contrast to the glorious sunshine she'd left in Caballeros.

She didn't take anything else. She'd known when she'd accepted Daniele's proposal that what she was agreeing to would not be permanent. But she could manage a few years, of that she was certain.

Daniele's *castello* was almost identical to how Eva had imagined it, sitting high in the rolling Tuscan hills. Evening was falling and the few lights on gave it an ethereal, gothic quality. Thinking of how it would look with all the lights blazing in the total darkness, she could easily see where it got its name. Castello Miniato, the illuminated castle, would have shone for miles in medieval times.

What had once been a castle of majesty and splendour in a bright salmon pink was now on the verge of being a crumbling relic.

'Are you renovating it?' she asked as she got out of the car, which the driver had brought to a stop in an enormous courtyard. She could just make out scaffolding poles along a far wall.

'My brother started on a renovation programme. He finished the south wing and now I need to think about what I want to do with the rest of it.' There was a distinct lack of enthusiasm in his voice.

'You don't like it here?'

He shrugged. 'I prefer modern architecture. If I could get away with it, I would pull it down and start again.'

She followed him through a wide solid oak door and found herself standing in a high-ceilinged room that, despite its size and grandeur, had a dank, cold feel to it.

The temperature change from what she'd been used to in the Caribbean hadn't bothered her until that point. The cold weather front had engulfed the whole of Europe, with Tuscany expecting its own share of the white stuff over the coming days, but it wasn't until she stepped into the *castello*'s reception room that Eva felt the cold in her bones.

'The chef has prepared a meal for us,' Daniele said, rubbing his hands briskly together. 'I'll show you to our living quarters.'

She trailed him for a good few minutes before he opened a door into a wide corridor lined with high, wide windows.

'This is the family quarters,' he said, then pointed to a door. 'That is my room, which will be our room once we're married.' He threw the glimmer of a smile. 'Of course, if you wish for it to be our room before then, you're welcome to join me in it.'

She threw back a smile that quite clearly showed hell would freeze over first. 'Which is my room?'

'Take your pick. Serena, who runs the place, got the staff to put fresh bedding in all the rooms. The only one off limits is Francesca's.' He indicated another door, this time his smile indulgent. 'If you want to make yourself a widow, just tell my sister I let you sleep in her room. She would kill me.'

'Does Francesca live here?' She'd assumed not but only now she was here did she realise she knew next to nothing about Daniele or his family, not on a personal, familiar level. All her dealings with them had been in Caballeros where medieval *castellos* and family trees had never cropped up in conversation.

'No, but she visits a lot. We all have our own keys and there's been a long-standing agreement that any family member can stay here whenever they like and for however long they like. Francesca spends more time here than any of us... I suppose that will change now she's getting married and moving to Rome.'

'Her fiancé seems nice.' Actually, Eva had found Francesca's fiancé, a security expert who was in charge of all the security for the hospital site in Caballeros, rather terrifying.

Daniele snorted. 'I don't think *nice* is the word you're looking for, but he'll look after her and that's all I care about.'

'You and your sister are close?'

He considered this and nodded. 'You've met her, haven't you?'

'Yes. I liked her.'

'Good, because you're going shopping with her tomorrow.'

'What for?'

He cast a critical eye over the outfit she was wearing, her usual uniform of old jeans this time topped with a thick jumper. 'Clothes. Francesca loves spending my money and is happy to help you spend it too.'

'Your money? We're not married yet.'

His smile was faint. 'You're here. You've resigned from your job. Judging by everything I've seen you wear, you need new clothes. Your allowance will kick in from the day we marry but I'm happy to give you a credit card now. We've got a meeting first thing at your consulate for the *nulla osta*.'

The *nulla osta* was the legal document she'd need to prove there was no impediment to them marrying.

'Then we have an appointment at the registry office to give notice of the wedding. Francesca will meet us there and take you shopping when we're done. She knows all the best shops in Florence.'

Eva thought better of warning Daniele that there was no chance of her being given the *nulla osta* straight away. He'd learn for himself that willing their marriage to take place immediately did not mean it could happen. Then she thought of her pitiful wardrobe, which hadn't even nearly filled her suitcase, and tried to remember the last time she'd gone clothes shopping. It had been before she'd joined the Blue Train Aid Agency. Working for them had required practical clothing. The only new stuff she'd brought for herself in the past four years had been direct replacements for items that had worn out. She couldn't remember the last time she'd worn something that hadn't been jeans or shorts.

'Choose the room you want,' he said when she made no verbal response. 'That door at the other end of the corridor takes you through to a living area where we'll have our dinner tonight.'

'Are there any other rooms off limits?'

'No. Francesca's the only one who kept her childhood room as her own personal territory. My mother has informed me she won't be sleeping here again. If she visits she'll return to her villa in Pisa. Pieta last slept here on the day he got married.' Daniele's nose wrinkled as if he'd detected a foul smell.

'Are we going to live here?' She knew he had a number of other homes. If they were staying here she definitely needed that shopping trip. The warm clothes she'd packed wouldn't be warm enough unless she wore them all at the same time.

'Only until all the paperwork is sorted out and I'm declared the legal owner. Choose a room and make yourself at home. I'll join you for dinner in half an hour.' And with that, he opened his bedroom door and disappeared inside.

Alone, she gazed at the doors along the right side of the corridor and opted for the one furthest from Daniele's. It was a relatively small room, with thick lined faded wallpaper and wood panelled ceiling. It had a four-poster bed, a wardrobe, a chest of drawers, heavy curtains for the windows and a cosy-looking fireplace. The door also had a lock with a key in it.

Yes. This would do her perfectly for the next three or four weeks.

She would worry about sharing a bed with Daniele when the time came.

They left early the next morning for the consulate in Florence. To Eva's utter astonishment, the *nulla osta* was produced immediately, and an Italian-speaking consular official was there on hand to translate copies of her other documents so there would be no unnecessary delays. Daniele's smug grin as they left the building made her shake her head, that feeling of not knowing whether to laugh or cry going through her again.

'Who did you have to bribe to get it done there and then?' she asked when they were back in the car and heading to the registry office.

'No one. I simply made a few calls before we left.' He flashed a grin at her. 'When I want something, I never take no for an answer.'

'So I've noticed,' she murmured.

His efficiency at getting things done was astounding.

She'd discovered that last night when she'd joined him for dinner and found the draft prenuptial agreement printed off for her to read. He'd stuck to his word on every aspect. Once they'd finished eating, he'd then produced a map of the *castello* for her, which he'd drawn himself, with every wing clearly marked and little comments like, 'Don't go in this wing unless you like getting rained on.' This random act of thoughtfulness had astounded her more than anything else.

It was such a short ride to the registry office that by the time they'd parked, she thought it would have been quicker to walk.

The registrar greeted them and took them straight to his office, where a pot of coffee sat on a sideboard, the fresh aroma filling the room.

For perhaps the tenth time since she'd joined Daniele on the terrace of his hotel suite, Eva wondered if she'd slipped into some kind of vortex. Here she was, sitting down to arrange a wedding with a man she barely knew and intensely disliked but it didn't feel real, felt like she'd slipped out of her body and was watching it all happen to someone else.

Daniele was keen to get on and forced a smile as the registrar, a plodding, laborious man, asked in hesitant English if Eva needed a translator.

'Italian will be fine, if you don't mind going slowly,' she said, speaking his language faultlessly.

The registrar beamed his approval and inspected the *nulla osta* she'd passed to him carefully. 'This seems to be in order. You both have your passports?'

They handed them over, Eva passing her translated documents with hers. They were all inspected with the same careful consideration.

Only when copies had been made were they handed back in a pile together.

Daniele took them and opened the top passport to

check whose it was, saw it was Eva's and passed it to her. About to pass her the other documents, which he'd not even glanced at until that point, his attention was caught by the top one.

In silence he scanned it, the beats of his heart turning to thumps that hammered loudly throughout the rest of their meeting, through the vibration of his phone alerting him to a message from his sister who'd arrived at the building, and through all the other formalities that would allow him to marry Eva Bergen, formerly Eva van Basten.

By the time Francesca and Felipe joined them in the room, his heart was like a crescendo in his ears.

He'd not had the faintest idea that the ice-cool, beautiful woman he'd chosen to marry was a widow.

'What do you think?' Eva asked the woman who was going to be her sister-in-law in five days.

Five days.

The registrar had agreed to reduce the banns notice to just five days.

She could hardly believe it would happen so quickly. She'd expected to wait for weeks. Had *hoped* to wait for weeks, figuring it might give her the time to get used to the idea.

She really needed to keep herself on high alert around Daniele. The man was more than just a magician. He could make anything happen.

As soon as their appointment had ended, Daniele had given Eva his credit card and a key to the *castello*, said something about needing to get on with his work and then disappeared in his car.

Confused at his abruptness, she'd watched him be driven away with a certainty that something had angered him. Then Francesca had whisked her away shopping and she'd pushed Daniele from her mind.

Or tried to. In five days he would be her husband. For better or worse, they were going to be legally tied together. Suddenly it all felt very real.

Now she stood in the changing room of an extremely expensive boutique surrounded by a pile of vibrantly colourful clothes in all shapes, sizes and materials, Francesca and her keen sense of style a welcome presence.

'When do you move to Rome?' Eva asked as she unbuttoned the silk electric-blue shirt she'd just tried on and adored. She'd balked when she'd first seen the price tag but Francesca had been insistent, pointing out that the money that would pay for these purchases had been legally earned. But, still, twenty-eight years of frugality would not be overcome by one shopping trip.

'We were going to move this weekend but are going to wait until after your wedding.' Francesca took Eva's hands to stop her undoing any more buttons. 'Keep this on. You look fabulous in it.'

'Will I be allowed to?'

'You've got Daniele's credit card in your pocket. You can do whatever you like.'

Eva laughed. She really did like Francesca. 'I'll be cold.'

'Then we'll get you a coat to go with it. Wear it with the black jeans and black boots.'

The black jeans were nothing like the jeans she usually wore. These were a real skinny fit and had little diamond studs ringing the pockets. The boots were like nothing she'd ever worn either, reaching her knees and with four-inch heels. Slut shoes, her mother would have called them. Her mother would turn puce if she could see them, then have a heart attack when she saw the price.

How would Daniele react to see her in such different clothing…?

'Have you thought of the type of wedding dress you

want?' Francesca asked, cutting through Eva's veering thoughts of Daniele.

Who cared what he thought of the clothes she bought and how she looked in them? Not her.

Yet those were her flushed cheeks reflecting back at her...

'I'm sure I'll find something,' she murmured, dragging her attention back to Francesca's question. As she didn't want to think of the actual ceremony, she hadn't allowed herself to consider what she would exchange her vows in.

'There's a lovely bridal shop in Pisa I can take you to. I found my wedding dress in it. Can I be your bridesmaid?'

'I don't think it's going to be that kind of wedding.'

'Don't be silly. A wedding's a wedding. And who knows—maybe you and Daniele will fall in love with each other! That would be brilliant.'

Eva was so shocked at this that for a moment she could only gape at the younger woman. 'You know?'

'That Daniele's paying you to marry him? Yes, I know. So does Felipe. And our *mamma*,' she added as an afterthought.

'It doesn't bother you?'

'We need to keep the *castello* in the family. That's more important than ever after what Matteo and Natasha have done.'

'Matteo? Your cousin? The one who's a doctor?'

Francesca nodded, her face darkening in exactly the same way her brother's did when he thought of something unpleasant. 'Did Daniele not tell you about it?'

'Tell me what?'

'Matteo's been having an affair with Pieta's wife, Natasha. She's pregnant with his child.'

Eva's jaw dropped. 'For real?'

Francesca nodded grimly. 'We found out last week. It was in all the papers.'

'I don't follow the news,' Eva said absently as the pieces suddenly clicked together. Daniele and Matteo in Caballeros together… Daniele's busted nose… His grim mood… 'Last week? Did Daniele and Matteo get in a fight about it?'

'Yes. It's such a betrayal. I don't dare see him. I think I would be sick before I could punch him. He was like a brother to us. Natasha…we all loved her. We thought she loved us too. They betrayed us.' She took a deep breath, blinked a number of times then brightened. 'I'm very glad you've agreed to marry Daniele. I know he can be a pig but he's not all bad. And by marrying you the *castello* stays with our side of the family, otherwise if Matteo marries Natasha then he will be next in line to inherit.'

Eva swallowed, remembering Francesca's visit to Caballeros to purchase the land to build the hospital on. Eva had met her there, happy to impart as much of her local knowledge as she could to assist her. It was through that meeting she'd learned Daniele would be building the hospital and Matteo supplying all the medical equipment and overseeing the employment of the doctors and nurses who would work there. She'd seen the two men together, witnessed the good-natured ribbing and the easy familiarity. The family had put aside their grief over Pieta's death to pull together to make the hospital happen, and now they had been torn apart.

For the first time she felt a pang of sympathy for Daniele. He was human. He felt pain.

His brother had died and now he'd lost the cousin who'd been as close as a brother too.

CHAPTER FIVE

DANIELE WAS STILL very much on Eva's mind when Francesca and Felipe, who'd waited in a café while they'd shopped, dropped her back at the *castello* late that afternoon. He'd been in her thoughts all day, a shadow in her mind she couldn't rid herself of.

Felipe insisted on carrying her bags in but they both shook their heads when Eva asked if they would be staying for a drink.

'Thanks but we've got somewhere to be,' Francesca said, her eyes darting to her fiancé.

Eva suspected their 'somewhere to be' meant a bed. Their obvious love and desire for each other sent another little pang through her, this one of envy. She'd been in love once, with Johann, and it had been as sweet as a bag of sugar-coated doughnuts, but the desire had never been there.

She bit her lip. There was no point in wishing for something she had never felt and that she suspected she wasn't built to feel.

But then she thought of the man she'd be marrying and that little fluttery feeling set off in her stomach. He truly was the most attractive man she'd ever met. He had the looks of someone who, when she'd been a younger teenager, she would have wanted to pin posters of to her walls so she could gaze at him to her heart's content.

Her sister Tessel had once put a poster up on the bedroom wall they'd shared. Eva remembered begging her to take it down before their mother saw it but Tessel had been stubbornly brave and refused. She had paid for that stubborn bravery, and Eva had never been tempted to follow suit. She'd always learned from her sister's mistakes. Well, mostly. There had been so many rules that sometimes breaking the odd one had been inevitable.

Shaking the thoughts away, she pulled out the map Daniele had drawn for her from the bottom of the new handbag Francesca had insisted she buy. He wrote in precise block capitals, she noted, unsure why seeing his penmanship set the flutters in her belly off again.

It took her three trips to her new bedroom before she had all her new bags and boxes in there and strewn over the bed. The *castello* was shrouded in such silence she felt certain she was alone.

Thirsty, she studied the map again and saw the quickest way to the kitchen was through the huge family living area. Maybe she would find someone there, the chef who'd cooked their evening meal and provided them with fresh pastries before they'd left for Florence that morning.

The fluttery feeling turned into a buzz when she found Daniele at the large dining table they'd eaten at the night before. He was wearing a thick navy sweater and had his head bent over a large scroll of paper, a range of pens and pencils spread out before him.

She hovered in the doorway, a sudden shyness preventing her from stepping over the threshold. Whatever he was working on had his complete attention. She'd never imagined he could be so still.

Just as she thought she should cough or something, he turned his head.

She saw something pulse in his eyes as he stared at her before he straightened and put his hands to his ears to tug out a pair of earphones he had connected to his phone. 'My apologies. I didn't hear you. I always listen to music when I work but haven't got round to setting up a music system here yet. Have you been back long?'

'Twenty minutes. Am I disturbing you?'

'Not at all.' He pulled his sleeve up to look at his watch, revealing an intensely masculine forearm covered in fine dark hair. 'I didn't realise how late it was. How was your shopping trip?'

'It was okay.' She pulled her gaze away from his arm and saw his own gaze sweeping over her with an intensity that sent a burst of unexpected heat surging through her veins.

Utterly flustered but determined not to show it, she raised her chin. 'I'm sorry. I spent a lot more than I meant to.' She hadn't realised when she'd set out on her shopping trip that Francesca would only take her to designer boutiques. At the time, with Francesca enthusiastically encouraging her to spend as if there were no tomorrow, she'd allowed herself to get caught in the moment but was now dealing with a serious case of buyer's remorse.

Daniele shrugged then rolled his shoulders. He'd been hunched over the table for four hours and his back ached, but Eva's return had perked him up. Her new clothes looked amazing on her. She'd look even better if she let her hair down, something he looked forward to in both a literal and metaphorical sense. 'It's part of our deal—you get an unlimited credit card to spend on whatever you like.'

'Your sister's taking me to Pisa tomorrow to buy a wedding dress. I won't need to buy anything after that, not for a long time.'

'Need is not that same as want.'

Had she worn a wedding dress for Johann? he wondered moodily. He'd brooded over that man for hours, finally drowning the name by plugging his earphones in and cranking up the sound to lose himself in the plans for the refurbishment of the theatre that homed the Orchestre

National de Paris. 'I'm one of the richest men in Europe. Buy whatever your heart desires. It's part of our deal.'

'Being rich doesn't mean it's right to be wasteful.'

Was that a deliberate dig at him? He worked hard for his money. Why should he not enjoy the fruits of his labour? 'You sound like a puritan.'

Her pretty face tightened, fresh colour heightening her cheeks. 'You don't need to be a puritan to think being wasteful is wrong.'

'Maybe not,' he conceded. 'But if you have money then spending it is good for everyone. It boosts the economy for a start and filters down.'

She tilted her head as if considering his words then scrunched her nose and raised her shoulders, and stepped properly into the room.

He scanned her from head to foot all over again. *Dio*, her new skin-tight sexy jeans emphasised her curves beautifully; a Bernini sculpture come to life. If not for the flashes of colour on her face he could believe she was made of marble. His loins tightening to imagine the real texture of her naked form. When he got her naked he would discover the texture for himself and learn her natural colouring...

'I'm not an economist, only a woman who's lived and worked with some of the poorest people on our planet.'

He forced his mind away from the delights of imagining her naked. Soon enough he wouldn't have to imagine it...

'Marrying me means those people get the benefit of my money.'

'That's why I agreed to it.'

'Has your lawyer got back to you on the prenuptial agreement?'

She nodded. 'He's advised me to sign.'

'I'm not surprised.' Daniele had given his own lawyer instructions to make the agreement as simple and unambiguous as it could be. He had a loathing of complicated clauses allegedly there for protection but which were, to his eyes, a showcase of the drafter's self-perceived legal brilliance. The prenuptial agreement was three clauses long and didn't deviate from what they'd privately agreed on in Aguadilla.

'There was one thing…'

'What?' he asked when her voice trailed off and she gazed down at the floor.

'There was nothing in it about us sharing a bed.'

'You want me to put that in?' he asked, bemused.

'No,' she said quickly, shaking her head vigorously, her ponytail whipping through the air.

'Are you sure? We can have it spelt out that you and I are to share a bed every night of our married life if you want to hold me to it.'

She crossed her arms, pulling the new chunky cardigan she was wearing across her chest and covering the new silk shirt that was *extremely* flattering on her. He wondered if she was aware how the cut and the material clung to the fullness of her breasts. Crossing her arms hid the effect but, *Dio*, she was one sexy lady and knowing his reward for marrying her meant he got to share a bed with her every night meant there was heady anticipation mingling with his dread at the forthcoming loss of his freedom.

'I just assumed you would put it in the document,' she murmured.

'It's a private agreement between us. *I* assumed I could trust you to stick to your side of it. Are you telling me I can't?'

For the first time since he'd met her she seemed genuinely flustered but that didn't stop her raising her eyes to meet his with defiance. 'I will stick to my side of our agreement.'

'Then there is nothing else to say on the matter. I'll tell my lawyer to come here first thing so we can get it signed.'

She jerked a nod and, keeping her arms tightly crossed around her midriff, walked past him towards the door that led to the *castello* kitchens.

'When were you going to tell me you'd been married before?' he asked to her retreating back.

She stopped in her tracks and slowly turned to face him. Her face was an emotionless mask. 'You said you didn't want to know about my past.'

He kept his response emotionless too, although he acknowledged to himself the truth in her rejoinder. It was something he'd brooded on during her shopping spree. Eva was so cold towards him that he'd allowed himself to believe she was that way with everyone, even when he'd seen the evidence with his own eyes that with people she liked, she had the ability to be warm, like with those kids who'd come running to wave her off in Caballeros. To discover she'd been close enough to someone that she'd actually married them had been disconcerting, although he couldn't put a finger on why. 'That you've been married is something I should have known.'

'I am not a psychic. I cannot be expected to know what you think you should know when, as I just said, you expressly told me you have no wish to know anything about me.'

And he thought his sister was quick off the mark. The difference between them was that Francesca would fire her retorts back where Eva kept a veneer of icy calm around her that was both a thing of beauty and disturbingly infuriating. She really could be made of marble.

Realising his jaw was clenched so tight his teeth could grind wheat into flour, he concentrated on relaxing it to say as politely as he could, to let her know two could play at the icy calm veneer, 'Is there anything else important about you that I should know?'

Now her eyebrow rose a touch but she kept her defensive stance. 'How am I supposed to know what you think is important?'

Did you marry Johann for love?

He kept that question to himself. It wasn't important. So unimportant was it that he couldn't fathom why he would even have thought of it.

Instead, he lightened his tone, taking them away from this dangerous territory. 'Do you have a criminal record?'

Instead of the instant rebuttal he'd expected, she hesitated before shaking her head.

'You don't seem very sure about that,' he said.

'No criminal record,' she said with more decisiveness, then indicated to the door she'd been heading towards. 'I'm going to get a coffee. Can I get you anything?'

'I'll call a member of staff to get it for us.'

'I didn't think there was anyone here.'

'There's kitchen staff in.'

'Then I should go and meet them.' She raised her shoulders. 'If I'm going to live here for the foreseeable future I need to get to know them and learn my way around this place.'

'Follow the corridor to the second set of stairs then take your first left at the bottom. I'm afraid the service elevator's out of use. We need to get it repaired, like everything else in this bloody place.'

She gave a noncommittal shrug. As she reached the door he couldn't hold back the other question clamouring inside of him.

'What happened to your husband?'

'How did he die?'

He nodded. If he hadn't been so shocked to have the man's death certificate in his hands he would have read it more carefully.

'A brain tumour.'

'I'm sorry.'

Her chest rose as her lips pulled in together and she gave a sharp nod. 'Thank you.'

He paused before asking, 'How long were you married?'

'Four years.'

'You must have been young when you married.'

'We were both eighteen.'

He winced. Eva was a modern, independent woman. Why would a woman like her marry so young?

If he asked her she would tell him. The way she stood by the door, her blue stare not flinching from his, he knew she would tell him anything he wished to know. If he asked why she'd hesitated about having a criminal record she would tell him that too. She would answer any question he wished to ask.

But he didn't wish to ask. He didn't need to know anything more than had already been revealed.

He especially didn't need to know if she'd married Johann for love.

To Eva's consternation, the next four days flew by. Every time she looked at the clock, expecting to see ten or twenty minutes had passed since her last look, she would find another hour gone. She didn't see much of Daniele. He had a host of work to get finished before they exchanged their vows, leaving her to her own devices while he flew to Paris and then Hamburg and then on to somewhere else she didn't catch the name of. She knew that would all change when they married.

Francesca took her to the wedding dress shop in Pisa as she'd promised, then surprised her by taking her to lunch where Vanessa Pellegrini, the woman who in a few short days would be her mother-in-law, joined them. Much to Eva's relief, the elder Pellegrini woman was as warm and hospitable as her daughter and clearly thrilled her remaining son was going to marry. If it concerned Vanessa that her son was paying Eva to be his wife, she kept it to herself.

Eva spent the rest of her days exploring the *castello* and the estate grounds. The vineyards in the winter cold were barren and lifeless but she could imagine them packed full of fat, juicy grapes in the hot summer months. At least that was something to look forward to.

She also visited the *castello*'s private chapel in which they would marry. She had misgivings about marrying in a religious house, something she had shared with Daniele after they'd signed the prenuptial agreement. His response had been a nonchalant, 'If we're both committing to this marriage then there's no hypocrisy or sacrilege.'

'But we don't mean it.'

He'd fixed those green-brown eyes on her. 'My ancestor, Emmanuelle the third, married his wife Josephine of Breton in the chapel with her father holding her arms behind her back to stop her running away. What we're doing is tame compared to that and they were married for twenty years.'

'Were they happy for twenty years?' she'd asked cynically, while her heart twisted for the agony the long-dead Josephine must have lived through. She doubted she would cope with marriage to Daniele for twenty weeks never mind twenty years.

His laughter had been short but full-throttled. 'Unlikely. But you don't have to stay married to me for that long. You are free to leave whenever you like.'

'Which proves my point that we don't mean it. Why can't we marry in a registry office?'

'Because I *do* mean it. You will be my only wife. If you leave then you leave, but it won't be something I do again. It will make my mother happy to see me married here.' He'd run his fingers through his hair and stared at the frescoed ceiling. 'God knows, she could do with some joy in her life right now.'

And that had been the end of that conversation. After meeting Vanessa, Eva had found herself coming to Daniele's way of thinking. As warm and amiable as she was, Vanessa Pellegrini had a sadness to her that Eva saw in Francesca's eyes too. They put their brave faces on but she could see that inside their hearts had been torn over the loss they'd suffered with Pieta's death. If Daniele felt the loss of his brother as acutely as they did he kept it well hidden but he had to feel it too, didn't he? She'd seen his anger over Matteo and Natasha's betrayal of Pieta. She'd seen *him*, she'd patched him up. She hadn't witnessed it since though; on the contrary, his mood was generally flirty and affable but that darkness... Yes, there were times when she looked at him and glimpsed it hidden deep inside him.

Midnight struck. Eva saw her bedside clock mark the hour with a constricted chest.

This was it. She was officially getting married again, that very day. In twelve hours she would forsake Johann's name and become Mrs Pellegrini.

The fire in the room burned sporadically and mostly ineffectually. She'd snuggled down deep under the heavy bedsheets and was as warm as she could get in this freezing *castello* but, try as she might, sleep wouldn't come.

The floor was cold under her bedsocked feet as she slipped on her new dressing gown and left her room, intending to get a hot drink. Immediately she was struck with the scene from the condensation-covered windows that lined the corridor and which her heavy drawn bedroom curtains had hidden from her. She wiped a pane to see more clearly. It was snowing.

In wonder, she perched on the cold windowsill, wiped more condensation with her sleeve and pressed her face to the lead-lined window to stare out at the Pellegrini vine-yards and surrounding rolling hills encased in shining white, a magical scene that made her heart ache at the beauty of it all.

The living-room door opened and Daniele appeared, his dark hair dishevelled, a roll of architectural drawings under his arm.

Exhaustion lined his face and thick stubble covered his jaw but still her senses leapt with awareness at the sight of him.

'I thought you were in bed,' he said when he neared her.

Her heart suddenly battering her ribs, she tightened the sash of her dressing gown. 'I couldn't sleep.'

'Excitement about tomorrow?' he asked drolly.

'The excitement is killing me,' she replied, matching the drollness by the skin of her teeth.

Their eyes met. That pulse of electricity she was becoming far too familiar with flashed between them, a hung silence developing, only broken when he said with a glimmer of amusement, 'You'll catch a cold if you sit there too long.'

'It's snowing.'

He sat on the sill beside her and wiped condensation from a pane of glass. 'So it is. I can't remember when we last had snow here.' He swore as the pane misted up again. 'These windows are a disgrace.'

Twisting round so his back was to the window, he stretched his neck. 'I need an office. I can't keep working at the dining table.'

'There's enough rooms to choose from.' Her words were automatic, spoken without any input from her brain, which was as fixated as her eyes were on the muscular thighs wrapped in heavy denim only inches from her own thighs.

They were as physically close to each other as they'd ever been, close enough for her to smell the last vestiges of his cologne.

'They're all full of damp and cold. The living room's warm.'

She was no longer cold, she realised. Whether it was his physical proximity or some strange alchemy happening inside her, her body no longer felt the *castello*'s chill.

A burst of heat throbbed deep inside her to think that tomorrow night she would lie beside him and benefit from his body heat all night long...

'Why didn't your brother renovate the family wing first?' she asked with abrupt desperation.

Daniele was too attractive, too masculine. He smelled too good. No matter how hard she tried to keep it switched off, there was something about him the base part of her responded to and she *had* to get a handle on it.

She needed to keep a distance from this man as much as she could but how could she manage that when she had to share his bed and wake to his handsome face every morning?

His smile was tight as he answered, 'He saw it as the *castello* needing to pay for itself. Pieta renovated the south wing first because the largest state rooms are there and they bring the money in. Corporations hire them out. The bedrooms on that wing are hired out too. People come for romantic weekends and ghost hunts.'

She shivered but not with cold. 'Is it haunted?'

'If you believe in that stuff. Do you?'

'No.' She believed in what she could see and feel before her. But that didn't stop the gothic atmosphere of the castle from evoking her imagination in a way it hadn't for a long, long time.

'Good. It's rubbish. The *castello* has a bloody history so playing up to that is a good money spinner. I give Pieta credit there. He saw a market for murder mystery weekends and luxury ghost hunts and ran with it.'

'But...?'

'He didn't think of the family. Being the owner of the *castello* is like being a guardian. It's never yours. It's just in your keeping. My mother won't stay here any more because it's too cold for her. Not that she complained to Pieta about it,' he said with a faint hint of bitterness that he quickly shrugged off. 'I offered him the money to renovate the family quarters but he turned it down.'

'Why was that?'

His nostrils flared. 'He didn't want my money or my input. The *castello* was his and he was going to run it how he wanted.'

Daniele, feeling the old bitterness curdle in his guts, inhaled through his nose to drive the bad feelings out. His brother was dead and their fraternal rivalry dead with him. What did any of it matter any more? He should be above feeling slighted that all the accolades that had rained down on him and all the architectural awards he'd won had been received by Pieta with a patronising smile. Sure, Pieta would often open a bottle of the *castello*'s finest wine to celebrate Daniele's success but that had been the actions of a man behaving properly, in the manner expected of him, rather than anything heartfelt. Daniele had celebrated every one of his brother's successes as if it were his own, even if he always did secretly determine to smash it with his own success. When he'd made the Rich List for the first time, Pieta had murmured that a man should never measure his success in monetary terms but in the good they did in the world.

That was one area Daniele hadn't bothered trying to compete with his brother in. Pieta's philanthropy had been all his, and their family had thought him like a deity for it.

How could he compete with a deity? It was impossible. And he didn't want to. In every other aspect of life he used his brother as his benchmark but when it came to charity,

Daniele preferred his involvement to entail nothing more than writing out discreet large cheques.

'You can run it how you want to now,' Eva said softly, cutting through his cynical reminiscences.

He shouldn't be thinking like this. For everything that had wound him up about him, Pieta had been a good brother, even if that goodness had always felt as if it were for show, a display of his humility rather than sincere.

Dio, he was doing it again. He had to stop this.

'Yes, I can. And my priority will be to make our living quarters fit to live in.' He'd never wanted the responsibility of the *castello* and the rest of the estate but fate, along with Eva's consent to marry him, had put it in his hands...

He looked at the woman he would be marrying in a few short hours, her head resting on the window pane, intense blue eyes fixed on his. The velvet robe she hugged around herself was a deep indigo blue, setting off the redness of her plaited hair perfectly. She looked ethereal yet substantial. In the dark moonlight he could believe she'd been made to live in this gothic *castello*. If he were a sculptor, he would strip her naked but keep her in that pose and carve her likeness in marble. And then he would make love to her. He would kiss every part of that creamy skin and bring the marble to life until she was liquid in his arms.

His loins tightened and burned at his vivid imaginings.

'Just think,' he murmured, leaning his face close to hers. He could smell her skin, a delicate fragrance that made his blood thicken and his pulse surge. Her pink, sensual lips had parted a fraction, almost begging to be kissed. She really was incredibly beautiful. 'Tomorrow night you get to share my bed.'

Her eyes held his starkly, a glimpse of the fire he was experiencing sparking from them before they narrowed, her lips closed into a tight line and she pulled her robe tighter around her.

He laughed and reluctantly got to his feet. *Dio*, his groin *ached*. 'With that happy thought I bid you goodnight. See you at the chapel, *tesoro*.'

He felt her eyes follow him all the way to the bedroom that in one short night she would share with him.

It was the only bright thought for a day that filled him with dread.

CHAPTER SIX

FEELING LIKE THE biggest fraud in the world, Eva took a deep breath and opened her mouth to recite her vows to the kindly priest who was making short work of the ceremony.

She wondered if they were setting a record, not only for the quickest wedding ceremony in Italian history but for the lowest number of guests.

There were six of them in the pretty chapel, not including the priest. Her, Daniele, his mother, his aunt, Francesca and Felipe. He'd asked her if she wanted to invite anyone. True to form, he hadn't questioned her response to the negative.

She hadn't invited anyone to her first wedding either. She would have asked Tessel to that one but hadn't dared to in case her parents had found out. Now, marrying for a second time a decade later, her terror of her parents long done with, she couldn't ask Tessel for the simple reason that her sister no longer wanted to be contacted.

Those that were there today were all dressed in traditional wedding attire. At Daniele's request, she wore a traditional wedding dress, in which she felt ridiculous. It was beautiful but she was very much aware that white was not a colour that flattered her and she itched to get out of it and into something she felt comfortable in. She hadn't worn a traditional dress for Johann and she had meant her vows to him.

Would Johann understand what she was doing, marrying Daniele? She liked to think he would. He'd been the sweetest, sunniest person she'd ever known, an anomaly not just of men but people in general. He'd married her to protect her and keep her safe.

Daniele, wearing a black tuxedo, was marrying her for an inheritance he didn't want. He wasn't marrying her for his own sake. He was marrying her for the older woman sitting watching them with tears rolling down a face that teetered between joy and grief. He was marrying her to keep the estate that had belonged to his family for six hundred years intact. For all his many selfish faults she had to respect that in this instance he was behaving selflessly.

In truth, she hadn't seen any evidence of his selfishness since they'd landed in Italy. In marrying her he was behaving as selflessly as Johann had, albeit for completely different reasons.

The other difference was that she'd married Johann with relief flooding her veins and hope in her heart. For all Daniele's insistence that everyone would be a winner from their marriage, she recited her vows without a shred of hope for them. Neither of them meant them for what they should mean, even if her heart did thud heavily as she spoke the words that would bind them together.

Then it was Daniele's turn. He stared right at her as he said his vows but for once there was no humour in his stare. He spoke them like a condemned man with no hope of clemency. Yet something sparked between them as they went through the motions of marrying that Eva hadn't expected, like a bond was snaring itself around them, pulling them together as conspirators, uniting them in their mutual loathing of what they were doing. And something else was there too, something deeper that tugged at her stomach and made the thuds of her heart turn into a skip and her chest tighten.

We're together now, his look said. *This is it. You and I.* Only when he took her hand in his and slid the gold band on her wedding finger and she felt the weight of it on her skin did the bond fall apart and Eva come to her senses.

She'd worn a ring on that finger before. It had been the cheapest they could afford but had meant so much more. It had been given and received with faith and love. All that had been missing was desire. She hadn't known that. She doubted Johann had either.

When they were done and officially declared husband and wife, they left the chapel side by side but not hand in hand. There had been no kiss for the bride and that she would count as a blessing. If she ever had to kiss him she didn't want an audience for it.

A fresh smattering of light snow had fallen during the ceremony but the estate's groundsmen had been busy scattering salt to melt a pathway for them. Now the sun was out in the cold blue sky, the air crisp. Eva was thankful Francesca had insisted she buy a cream faux fur wrap to put over her shoulders. It staved off a little of the December chill.

'Let's get the picture taken here,' Daniele said.

'In front of the chapel?' she asked. This would be the picture they would send to the media. She still didn't know how she felt about having her photo given to the press but accepted that she was marrying—*had* married—a famous man and that their marriage would be deemed news. The odds of any of her family seeing it were slim and even if they did...what did it matter? They couldn't touch her or hurt her now.

He nodded. 'Let's keep it simple. One picture. A brief announcement of us having married and leave it at that. We only need to feed the wolves, not give them a banquet. Felipe, can you take it for us?'

'*I'll* take it,' Francesca said, beaming at them. 'The camera on my new phone is amazing.'

Eva noticed the indulgent eye roll Felipe gave his fiancée and felt another of those envious pangs in her stomach.

'Right, you two, stand in front of the door—Mamma, can you close it for them, please? Perfect. Daniele, put your arm around your bride.'

Eva met Daniele's eye and the pang turned into a flutter.

Amusement quirked on his lips at his sister's bossiness but there was something quite different in his eyes, a challenge to her.

Touch me and look adoringly at me, they said. *I dare you.*

And then he slid an arm around her waist and pulled her to him.

His physique had been a good indication that he was strong but she would never have guessed the solidity behind it, or the warmth that radiated from him, which seeped into her skin at the first touch.

'Get closer,' Francesca ordered. 'You've just married. The whole of Italy and much of the rest of the world is going to be looking at this picture.'

Eva inched a little closer so that her breast pressed lightly against his torso.

She blinked, shocked at the instant flash of sensation that pulsed through her.

'Now put your hand with the flowers to his chest.'

Breathing heavily, her heart hammering louder and more painfully than it had ever done in her life, Eva did as ordered, resting her hand as lightly against him as she could.

'Daniele, take her hand so you're both holding the flowers.'

A warm hand enveloped hers, the movement pressing her closer so she found herself flush against him. She could hear the heavy beats of his heart. The scent of his cologne was no longer a trace that she caught but right there, firing into her senses, setting them alight. The hand around her waist slid over to cup her hip, his fingers digging painlessly into her.

Lifting her eyes, Eva gazed up at him.

The returning green-brown stare swirled and pulsed, boring into her, explicit confirmation that his desire for her was more than just words, that when he got her into his bed he had every intention of seducing her and that it would be down to her own resolve to stop herself from succumbing.

An ache spread out low inside her as her gaze drifted to his lips. There was such sensuality in that mouth…

'Perfecto!'

Francesca's shout of approval brought Eva back to her senses and she pushed against Daniele's chest and stepped back.

'You're done?'

'Yes. Do you want to see it?'

'Can we wait until we get back inside? I'm freezing.'

But she wasn't cold. Being held by Daniele had warmed her so thoroughly she needed to lie on the white ground and make snow angels to cool down.

Daniele finished the last of his wine and grimaced.

So, it had been done. He was now a married man.

They'd returned to the *castello* for a short celebratory meal with his family that, for Daniele, had felt like a wake. Not only had he done the one thing he'd sworn he'd never do but as the day had gone on a Pieta-shaped absence had emerged. This was the first family event without him. He'd missed him and he knew his mother and sister had too. The two women had smiled and laughed and celebrated his marriage but neither had been able to hide the sadness in their eyes.

And now it was time for them to leave, his mother and aunt back to their villa in Pisa, his sister and Felipe flying on to their new home in Rome.

As they left, his mother cupped his cheeks and said, 'Thank you for doing this, Daniele. I know marriage is not what you wanted but I think, with Eva, you've found someone you can be happy with.'

He wanted to laugh at the irony of it. Since when had his happiness been a factor in his mother's thoughts towards him? Even the success he'd made in his professional life, which had far exceeded his brother's, had come second place in their minds to his absolute refusal to settle down and marry. But he'd always known his own mind and followed his own path and every nudge by his parents to 'be more like your brother' had only driven him further up that path, and driven him in a number of extremely fast and extremely expensive sports cars that should, according to his parents, have been replaced by luxury cars like the Bentley his brother had driven. At the time of his father's death just over a year ago he'd barely been on speaking terms with him, his father's fury at a kiss and tell by another of Daniele's girlfriends driving the semi-estrangement.

Why can't you be like Pieta? He would never bring such shame on our family.

It had been a constant refrain throughout his life. Be like Pieta. Be sensible. Make the right choices. Think of the family name. Be like Pieta.

He'd never wanted to be like Pieta. The only person he had ever wanted to be was himself, but in his family's eyes he hadn't been good enough as himself.

But the estrangement was something Daniele deeply regretted. He couldn't lay all the blame for it at his parents' door. He was an adult. He had to take responsibility for his own part in it. His mother was grieving for her firstborn and in emotional disarray at the betrayal of the nephew she'd raised as her own from his teenage years and the daughter-in-law she'd so wholeheartedly welcomed into the family.

So instead of laughing or making a sarcastic retort, he kissed his mother and embraced her tightly.

Marrying Eva had kept the *castello* and the rest of the estate in their branch of the family and eased a little of his mother's pain. He didn't deny that it made his chest swell to know he'd done something that brought her comfort and happiness. Pieta, and to a lesser degree Matteo, had always been the one to do that before.

Eva hung back while he made his goodbyes. He caught the startled pleasure in her face when his mother moved from him and took her new daughter-in-law in her arms.

The day had been as difficult for her as it had been for him but she'd coped stoically. He had no doubts that he'd made the best choice of wife that he could. She hadn't put a foot wrong, had made a concerted effort to smile and at least pretend that marrying him wasn't her idea of purgatory, even if it had been for his family's sake and not his.

That look in her eye, though, when they'd pressed themselves together for the photograph... He'd seen those ice-blue eyes darken and the tinge of colour spread over her cheeks. He'd felt her curvy body quiver against his.

Once his family had gone and they were alone in the armoury where they'd had their meal, she sighed heavily and said, 'Is there any wine left?'

'I'll get another bottle brought in.'

'Don't worry about it. I'm going to get changed.' There was a slight wrinkle in her nose as she looked down at the wedding dress she'd been in for hours.

He let his gaze drift over her. The dress she'd married him in was long and white with a high lacy neck and long lacy sleeves. Her long scarlet hair was wound in a coil at her nape and she'd applied minimal make-up. While she looked beautiful he thought Eva was made for dark, bold colours, not something as insipid as white.

'Let's go out,' he said impulsively.

'Now?'

'We'll change out of these monkey suits first.'

Their eyes met, understanding flowing between them. A glimmer of amusement played on her lips. It didn't need saying. The charade they'd been acting was over.

'Where do you want to go?'

'Club Giroud will do. We can dress up in clothes that don't look as if we've just got married, have a drink, and pretend for a few hours that we haven't thrown our lives away.'

'Your whole attitude to marriage stinks, did you know that?'

'Do you feel any different?'

She shrugged. 'I didn't have a life to throw away. But, yes, let's go out. See if you can convince me over the next few hours that you're worth the commitment I've just made to you.'

'I thought it was my money you'd committed to.'

Now she bestowed him with one of her rare smiles. It was like being shone on with starlight. 'It was. Unfortunately getting that money means I'm now tied to you.'

'Then let us hope the ties don't cut either of us.'

An hour later Daniele was showered and changed into a suit of a very different hue that made him feel like himself and not a man playing dress-up. He normally liked wearing a tuxedo but marrying in one had made it feel like he was wearing a straitjacket.

Now he waited in the large reception room for Eva to join him. He'd tapped on her bedroom door—it would be the last time she used it as a bedroom—and she'd called out that she would be ready in ten minutes.

While he waited, he fiddled with his phone. After a few minutes swiping through the news outlets, and coming across an article about Matteo and Natasha, he chucked it to one side and sighed.

The torrid affair his cousin and sister-in-law had begun

before his brother was even cold in his grave was a matter of greedy public consumption.

His anger for what they'd done was still as fresh as it had been when he'd first learned about it, but a little time and distance had given him time to think. That time and distance had only increased his anger towards them. The rumours his sister had whispered to him earlier that they'd broken up did nothing to quell it. They were having a baby together. They'd spent the two months since his brother's death secretly screwing each other while pretending that Natasha had travelled to Miami for a break. He would never have believed his cousin could behave so dishonourably or tell such bold-faced lies.

Had Pieta meant so little to them that they could betray his memory and everything he'd been to them? He'd never believed in his brother's saint-like persona but that didn't mean his brother hadn't been a good person. He hadn't deserved that from his wife and the man who'd been closer than he, his own brother, had been to him.

Then he forgot all about his brother and the rest of his family for the clacking of Eva's heels introduced her appearance.

And what heels they were too, black stilettoes that supported legs he could have been forgiven for thinking didn't exist as she always kept them covered up. Her long black winter coat was buttoned up and covered whatever else she was wearing but her smooth, shapely calves were on show and he had an almost irresistible urge to get on his knees and kiss the arch where they met her pretty ankles.

He let his gaze drift up to her face. The collar of her coat was up and around her ears to protect her from the chill but it looked to him as if she'd left her hair loose.

He'd never seen it loose before.

Her usually bare lashes were thickened with dark mascara, a sheen of glittery eyeshadow on the lids, her lips…

Her lips were painted a deep, utterly kissable red.

He couldn't wait to see what lay beneath the coat. And then he couldn't wait to see what lay beneath that.

Eva was his wife now. Which meant she was fair game for him to seduce. And from the challenge firing from her eyes, she remembered that part of their deal as well as he did.

Try it, those ice-blue eyes said. *Try it and see what happens. Try it but remember that I have the right to say no.*

His loins tightened and heated to think of all fun he was going to have in making those eyes fire at him with a desire that screamed *yes*.

He had no doubt at all that he would succeed.

Sooner or later his wife would be putty in his hands.

CHAPTER SEVEN

THE EXTERIOR OF Florence's Club Giroud looked a typical Renaissance masterpiece, a beautiful piece of architecture as beautiful as the rest of the city. But inside...

Once they were admitted by the bouncers who guarded it like a pair of Rottweilers, scanning Daniele's card and returning it with a nod of respect, the inner sanctum was like stepping inside a classy, sensual courtesan's boudoir.

In the entrance room Eva gazed at deep mahogany stained walls and the fleshy nude Renaissance paintings that lined them. Florence was a stunning city rich in history and heritage and this one room encapsulated its earthier history while retaining its expensive class.

The concierge greeted them with a wide smile. 'Good evening, Mr Pellegrini,' she said in Italian, before nodding politely at Eva. 'May I take your coats?'

When Daniele had suggested going out her instinct had been to tell him to go without her. The day had been long and far more emotional than she'd anticipated. In truth, she'd felt dead inside for so long that she hadn't expected to feel any emotion other than maybe some guilt, even though she knew Johann wouldn't want her guilt. He'd been gone so long that if she were ever to allow herself to be vulnerable again, which she never would, it wouldn't be a betrayal to him. She'd mourned him. She'd picked up her life and carried on without him, slowly becoming anaesthetised until she felt nothing at all.

Perhaps she'd been naïve thinking she could get through

this day with her emotions buried. Emotions had been flickering inside her since her arrival in Italy, heightening whenever she was with Daniele. But even so...

She hadn't expected to feel like she was choking. She hadn't expected her lungs to cramp so tightly that breathing had taken effort.

She hadn't expected that she would feel differently to have his ring on her finger or that she would look at his bare finger with resentment. Whether Daniele wore a ring or not shouldn't matter to her. She hadn't asked him to.

But they were married now. They needed to get to know each other. They didn't have to know each other's deepest secrets but if their marriage was to be painless, they deserved to at least see if there was a chance they could live in harmony, if not friendship.

Escaping the *castello* for a few hours to let their hair down together had sounded like the ideal way to start.

She'd opened her wardrobe and fingered the deep red dress that had caught her eye the moment she'd walked into the second boutique with Francesca. Slipping it on in her bedroom she'd sent a mental word of thanks to Francesca for insisting she disregard the price tag and buy it.

It was like nothing she'd ever worn before.

Strapless and sleeveless, it showed only the tiniest amount of cleavage and hugged her curves to fall just below her knees. Unlike the wedding dress that had made her feel like a washed-up china doll, this dress made her feel elegant, something she hadn't had the opportunity to feel for more years than she could remember.

It made her feel like a woman.

By the time she'd finished getting ready and met up with Daniele in the cold *castello* entrance room, tendrils of excitement had curled in her stomach. The look in his eyes when she'd walked in had reinforced that new feminine feeling inside her.

She'd never suffered from vanity before but with Daniele...

For reasons she couldn't begin to understand, being with him made her want to check her appearance every five minutes. She brushed her hair with extra care then became irritated with herself for it and pulled it back into a ponytail or a bun. She kept her make-up minimal. She didn't want him to think she was making an effort for him. She would deny her attraction to him until she was, as he'd once suggested, blue in the face.

But she couldn't deny it to herself. All she could do was contain it.

A night out, though, was a different kettle of fish from being alone in the *castello* with him. She remembered all too vividly her humiliation during their 'date' in Aguadilla when she'd been in her work clothes and everyone else had been dressed in their finest.

She'd chosen this dress because she liked it. She'd put the red lipstick on because it complemented the dress, *not* for him.

Now she carefully removed her coat and handed it to the concierge, doing her best to appear confident and not betray her nerves.

Then she met Daniele's eye.

Her feminine vanity bloomed to see the unadorned appreciation in his stare.

He'd removed his own coat, revealing a sharp light grey pinstriped suit and navy tie. His hair was mussed in the way she liked and...

Mussed in the way she *liked*?

Since when had she liked anything about him other than the money he would give to her charity?

But, gazing into those hypnotising green-brown eyes, she had to admit that she didn't dislike him any more.

His eyes glimmering, he held his arm out for her. 'Ready to go in, Mrs Pellegrini?'

She couldn't fight the smile that spread over her face at his insouciance.

Slipping her arm through his, she said, 'I thought this evening was all about trying to forget we were married.'

He walked her to the elevator, his voice dropping into a caress. 'With you looking like that? I've changed my mind. Tonight I want everyone to know you're mine.'

Her jaw dropped open at his arrogance while a pulse of heat melted her core in a way that flustered her as much as his words infuriated her. 'Just as I was starting to like you, you say something like that?'

'You're starting to like me?' he asked with interest, tightening his elbow so she couldn't remove her arm from the crook of his. The elevator door pinged open.

'I *was*, but then you went and ruined it by saying I'm yours. I'm not *yours*. I belong only to myself.'

He steered her inside and pressed the button for the third floor.

It was an old, creaking elevator and took a few moments to get going, time enough for Daniele to release his hold on her arm and somehow pin her in the corner, his hand resting on the wall by her head, not quite touching her but close enough for the scent of his earthy cologne to play havoc with her senses.

A smile played on his lips, amusement and something in his eyes that made her belly squelch. 'You know that every man who sees you tonight is going to want you.'

She had to swallow to get her throat working. Her words were hardly above a whisper. 'I know no such thing.'

'They will,' he said with authority. 'They will *all* want you, but I can guarantee that none of them will want you more than me.'

She felt colour crawl over her face that deepened when he traced a thumb over her cheek.

Her throat moved but she couldn't find the words she wanted to say; couldn't say them or think them. Her brain had turned to mush.

'And you want me too.' He brought his mouth close to her ear. 'You cannot tell me you didn't choose that dress and imagine what it would feel like for me to strip it off you.'

She wanted to deny it and throw his arrogant assertion back in his face with a cutting retort that would wipe the conceit off it.

'Stop it,' was all she could whisper.

'We are married now, which means that you, *tesoro*, are fair game for me to seduce. But I am a man of my word and I gave you my word that whenever you told me to stop, I would.' He took a step back and raised the palms of his hands. 'And now I stop.'

The elevator doors pinged and began their slow slide open.

The amusement that had been on his face lessened, a serious expression forming on his chiselled features. 'When I said they would know you are mine it's because that's the assumption people make about couples who are married. We will never belong to each other but we *are* married now and you are an incredibly beautiful woman. There isn't a man alive who wouldn't walk with a swagger with you on his arm.'

Fresh colour suffusing her, Eva had to fight to keep her stare level with his and not let it drop.

No one had ever spoken to her like that before. No one had ever looked at her the way he did.

No one had made her stomach melt with a look before either.

The door now fully open, Daniele took her hand in his. 'Come on, Mrs Pellegrini. Let's have some fun.'

The floor they walked out onto in Florence's Club Giroud was like stepping into an idealised magazine spread of what a billionaire's playhouse should look like. Trying to ignore the tingling sensation that having her fingers laced so tightly in Daniele's as they walked the narrow, higgledy-piggledy corridors evoked, Eva didn't doubt for a minute that the people spread out in the vast array of rooms were from the ranks of the filthy rich. It wasn't just the expensive cut of their clothes or the diamonds that sparkled from every woman's fingers, earlobes and neck but the confidence they carried. It was a confidence she'd seen before, from the guests that had made her feel so inferior at the Eden Hotel in Aguadilla.

Tonight, dressed as she was, she could hold her head high and meet the curious yet surprisingly friendly eyes that caught hers.

All the rooms seemed to serve a specific purpose whether as restaurants or gambling rooms or bars. Some had only a handful of people in them, others were packed. Some were quiet, others filled with raucous laughter.

Daniele led her into a bar that had a pianist in a lounge suit playing contemporary music in a jazz style in a corner and an abundance of dark leather sofas and low round tables.

As they took their seats on a sofa that managed to be supportive and also incredibly soft and luxurious, a hostess in a surprisingly smart uniform approached them with a welcoming smile on her face. Eva had formed the wrong impression that the hosts would all be squeezed into gold leather or something equally vulgar.

'It's a delight to have you here again, Mr Pellegrini,' she said. 'What will be your pleasure this evening? There's a poker tournament starting in an hour.'

'Just drinks for us tonight, Anita,' he answered smoothly, then said to Eva, 'Champagne?'

'I'd prefer a gin and tonic,' she admitted.

'Two gin and tonics,' he said to the hostess.

'I had no idea a place like this even existed,' Eva murmured as the hostess bustled away, a little overawed but very much intrigued.

'It's a private members' club and the best-kept secret in Italy. There's quite a few Clubs Giroud around the continent. My personal favourite is the Vienna one.'

She cast her eyes around the walls, tastefully covered in framed photos of famous musicians.

'If you don't like this room we can move somewhere else.'

'No, this is fine,' she said, then almost felt her eyes pop out of her head to see a famous movie star sitting on a sofa across the room from them.

Daniele, seated beside her but with his head to the back of the far end of the sofa, followed her starstruck gaze. 'I heard she was filming in Florence,' he mused. 'Now stop staring.'

Eva cringed at her own gaucheness. 'Sorry.'

'The members come to relax and enjoy themselves away from the spotlight.'

'Message understood.'

He grinned. 'I brought Francesca here once and she nearly fainted when she spotted her favourite singer in the champagne bar.'

'It's good to know I'm not the only one.'

'You'll get used to it. Many of the Club Giroud members are well-known faces. Just remind yourself they're human and all have the same basic needs as every other human and you'll be fine. Either that or work on your poker face.'

As he said that, Daniele thought that on the whole Eva had an excellent poker face. It was very hard to read what was going on in her head or guess what her thoughts were. He'd learned the best way to read her was through her eyes. They never lied.

Their hostess returned with their drinks, their tall glasses filled with ice and a slice of lemon. Eva took hers and sipped at it then nodded her appreciation.

'It's good?' he asked.

She nodded and settled back in the sofa, carefully crossed her legs then looked around the room again. 'When I woke up this morning I didn't think I'd be finishing the day somewhere like this.'

'It's not finished yet,' he said, loading his contradiction with meaning.

'Did you have to remind me?'

'Why not? It's all I can think about. Is it not the same for you? Have you not spent the day thinking that tonight is the first night we spend together in my bed?'

'Actually, I've been trying very hard to forget.'

'You're a terrible liar.'

'And you're a terrible egotist.'

'And you're reduced to insulting me because it's easier than admitting the truth that you want me.'

The tiniest flash of colour seeped across her cheekbones. 'Oh, suck on your lemon.'

'My point is proved.'

'Your point is invalid.'

He shifted to settle against the back of the sofa so he could face her properly. 'There is no shame in desiring your husband.'

'You're not...' Then she checked herself and shook her head. Her loose hair, which was far longer and thicker than he'd imagined, swished with the motion. The scarlet colour suited the dress she wore and her lipstick so well they could all have been made for each other. He could spend the evening doing nothing more than stare at her and not feel any boredom.

'I was going to say that you're not my husband. But you are.' And then she laughed and drank half her gin and tonic in one go. 'You're my husband. God help me.' She said the latter with a sigh and a roll of her eyes but with a definite trace of resigned amusement.

'God help us both,' he said drily before raising his glass. 'To us and a marriage of the absurd.'

She chinked her glass to his and in unison they drank.

They had hardly placed their empty glasses on the table when their hostess returned with fresh drinks for them, placing them on the table before disappearing as unobtrusively as she'd arrived.

'Excellent service,' Eva commented idly. 'I can see that being rich has it perks.'

'And you will come to love those perks.'

She pulled a wry face.

'What would you rather be? Rich and miserable or poor and miserable?' he asked.

'Rich. But anyone would answer the same. Being poor is a horrible state to be in.'

'Have you ever been poor?'

'Not in the way the people of Caballeros and certain other countries are, but Johann and I struggled for years. I know what it's like to wonder if there's enough money to feed you until payday.'

'I'm surprised an intelligent woman like you didn't go to university.'

She glowed at the compliment in a way she never glowed when he complimented her on her looks.

'I *did* go to university. I did a degree in International Business and Languages in Amsterdam.'

'I thought you said you got married at eighteen?'

'I did. Being married and going into higher education aren't mutually exclusive.'

'How could you fund and support yourself doing a degree?'

'Johann worked.' She shrugged. 'I worked weekends and

holidays. It wasn't easy but we managed. When I graduated I got a job as a translator at the Ministry of Foreign Affairs in The Hague and we stopped having to struggle so much. We could even afford to buy our own little apartment.'

'What did Johann do?'

'He worked in a bicycle shop.'

'He didn't have ambition for himself?'

'He had lots of ambition,' she said with a trace of sadness. 'He wanted to be an engineer but we couldn't afford for us both to study and support ourselves. He had so many dreams but he put them on the backburner so I could pursue mine and never got the chance to realise his own.'

Daniele's heart gave an unexpected lurch at the melancholy in her voice for her dead husband.

Did she still miss him? Was it because of her great love for him that she'd vowed never to remarry?

Why did that thought make him feel so inadequate? He'd worked hard for his money. He'd been fortunate to have wealthy parents who could afford to put him through university but he hadn't taken a cent from them since he'd graduated. He'd made a great success of his life and had the satisfaction of knowing everything he had he'd earned for himself.

But deep down he knew that whatever he did, he would never inspire anything like the loyalty and affection Eva held for Johann. She would always compare him to her first husband and find him wanting, just as his mother would always compare him to her first son and find him wanting.

It didn't matter. He would demand Eva's loyalty as his wife but he didn't need her approval. He didn't want her affection in any place other than the bedroom.

Just as he was telling himself he didn't care, that Eva's past meant nothing to him and was irrelevant to their own marriage, he heard himself say, 'You know what I don't understand?'

She shook her head and reached for her drink.

'Why you married so young.'

She contemplated him as she drank, this time through the straw, her eyes clearly saying, *I thought my past was irrelevant to you.*

'I'm curious,' he said with an affected nonchalance to overshadow the heavy thuds of his heart. 'Most intelligent modern women like yourself choose to marry later in their lives—my sister is an example of that.' At least she had been until she'd met Felipe and fallen madly in love. 'But you bucked that trend.'

She drank a little more, then cradled her glass in both hands.

He prepared himself for tales of teenage hormones and rebellion.

'We married to protect me.'

'What did you need protection from?' he asked with astonishment.

She contemplated him some more but now he couldn't read the meaning in her piercing eyes. A shutter had come down on them.

Then her chest rose and she gave the slightest nod before saying, 'Not what. Who. My parents.'

His astonishment doubled. 'You needed protection from your *parents*?'

Her lips pulled in before she gave another nod. 'I would say I left home on my eighteenth birthday but I didn't—I ran. Turning eighteen meant their authority over me ended but I wanted the protection marriage would give me. I didn't know what they would do to find me or the lengths they would go. Johann and I knew that if we married and I took his name it would make it harder for them, whatever they did. I was scared that if they found me they would go to the courts to try and force me back.'

Scared? Eva? He hadn't thought anything frightened her. 'Would they have been able to do that?'

'Legally no, but I know my parents. They would have tried anything they could. They would have had me declared incompetent or…anything, really.'

'But why?'

'Because I *belonged* to them. We all did. They gave us life and therefore they owned us. It was for them to choose what we wore and where we went and who we saw. They knew best about everything and their rules were rigid. If we didn't obey it was because there was something wrong with us and we needed to be punished.' She took another sip of her drink. Somehow she'd kept her composure throughout this brief retelling of her childhood that he knew hadn't even scratched the surface, seemingly relaxed into the sofa, her legs curled beneath her bottom, her eyes on his. She'd managed to keep her dress from riding any higher than her knees.

This composure was all surface, he was sure of it. There were little signs to confirm it, the way her throat now moved of its own accord, the way her back teeth seemed to be grinding together.

Eva's family…

He'd wondered briefly why she hadn't invited them to the wedding but, assuming it was down to her not wanting to put her family through what they both considered to be a charade, hadn't questioned her about it.

A loud, booming voice suddenly chimed in his ear. 'Daniele Pellegrini! It's good to see you, man.'

Standing above them was the mountainous form of Talos Kalliakis.

Delighted to see him—and, he had to acknowledge, more delighted at the interruption of a conversation that had veered dangerously close to too personal and which he had been on the verge of taking further—Daniele got to his feet and embraced his old friend.

'What are you doing here? I didn't know you were planning a trip to Italy.'

'Amalie's playing at the Opera di Firenzi this week,' Talos replied, referring to Florence's new opera house, designed by an architect Daniele had long admired. He wasn't interested in the arts and culture itself but the buildings that housed them had sparked his imagination from a very young age. He remembered being dragged every few months to some production or other at the *Teatro di Pisa* as a child and spending all his time gawping at the brilliant interior rather than paying attention to the on-stage production.

Talos's wife, Amalie, was a violinist who played so movingly that even Daniele could appreciate its beauty.

'You're on your own? Come, join us.' Then, turning to Eva, he made the introductions. 'Eva, this is my old friend, Talos Kalliakis. Talos, this is Eva...my...wife.'

'Your *wife*?' Talos didn't bother hiding his shock. 'You dark horse. I didn't know you'd got married.'

'That's because we only married today,' Eva piped up, getting to her feet and sticking her hand out to him. She'd had a few breathless moments there when she'd wondered exactly how Daniele was going to introduce her. 'Nice to meet you.'

It was *very* nice. The interruption was exactly what they'd needed.

Despite her best efforts over the years to move on and forget her torrid childhood, discussing her family and her past still had the power to hurt her. She could lay the facts out in simple, unambiguous language but the memories that lay behind them...

That was an area she would prefer not to delve into, especially with the man who'd explicitly told her that he had no interest in her past, hence no interest in *her*. Daniele desired only her body. She was a means to an end for him and she would do well to remember that, just as she had to remember that he was nothing but a means to an end for her too.

Ignoring her hand, the giant planted an enormous kiss on both her cheeks and embraced her tightly. 'Congratulations to you both. Are you sure it's okay to join you? I won't be offended if you'd rather be alone.' He looked quizzically at Daniele as he said this, clearly wondering why a married couple would spend their wedding night anywhere other than in bed.

'Not at all,' Daniele insisted in that relaxed, good-natured manner he had that Eva knew she would never be able to emulate. He took her hand and brought it to his lips. 'Eva and I have the rest of our lives to be alone.'

Talos called for champagne to be brought over and, before she knew it, the three of them had formed their own little group that slowly expanded as more people drifted over to join them, including the movie star Eva had been enraptured by earlier, more bottles of champagne were ordered as word got out that the notorious bachelor Daniele Pellegrini had finally settled down.

CHAPTER EIGHT

EVA STARED AT the eclectic mix in which they were the
star attraction with that old feeling of falling into a vortex
engulfing her again. It didn't help that Daniele kept her
so close to him for the rest of the evening that she ended
up squished against him on the sofa with his arm around
her and his large warm hand resting possessively on her
thigh. He made sure she was included in all the conversations and, to the natural question asked *ad infinitum* of
how they'd met, he proudly told them all about her work
in Caballeros. He even sounded genuine about it, which
thrilled her more than she cared to admit.

These were some of the richest and most famous people in the world and they were treating her as their equal.
She almost choked on her champagne when she realised
Talos was, in fact, a prince and that his wife was the violinist whose latest album Eva had downloaded. When they
finally left it was with a dozen invitations to parties and
dinner ringing in her ears.

'What did you think?' Daniele asked when they were
in the back of the car, his driver taking them back to the
castello. 'Did you enjoy yourself?'

'It was surreal but, yes, I did.' She'd surprised herself by
how much she'd enjoyed it. She'd felt like a fish out of water
but his friends had been so hospitable and welcoming—
even if some of the women had looked at her a little bit too
pityingly for her liking—that she'd almost relaxed.

'I thought you did amazingly.' His admiration sounded

as genuine as his pride when discussing her work. She hadn't expected that, not for a minute.

But Daniele was proving to be nowhere near as shallow as she'd thought when she'd first met him. She'd formed preconceptions about him, which his behaviour on their 'date' had confirmed for her. She hadn't given him any credit for what he was doing in Caballeros; a project that his brother had set in motion. The brother who had died just a month before their date.

Other than the flirting, she hadn't seen any sign of that selfish, shallow behaviour since. Quite the opposite if she was being honest. On the whole, he was a perfect gentleman.

'Thank you,' she said softly.

'For what?'

'For including me. For not ignoring me.'

'Why would I do that?' he asked, seemingly bemused.

Suddenly she realised they were still holding hands.

She carefully disentangled her fingers from his and put her hands together on her lap. Her fingers tingled their disappointed resentment.

'I don't know.' She took a long breath. 'I hadn't thought about what would happen when we met your friends. It just surprised me that you included me in the conversations. I guess I had an image in my head that when rich men get together the cigars come out and the little women are banished to another room.'

'If that still happens it's not in the circles I mix in.' He didn't sound put out by her less than charitable preassessment.

'Have you taken many women there before?' She couldn't summon the courage to ask if any of the women with the pitying stares had been ex-girlfriends of his.

Had they pitied her because of their own pasts with him or were those looks based solely on his reputation?

Why did it even matter? It shouldn't. His past held no more interest to her than hers did to him...

She felt his hand cover hers and had to close her eyes and will herself not to take hold of it again.

'*Tesoro*, would you do me a favour?'

'If I can.'

'Stop assuming the worst of me. I'm not an angel. I know my reputation with women isn't good—and deservedly, I admit—but I'm not the pig you think. I meant what I said when we first discussed marriage, about it being based on respect. I would never be so disrespectful as to take you somewhere I've taken other women.'

She opened her eyes and turned her head to face his intent stare. 'I'm starting to believe that,' she murmured.

'Good.' Then he ruined it all by grinning lasciviously at her and kissing her knuckles. 'And I also meant what I said when I promised to try and seduce you at every given opportunity.'

She glared at him but couldn't quite summon her usual force, not when her whole body now ached to be kissed in places far more intimate than her hands.

'You can let go of my hand now,' she said, hating that her voice pitched itself so low.

He laughed in as low a pitch but did as she said. 'I'm starting to think that marriage to you is going to be fun.'

She flexed her fingers. 'I'm a laugh a minute.'

'You're a lot more fun than I thought you would be,' he admitted, twisting so he faced her with his whole body.

'I've never had much time to explore my fun side,' she said drily. 'I've always been too busy studying and working.' She didn't add that the concept of fun had been banned in her household when growing up. Fun was something other families had, not the van Bastens.

'I've always studied and worked hard too,' he pointed out. 'It never stopped me having fun.'

'I don't imagine there's anything that would stop you in your pursuit of pleasure.'

'*You're* stopping me,' he said, dropping his head a touch to look woebegone, but then his eyes sparkled and he inched closer to her. 'But not for much longer, and I can promise you the pleasure will belong to us both.'

'Do you only think of sex?' She shouldn't be encouraging this conversation but sense seemed to have gone out of the window. And she shouldn't be leaning closer to him…

'Have you not looked in a mirror? What man wouldn't look at you and think of sex?'

'I am more than just my body.'

'And I am more than just my sex drive. I'm learning to appreciate all your other qualities too.'

'If you're more than just your sex drive, why do you hate marriage so much?'

'I don't hate marriage. It's just an institution I never wanted to join. But now that I have joined it, I mean to make the most of its positive aspects, which involves sleeping beside your warm, delicious body every night.'

With her body leaning ever closer to his, Daniele's gorgeous mouth near enough that one quick push forward would link their lips together, it was with great relief that Eva saw the lights of the *castello* glowing brightly in the night sky.

She snatched a breath and forced herself away from him.

They were home. It was time to go to bed.

Daniele stoked the fire before getting into the four-poster bed that had been a feature of the *castello* for so many years it was considered an antique. He'd already replaced the curtains on the high window with the thickest available, and made a mental note to call his head contractor in the morning. He wasn't prepared to wait a day longer. The renovation of this wing would start immediately.

His thoughts puffed away when Eva emerged from the bathroom with her thick robe wrapped around her.

Her composure, as had become her trademark, was exactly as it always was. It had been the same when she'd first stepped into his room and looked around it coolly before giving a little nod that he took to be approval.

He'd arranged for the staff to move her stuff over to his bedroom while they were out, and she'd opened the doors to her new dressing room, which had been used by his ancestors as a prayer room, as if she'd opened them a hundred times before. She'd selected her nightwear then gone into the bathroom as if it were something she'd been doing for years.

It was only as she walked barefoot to their bed that he saw a faltering in her step.

She slid under the sheets and gave a little gasp. 'You don't use any kind of bed warmer?'

Not tonight he didn't. Tonight he'd left deliberate instructions to the staff not to warm the bed for them. Underhanded but necessary. 'If you're cold I'm very happy to warm you.'

'I'll get warm without your help soon enough.' She flashed a knowing smile at him. 'Especially if I keep my robe on over my pyjamas.'

'Are they sexy pyjamas?'

Settling onto her side and burrowing under the covers so only the top of her vibrant red hair peeked through, she said, 'If you won't use a bed warmer you'll never find out. Goodnight, Daniele.'

'No goodnight kiss for your new husband?'

'No.'

'It *is* our wedding night.'

'Happy wedding night.'

Laughing softly, Daniele switched the bedside light off, pitching the room into black. Done, he settled himself down as close to the middle of the bed as he could without encroaching on her space in a way she could complain about, facing towards her. Well, facing towards her back, which his eyes took a while to adjust to the darkness to see with any form of clarity.

He could smell the faint trace of her shampoo. And the mint of her toothpaste. And the remnants of the perfume she wore, which he was coming to adore.

She shifted a little, her movements those of someone trying to get warm.

'Still cold?'

'I'm warming.'

They fell into silence, the only sound the rustling of the sheets where Eva had entangled herself.

'Are you always such a fidget?' he teased.

'Do you always talk so much?'

'I can get you warm.'

'I'm fine.'

'Prove it and stop fidgeting.'

'I don't have to prove anything.' But she stopped moving. For almost a whole minute before the rustling started again.

Grinning to himself, Daniele inched closer and lifted the sheets where they were tight across her back.

'What are you doing?' she asked sharply.

'Using my body heat to warm you. Don't worry, you're perfectly safe.'

'Touch me inappropriately and *you* won't be.'

Taking full advantage of her tacit, if reluctant agreement, Daniele hooked an arm across her belly, taking great care not to touch her anywhere she could deem inappropriate, and pulled her so she was spooned against him.

'Better?' he asked into the top of her head. The strands

of her hair brushing the underside of his chin had the texture of silk.

She gave a noncommittal mumble. She was hardly melting into him but neither was she attempting to escape.

It surprised him how good this felt, just holding her. He wasn't going to try anything else—though he wouldn't mind in the least if she turned over and jumped on him—and found himself content to simply lie there with her voluptuous curves nestled against him, all the scents that combined to make *her* filling his senses.

It was too much to expect his loins to behave with the same decorum as the rest of him. He'd fantasised about getting Eva into his bed for weeks and having her in his arms, even as chastely as this, was playing havoc with his reactions to her.

He heard an intake of breath and knew she could feel his lack of decorum for herself.

'Relax,' he murmured. 'You're safe.'

She must have believed him for she sighed but stayed exactly where she was. When he moved his hand over her belly and the tie of her robe knotted around it, and found her hand, she didn't resist when he covered it with his own. When he laced his fingers through hers he felt the lightest of pressure in return.

Her fingers were cold.

A smattering of guilt settled in him. Eva had lived in the Caribbean for...how long, he didn't know. He hadn't asked. But he knew it had been a long time. The only thing Caballeros had going for it was its year-round sunny climate. She must have adjusted to that and now she was living here in this draught-ridden ancient castle in a winter far colder than was the norm for this region, she was having to adjust again.

She hadn't complained. She'd simply got on and coped with the cold draughts and mostly ineffective log fires. If he'd known how much she felt the cold he would have got his tradesmen in immediately to sort their living quarters out, not decide to concentrate on getting as up to date with his work as he could before their wedding.

And he would have got the bed warmed up for them too. Wanting her to be a little bit cold so he could take advantage of it was a different matter from making her body temperature plunge to that akin to a fridge.

But she *was* warming up now. And relaxing.

His heart beating harder with every passing second, Daniele willed himself to relax too.

It was a long struggle, one he knew he'd brought on himself by holding her so close, even with that thick robe separating their bodies. The only parts of their flesh that touched were their hands, which neither of them seemed to be in any hurry to part.

'Can I ask you something?' she whispered just as his brain was starting to switch off.

'Sure.'

'You've had so many lovers…didn't you have feelings for *any* of them?'

So she was thinking of him with lovers…

He didn't know if that was a good thing or a bad thing. Probably the latter, which he couldn't blame her for.

'There were some I liked more than others,' he answered honestly, his mind flickering to a few years back when he'd been dating a French model who'd been capable of holding a decent conversation. Not a decent conversation like he could have with Eva but compared to his other girlfriends she'd been an Einstein. He hadn't bored of her as quickly as he usually did. A few weeks into their relationship—a record for him—he'd taken her to a party at an embassy in Paris that his brother had also attended. She'd spent the entire night flirting with Pieta, who'd made no effort to discourage her even though he'd been engaged to Natasha, who in turn had been absent from the event. Daniele had dumped her without a backward glance. Whenever he thought of that night it wasn't her he thought of but his brother.

Daniele had been the one with the reputation of a Lothario but he would never have flirted with Natasha or any of Pieta's girlfriends that had come before her. He would never flirt with any woman who had a partner. His sense of honour might be warped in some people's view but his loyalty was absolute. It had angered and astounded him that Perfect Pieta's honour and loyalty could be so fickle and that he could have been so blind to it.

'But none you would have considered marrying instead of me?' she asked in the same soft whisper.

'No.' His fingers tightened against hers reflexively. He didn't want to think of his brother and his less than perfect behaviour. He needed to remember the good, not the bad, and there had been far more of the former. 'You are the only woman I could have taken this step with.'

He knew with a certainty that he couldn't explain that Eva would never demean herself or be so insensitive as to flirt with a man when she belonged to someone else.

Not that she belonged to him, he quickly reminded himself. Of course not. And if she could read that thought he was quite sure she'd kick him.

But none of this did anything to alter the proprietorial feeling in his chest as he held her so tight against him.

Eva awoke feeling as snug as she'd ever felt in her life, so warm and dreamy that she was reluctant to open her eyes and break the spell.

Daniele's large warm body was still pressed against hers, keeping her warm as if he were her own life-sized hot-water bottle. At some point in the night their fingers had unlocked and his hand had burrowed under the knot-

ted tie of her dressing gown and through its gap to rest
over her pyjama top on her belly.

She hadn't thought she'd be able to sleep in the same
bed as him but she'd slept as deeply and sweetly as a baby.
She'd felt his erection pressing against her. The heat it had
conjured... It had been enough for her to move away from
him with the truth that she was no longer cold.

But she'd stayed exactly where she was. She hadn't
wanted to move. She'd ached to press back against him
and tempt him into acting on his desire and kiss the word
'no' away from her lips...

That same feeling was in her now. An ache that had
spread into every part of her, heat pooled so low and so
deep inside that she had to fight to remember all the very
good reasons why she was determined to keep their marriage platonic.

She inhaled deeply through her nose then opened her
eyes. The darkness that had cloaked them throughout the
night had turned into a grey haze, the morning sun struggling to filter through the room's thick heavy curtains as
much as she was struggling to understand the depth of her
craving for the man she'd married.

Pushing the covers off her in one decisive movement,
Eva climbed out of bed and hurried to the bathroom.

Once safely locked inside her temporary sanctuary, she
stepped into the shower and prayed for the steaming water
to rinse her of these feelings that had broken through the
shell she'd erected around herself.

'Did you sleep well, *tesoro*?'

Eva looked up from the cup of coffee she'd just put to
her lips and felt her heart lurch dangerously. After finishing in the bathroom she'd slipped into her dressing
room. As she'd been deciding what to wear she'd heard
the shower start and known Daniele was up and about.

Suddenly feeling shy for reasons she couldn't comprehend, she'd dressed quickly and shoved her damp hair back in a ponytail, wincing to see her dark roots poking through on her hairline. In a couple of days it would be noticeable.

She'd then hurried through the bedroom before he could appear from the bathroom and had taken herself to the dining area. A member of staff had arrived with a tray of coffee and a selection of fruit, cold meats, cheeses and fresh pastries for breakfast, looking disappointed when Eva had turned down the offer of something cooked.

This was the first she'd seen of Daniele since she'd hightailed it from his bed.

Was she imagining it or did he get even more handsome every time she looked at him?

Today he'd dressed casually in black chinos and a round-necked chunky grey flecked sweater. His mussed hair was still damp and he carried the strong scent of shower gel and fresh cologne.

His eyes sparkled as they met hers.

She cleared her throat discreetly and stopped her hand from pressing against her racing heart. 'Well enough, thank you. And you?'

'Well enough for a man who feared his balls turning blue,' he said with a grin that could only be described as sinful.

She cleared her throat again. 'Perhaps you wouldn't have that problem if you slept on your own.'

He shook his head with mock regret. 'I have been suffering from chronic unfulfilled desire since you moved in with me. Just thinking of you in a bed is enough.' He tilted his head as if considering this assertion. 'Actually, just thinking of *you* is enough.'

'Coffee?' she suggested pointedly.

'I don't think that works as a cure for Chronic Unfulfilled Desire syndrome but, yes, please.'

Trying to disguise the tremors in her hands, she poured him a cup and pushed it across the table to where he'd just sat down and helped himself to a Danish pastry.

'Thank you,' he said with a grin. 'Now eat up and pack a bag.'

'Are we going away?'

'Only to my house in Siena for a couple of days. The weather's not any better but the house has proper insulation. I've got my men coming in to make some changes here so you don't feel like you're sleeping in an igloo.'

But that was the problem, she mused a short while later while selecting some clothes to take with her. She'd liked sleeping in an igloo. She'd liked that it had meant she could accept the warmth of Daniele's body insulating her.

CHAPTER NINE

DANIELE'S HOME ON the outskirts of Siena turned out to be a sprawling villa of his own design, sympathetic to the city's heritage yet undeniably modern. It was so well insulated Eva could have walked around naked without feeling a chill.

They took a leisurely drive there, stopping at a traditional Italian restaurant in a hillside town for some lunch, spent the afternoon touring around the cathedral; the evening in yet another restaurant where they dined on *ribolitta* soup and *pappardelle* pasta and a Chianti so smooth Eva had to resist drinking more than two glasses.

As the climate in his home was so constant, she got into the bed without her dressing gown on but with her pyjamas fully done up. Refusing, again, Daniele's seductive request for a goodnight kiss, she'd again slept with her back to him.

In the morning, though, she'd awoken to find herself spooned against him, his hand holding her belly and a heavy thigh draped over hers, and the warm sensation of desire curling through her veins.

Not until she'd slipped out of the bed without waking him did she notice where on the bed they'd slept curled together. She must have inched her way back to meet him in the middle.

The same thing happened the next night too, but this time Eva woke to find herself curled in his arms with her face pressed against his bare chest, breathing in his warm, musky scent. She'd gone from feeling like she was in some kind of drugged state to being wide awake in an instant and shot out of the bed quicker than a rocket. When her pulses had finally calmed enough for her to leave the sanctuary of the bathroom she'd pretended not to see the knowing gleam in his eyes.

She would deny this attraction for ever if she could. She would ignore her surging heart rate evoked by a simple look and her raging pulses whenever his hand brushed against her.

After two nights and a lazy morning spent wandering around a museum, they made the drive back to the cold *castello* so they could get ready for a night out with Francesca and Felipe, who were in Pisa for the day.

As soon as they drove into the courtyard Eva could see something major had happened in their absence.

Scaffolding had been erected around their wing, an army of men working against the cold December air repointing the stonework.

The first thing she noticed when they reached their quarters was the lack of draught.

'New windows,' Daniele explained with a grin. 'Wait until you see our bedroom.'

She took one step inside and came to an abrupt halt.

Daniele watched her reaction closely. 'What do you think?'

'I had no idea you were doing this,' she said a little breathlessly, turning to him with a look of wonder.

In the short time they'd been gone his team of contractors had redecorated, replacing the old wallpaper with a gold-leaf pattern that remained sympathetic to the *castello*'s heritage but with a much more modern twist, and new, thicker carpet put on the floor. The hearth had been cleaned out and heavy curtains that matched the ones he'd had put up on the window were tied back on the posts of the bed.

'I think you'll find the insulation in here much more effective now,' he said, breaking the silence. 'I figured I had to do something to warm the *castello* just in case the cold spurred you into running away with all the money I give you.'

'We've only been married for three days. Give me time.' But the softness in her eyes suggested that any thoughts of ending their marriage quickly had been put aside.

She was softening towards him like a snowman melting in the thaw.

'Do I get a thank-you kiss for doing all this?' he asked.

Expecting her to pull a face or make a sarcastic retort, he was taken aback when she closed the space between them, rested her hands lightly on his shoulders and pressed her lips on his cheek.

Her lips were as soft as he'd imagined but she pulled away too quickly from him.

'You call that a kiss?' he demanded, snatching at her wrists and holding them with enough strength that she couldn't wriggle out.

Colour slashed her face and the blue of her eyes darkened. 'What kind of a kiss were you thinking of?'

Never one to look a gift horse in the mouth if there was the chance delay or further conversation might make it bolt, he tugged her so she was pressed flush against him, close enough for him to feel the little quivers of excitement racing through her.

'One like this,' he whispered, releasing her hands and sliding his fingers up her arms and over her shoulders to cradle her face and fuse his mouth to hers.

There was only the slightest resistance from her, a quick

inhaled gasp of shock that turned as quickly into a sigh before she almost seemed to sink into his kiss.

Desire, never far from the surface these days, bloomed through his veins, the heat of her mouth and the heat of her response stoking it. Her tongue darted into his mouth, all the encouragement he needed to deepen the kiss and move his hands from her face to tug out the band holding her ponytail in place and spear her silky hair and cradle her head tightly.

But then, all too soon, Eva broke it, turning her face so his lips lingered on her cheek.

'You can stop now,' she said in a voice that seemed to be searching for air and not at all as confident as she usually sounded.

His groin aching, Daniele closed his eyes and breathed in deeply, which only made things worse as he inhaled her wonderful unique scent.

'You're killing me,' he groaned.

She gave a short laugh. 'I think I might be killing us both.'

'Then what's stopping you?'

Backing away from him and gathering her hair at the back of her head, ready to tie it back but either forgetting or not realising he had it in his hand, she bit into her lip.

'Daniele,' she began, her voice still not quite working properly. She took another breath then said, 'I've only been with one man. I've been celibate for six years. I'm…' She blinked, clearly struggling to find the word to explain what she was feeling. 'I'm scared, okay?'

'Of me?'

She shook her head and looked away from him. 'Of how I feel.'

His stomach lurched. 'And how do you feel?'

'Confused.' She dropped her hold on her hair and it fell softly over her shoulders and down her back. 'I've never experienced desire before. I didn't know it could make a sensible head want irrational things.'

His brain pulsed at the admission she'd never felt desire before him and with it came the instinct to put a stop to this conversation. He didn't need to know any more details.

He already knew she'd been married for four years and that she'd married Johann to escape from her parents. That was more than enough. He didn't want to complicate their marriage with feelings. Especially not his own.

But to hear that she'd never felt desire for the man whose memory he'd been fighting against thinking of as a rival...

To hear *he* was the first man she'd ever experienced desire for...

'There is nothing irrational about wanting someone,' he said carefully, knowing he was avoiding asking the question of what irrational things her head wanted and knowing it had to be this way. 'Desire is what makes the world turn, whether it's the desire for money or power or for another person; it's what drives us. I want you. You want me. We're married. What's irrational about any of that?'

She looked back at him with what looked like a touch of sadness. 'You make it sound so simple.'

'It's only complicated if you make it so.'

After holding his gaze a moment longer, her shoulders dropped and she gave a short laugh. 'Yes, you're right. I do have a tendency to overthink things.'

He held his arms out wide. 'Then stop overthinking and come here.'

But she stayed where she was, a smile playing on her lips. 'I'll think about it.'

Strolling to her, he took her face in his hands and planted a firm kiss on her mouth. 'There,' he whispered in her ear. 'That will help you think.'

Then he let her go and strode to the bathroom. 'And when we go to bed tonight… I promise to help you think some more.'

Francesca and Felipe were in excellent spirits at the exclusive but friendly restaurant they met up at in Pisa. Exclusive but friendly, Eva was coming to think, perfectly summed up the Pellegrinis.

Listening to Francesca speak nineteen to the dozen about their new home and all their wedding plans almost took Eva's mind off the kiss she and Daniele had shared…

She shivered just thinking of it.

She mustn't think of it. Not here. Not now. Not in a restaurant where people would notice the heat she still felt from it spreading over her neck and face.

So she made a concerted effort to forget all about it and forget about what the night would bring, and relaxed into the warmth and camaraderie, heightened at the waves and hails from other diners recognising them, some stopping to exchange a few words. Daniele knew so many people; had so many friends.

It felt that she'd spent her entire life keeping people at arm's length. Most people learned to make friends in childhood but Eva had never acquired the skill. Friendships had been discouraged. Inviting a fellow child over for a playdate had been a non-starter. It had taken her a year to pluck up the courage to return one of Johann's shy, sweet smiles. After they'd married and with his help, she'd become better at socialising but he'd remained the only real friend she'd ever had. Until now. Daniele had a wide circle of friends all eager to welcome her into it.

A couple with a sleeping baby heading for the exit spotted them and came over to say hello, the father introduced as an old friend of Daniele's. The baby, on the verge of becoming a toddler, shifted in his arms, yawned widely then opened her eyes and fixed them on Eva.

Eva smiled automatically and found herself on the receiving end of a smile so wide and adorable that she couldn't resist reaching out to stroke the little girl's chubby cheek.

'She likes you,' the mother observed with an indulgent smile at her daughter.

'She's beautiful,' she said simply, her eyes soaking in the plump wrists now waving at her and the small tuft of blonde hair, and felt something move in her heart strong enough to steal her breath.

Such a beautiful, beautiful child...

She'd never thought of having children before. When she'd been married to Johann it had been hard enough scraping the money together to feed themselves, never mind bringing a child into their world. Since he'd died, she'd been on her own, closed off from everyone, so shut off from her own emotions that the thought of children hadn't even entered her head. She loved the children at the camp in Caballeros but in the detached way infant teachers loved their little charges.

Since Daniele had steamrollered her into his life all those shut-off emotions had started seeping out, a gentle trickle that she could feel building momentum inside her.

For the first time she allowed herself to imagine what it would be like to have a child of her own. Someone to love. Someone to love her.

Then she looked at Daniele and saw his gaze was fixed firmly on her, just as it always seemed to be, and her heart moved again.

They could have a baby together.

As quickly as the thought came, she pushed it away.

They'd only been married for five minutes, far too soon to be thinking of having a child together. A child meant a lifetime commitment and that was one thing she hadn't promised him. She could walk away whenever she wanted.

Her eyes flickered to his again. He was grinning at something Francesca had said. He must have run his hands through his hair since she'd last looked for the top was sticking up. She longed to reach out and smooth it down, then let her hand move down to the nape of his neck.

Another delicious anticipatory shiver raced up her spine.

Their marriage would last as long as she wanted and right then she knew she had no intention of walking away from it.

Daniele held Eva's hand in the back of the car as they were driven back to the *castello*. Rather than delight that she seemed content to let him hold it, he found his mind going over everything he'd discovered about her that evening courtesy of his nosy sister's incessant questioning.

He'd learned Eva had spent her first three years with the Blue Train Aid Agency working in the poorest countries in Africa, co-ordinating food aid and medicine and making sure it got to the people who'd needed it. As she'd put it, 'Lots of paperwork.' She'd been transferred to Caballeros a year ago on the basis that she spoke Spanish, again co-ordinating food aid and medicine to those in need, which in that country was a significant percentage of its people. When the hurricane hit, she'd been fortunate to take shelter with her colleagues in the concrete building they'd been using as an office. That Eva and her colleagues had been right there, ready to swing into action and get working on the refugee camp, had been sheer luck.

That's what she'd called it—luck. Luck that she'd been stuck in the middle of one of the most powerful hurricanes on record. She'd related it so matter-of-factly that he could believe she hadn't experienced any fear during it. Eva had said as much when questioned about it by an agog Francesca.

'There was nothing for me to be scared of,' she'd said with a small shrug. 'If it was my time then it was my time.'

That she could be so blasé about her own safety, her own *life*, had sent chills up his spine and through his bloodstream. Those chills were still there in his veins.

What kind of life had she lived where she could see no value to it?

He released her hand and ran his fingers through his hair.

'I've been thinking, you could start your own consultancy business advising the rich and famous how best to help those in need.'

She blinked at him in surprise. 'Really?'

'Why not? You didn't want to give up your job and I know you were bored in the days running up to our wedding. It can be as formal or as informal as you like. People like to be philanthropic but it's not always easy knowing where to start or knowing that the money they give is going where they think it's going. You must have lots of contacts in the charity world.' He raised his palms. 'It's something to think about.'

She nodded slowly. 'You continually surprise me.'

'In what way?'

'When we met I thought you were nothing but a selfish playboy but you're not, are you? Beneath your don't-care exterior I see a man who does care and does want to help. You've donated money to good causes before, haven't you.'

It wasn't phrased as a question.

'Guilt money. I leave the true philanthropy to others.' Like his brother.

She twisted a little in the seat, her eyes holding his and studying him as if she was trying to read him. 'At least you're honest about your motives and don't use it to further an agenda or because you crave adulation.'

'You know people who do that?'

She nodded. 'For some, I get the impression that their philanthropy is an act.'

'An act? In what way?'

She grimaced. 'Please, don't think I'm speaking badly of them. What they do is wonderful, whatever their motives. It's just that there's some I never think mean it on an emotional level. You understand what I mean? That it's all for show? That it's the adulation and plaudits they crave, not a genuine, emotional desire to help or make things better. Only some of them, I should add. I met many you could see genuinely cared.'

'What about my brother? What category did you put him in?'

Expecting the usual waffle of what an amazing man Pieta was, he was slightly thrown when she hesitated and bit into her lip.

'You put my brother in the category of doing his great acts of philanthropy for the adulation?' he asked slowly, a prickle of anger setting loose inside him.

'I didn't say that.'

'You don't deny it.'

'I only met him a couple of times and never on a one-to-one basis. I hardly knew him.'

Her evasive non-answer made the prickles deepen. 'You thought you knew him well enough to judge him.'

'I didn't judge him,' she protested. 'He was an amazing person—what he did to help those in need was incredible...'

'But you still felt he did it for show.' His heart battering against his ribs, Daniele leaned forward. 'My brother did more than anyone I know to help others. He spent so much time fundraising and organising projects for his foundation and going into dangerous situations with little thought to his own safety because he wanted to help and he knew he was in a position to help, and he never took a cent for himself, unlike charity employees such as yourself who are paid a salary for your good works. And you have the nerve to criticise him?'

Eva remained incredibly still during his tirade. He didn't know where that had come from, spoken even as the rational part of his brain knew he was being unfair to her but unable to stop.

In his entire life he had never heard a word of criticism towards his brother. Not one word.

'I didn't criticise him,' she refuted steadily but with a tremor in her voice. 'You asked for my thoughts and I gave them. Your brother did incredible things, and nothing can or should change that, certainly not my private opinion, which isn't worth anything.'

Daniele breathed deeply and dug his fingers into the car seat.

Painful as it was to acknowledge, Eva's opinion matched precisely his own. He'd always thought Pieta's good deeds were for show, a way to display to the world what a magnificent man he was. He'd never believed it had come from the heart.

But his private thoughts towards his brother were one thing. He was his brother, it was his job to pick faults and criticise. No one else's.

'You have a right to your opinion,' he said, doing his best to modulate his tone. 'But you should remember that he was my brother and I will always defend him.'

'I understand,' she said quietly. 'Families are complicated but the bonds can be very powerful. Even when they're the worst kind of human, the instinct to protect them is strong.'

He didn't have to ask to know she spoke from experience and that fired the stabbing prickles in his blood off again.

He wouldn't ask for details. He didn't want to know any more about her. Their marriage was supposed to be a long-term parlour game where emotions were placed in the box labelled 'no', a marriage that was a means to an end for them both.

Their vows were supposed to tie them together in a figurative sense.

He wasn't supposed to feel anything for her but desire.

CHAPTER TEN

EVA COULDN'T UNDERSTAND why she felt so wretched. She hadn't said anything derogatory about Daniele's brother but she knew she'd angered him.

She wished she'd kept her mouth shut. She hadn't been thinking of his brother when she'd mentioned the philanthropists who did their good deeds for the adulation. She'd been thinking of Daniele and how beneath the seemingly egotistical, selfish outer layer lived a good, thoughtful man who had no need for adulation. She was coming to think adulation was something he actively worked against receiving.

The last ten minutes of the drive back to the *castello* had been conducted in silence. When they'd pulled up in the courtyard, he'd got out first and offered his hand to help her, but instead of taking the opportunity to keep hold of it as he usually did, he'd dropped it as soon as she was on her feet.

The silence had continued all the way to the now warm bedroom. He'd offered her the use of the en suite, muttering something about using the bathroom next door before walking back out again.

So she'd taken a shower, wishing she knew the words to say to make things right between them again.

After drying herself, she stared at the clean pyjamas she'd brought in to change into and swallowed, indecision racking her.

It amazed and scared her how quickly her feelings towards Daniele had changed. Her relationship with Johann had developed over many years, sweetly and shyly. In his own way, Johann had been as sheltered as she had, a small-town boy with big dreams and an even bigger heart. Love and friendship had been their driving force, not, she was sad to acknowledge, passion. When she'd looked at him she would feel content and safe. When she'd kissed him she'd felt comfort.

When she looked at Daniele she felt as if she had two hearts beating in her chest. When he'd kissed her she'd felt her desire for him like it had a heart and life of its own, a blazing force of nature she'd only just managed to tame.

Not tame. No, that was the wrong word. How could you tame a force of nature? All you could do was run away and hope you ran fast enough to beat it, or hide somewhere and hope your hiding place was good enough to save you. All she had done to escape the feelings that had roared through her with their kiss had been to run, but she knew she could never run fast enough to escape it. For as long as she was with Daniele, it would be there, glowing red-hot between them, provoking and tempting her to fight her fears and confront it.

But what was she even frightened *of*? It was only sex.

She was overthinking things again.

Sex had always meant so little to her before so why blow it up out of all proportion now? She'd told Daniele right from the beginning that she would never have sex with him because she'd needed to keep some power in her own hands and because their marriage was a contract based on money and she could never countenance having her body used as a form of return payment. To her, it would have been nothing short of prostitution.

Her feelings had changed. *They'd* changed. Making love with him… It wouldn't be prostitution. What power would making love give him over her? She was free to leave whenever she wished.

Suddenly she snatched at her robe hanging on the door and, still naked, slipped it on, tying it securely around her waist.

No more thinking. No more worrying. No more complicating things in her own mind when the facts of the matter were simple.

She wanted Daniele and he wanted her. What was there to fear about that? What was there to fear about acting on it?

Not prepared to hang around in the bathroom a moment longer and give her imagination the time to answer, she opened the door and stepped into the bedroom.

Daniele was already in bed, lying on his side under the covers, facing the wall. He'd turned the main light off, leaving her bedside one on.

There was no movement from him, no acknowledgement of her presence.

Softly she stepped over to her side of the bed. Instead of climbing in, she untied the curtain tied to the post and pulled it to the centre of the bar connecting the posts together.

He turned over slowly onto his back.

With Daniele watching her wordlessly, she made her way around the bed, untying the curtains and drawing them shut until the entire bed was surrounded by the heavy maroon drapes. Then she slipped between the two that had come together on Daniele's side. They fell back into place with a swoosh, enclosing them in.

It was like stepping into the past. She could imagine his ancestors doing the very same thing centuries ago, closing off the world along with the chill of the night air. The utmost in privacy. The only illumination came from the soft glow of tiny lights running atop the wooden headboard, which he must have switched on while she'd been closing the drapes, bathing them in a flickering red glow.

Daniele now had a hand behind his head and was staring at her with an incomprehensible expression in his eyes.

Eva stood beside him and placed her hand on the bedspread that covered the rest of the sheets on the bed, all resting on his chest. Working from his stomach, she smoothed her hand up the sheets until she reached the top and then, not giving doubt or fear any space in her head, pulled them down to his feet.

Then she just stood there and drank him in.

In all the time they'd been living together she'd only seen him fully clothed, never bare, not even those nights they'd slept together and he'd slept nude beside her.

He was naked now and he was glorious.

Muscular legs and thighs led up to snake hips between which jutted an erection so huge she almost blinked to make sure it wasn't a trick of the flickering light, reaching up to his flat navel. His chest was muscular and defined with a light smattering of dark hair in the space between his brown nipples.

Deep inside her something throbbed and pulsed, the force of nature she'd been running from awakening and curling its tendrils through her veins. She welcomed its hold, her resistance a thing of the past.

This was now. This was what she wanted; what they both wanted.

Her gaze drifted back down to his large and surprisingly handsome feet. She'd never known feet could be handsome. She reached out and placed her hand flat on the right one. His toes made a little wiggling motion. Slowly and gently she traced her fingers over his ankle and up the leg and thigh, over the washboard stomach covered in fine dark hair that pulled in at her touch, past the straining erection, up over his rapidly rising and falling chest and collarbone, up the side of his neck to his jawline, coming to a stop when she reached his mouth.

His lips parted and he strained towards her. Pressing her forefinger down on his lips in lieu of a kiss, she then, finally, sat on the edge of the bed beside him.

Keeping her gaze on his now darkly hooded eyes, she unknotted the sash around her waist.

Her robe fell open, exposing her to him as he was exposed to her. The widening of his eyes and the movement of his throat drove away any shyness she might have felt.

She took the hand resting by his side and held it between hers. He made no movement, letting her run her fingers over the length of his, so much longer and thicker than hers, and stroke the smooth palm before brushing her lips over it and tracing the lifeline scored on it with her tongue.

His breathing had deepened, become ragged.

Then she placed his hand on her aching breast.

The sensation it evoked was like heated darts firing through her skin and her head rocked back with the force of it.

Daniele felt as if he'd fallen asleep and woken to the most erotic dream he could have wished for.

All the tormented emotions he'd carried up to the bedroom were forgotten.

With the bed curtains drawn around them it could be only the two of them in this world.

Eva was seducing *him*.

He could hardly believe it was real.

The heavy weight of her breast in his hand felt real. The breathless sigh that escaped her mouth when he gently squeezed it sounded real. It sounded like his dreams come to life.

He'd never seen such concentrated desire as he did then from the ice-blue eyes that had become so heated they could be molten.

He'd never felt such desire within himself.

Such beautiful breasts, he thought dimly. He'd imagined them more times than he could ever count but they surpassed everything his feeble brain could conjure, as white as snow with nipples as pink as pale raspberries, and the texture…the texture of satin.

All of her was beautiful. Exquisite.

He stared again into her eyes and felt the connection between them flow like a running tide.

Raising himself up, he put a hand to her slender waist and took her breast in his mouth.

Her head rocked back again, a mew escaping from the lips he suddenly hungered to kiss.

He caught hold of the robe hanging open on her and tugged it off so she was as naked as him and then turned his attention to her other breast, kissing and licking it, his desire heightening when her hands cradled his head, her fingers digging into his skull, and she arched into him, silently asking for more.

He needed to kiss her.

But first he wanted to look at her again.

Taking hold of her hips, he used his strength to lift her so she straddled him, then lay back down.

One small adjustment and he could be inside her.

His erection gave a powerful throb at the thought and he concentrated his mind away from the ultimate pleasure that would come soon enough.

Eva's long red hair had spilled over her shoulders and over the heavy yet pert breasts that tasted like nectar. Her stomach had a rounded womanly softness to it…*she* was soft. All of her, a complete contrast to the hardness of his own body. The perfect complement to him.

How could he have imagined her like marble?

He reached out to palm her stomach then walked the tips of his fingers lower to touch the dark downy hair between her legs…his instinct that she was a natural brunette had been proven right. She quivered and closed her eyes.

Then she leaned down and her hair spilled over him as her mouth found his and he was pulled into a kiss so deep and full of meaning he could drown in it. Her tongue swept into his mouth and he caught that taste again, one he could never describe but that was as uniquely Eva as her scent was and had played on his tongue like a remembrance since their earlier kiss. As their fused lips and tongues devoured each other, he wrapped an arm around her neck and swept a hand over her back and then down to her bottom, which was as ripe as the most succulent of peaches.

He tightened his hold and rolled her over so she was the one flat on her back and he on top. The feel of her breasts close against his chest was simply incredible.

Pulling his lips from hers, he stared in wonder into eyes that returned everything he was feeling.

It was as if his entire life had been a dress rehearsal for this moment.

He ached to be inside her but he wasn't ready, not yet. First he needed to discover Eva's final flavour, the only one he had yet to experience.

With one last passionate kiss, he began his exploration of the woman who had driven him mad for so long, using his tongue and his fingers to touch and feel and taste, her moans and writhing body urging him on. When he reached her most intimate, feminine part and gently parted her thighs, she gave a shudder before he'd even put his lips to the beautiful folds.

This taste… This was Eva. This was her muskiness, her desire. And it belonged to *him*.

At the first press of Daniele's lips to the part of her that had never been kissed before, Eva thought she was going to lose her mind and clenched her hands into fists to stop herself from jerking away.

She hadn't been prepared for any of this. She could never have been. It would have been impossible.

Intimacy such as this couldn't be real.

But it was very real.

Shivers and sensation had bloomed into every part of her, burning her with such a craven need for everything Daniele was doing to her and for…

His tongue found her most sensitive part.

Lieve God…

It felt as if the pleasure surging through her had been gifted by a benevolent creator.

She could feel the sensations massing together into a heavy tightening cluster that throbbed and burned. A moan echoed softly in the den they'd created…that wanton sound had come from *her*.

Just as the cluster reached a point that had her breaths shorten in anticipation of something, she didn't know what, Daniele shifted and kissed her inner thigh. Her cry of disappointment was muffled when fresh sensations started over her skin and he dragged his lips back up over her belly and breasts…she had never known her breasts could ache so much…and up the sensitive skin of her neck, his body moving with the motion until he was positioned between her legs, his erection prodding between her thighs, staring down at her.

The heady desire she read in his eyes made her throat close and her chest expand.

When his lips came back on hers for a kiss that was almost restrained, she tasted something new and realised with a jolt that the taste belonged to her.

Sliding a hand around his neck, she dragged her fingers through his hair and deepened the kiss and as his tongue swept into her mouth his buttocks moved and he slowly inched his way inside her.

Lieve God…

He made love to her slowly, groaning into her mouth, bodies entwined, their chests crushed together, as close as two people could ever be. She wrapped her legs tightly around him, all the sensation flowing through her thickening and gathering into a mass again, but this time he didn't pull away, driving slowly and languidly inside her. Her cries became louder yet somehow muffled to her ears, the mass tightened and tightened until, without any hint of what was going to happen, it exploded and the purest, headiest form of pleasure imaginable burst through her.

As if he recognised what was happening to her, Daniele stilled, breathing heavily into her ear, allowing her to cling to him and ride the waves until they lessened, and then, with a groan, he started again, this time harder, as if he'd been waiting for her release of pleasure before taking his own.

His thrusts became more frenzied, his groans deeper and then, with one last long, forceful drive, he shuddered wildly and then collapsed on top of her.

With the echoes of her own climax still pulsing through her, Eva held him tightly in her arms, welcoming his weight and his hot breath dancing on the skin of her neck.

Drums beat loudly through her, in her head, in her ears, so loudly he must be able to feel it too.

It seemed to take for ever for all the sensations to evaporate but even when the throbs in her core had stopped she could still feel the remnants of what they'd just shared, a newness in her veins that she'd never known before.

Brushing her lips against his damp cheek, a feeling of blissful contentment settled in her chest and she took a long breath.

'Am I hurting you?' he asked hoarsely, his voice muffled against her neck.

'No.' She stroked her fingers over his back and breathed

again. Her throat was closing and her lungs tightening but it wasn't Daniele's weight causing it. She swallowed and felt her chest hitch, felt hot tears burn in her eyes that she blinked back frantically.

She was going to cry.

She *mustn't* cry.

But as soon as she thought it, a tear leaked out and landed with a soft plop on the pillow.

There was a delicious languidness in Daniele's limbs. Sleep was snaking its way in his brain but he resisted the need to switch off, certain he must be crushing Eva with his weight. Reluctantly, he moved off her and rested his head on the pillow beside hers, and hooked an arm around her waist.

He'd never experienced before in his life anything like what they'd just shared.

It had been more than just sex, although he couldn't have said why, just knew that it had been incredible. He felt different…

As he was trying to pinpoint what felt so different inside him he saw with a start that Eva's eyes were shining with tears.

'What's wrong, *tesoro*?' Instinctively he gathered her to him so she was draped against him with her face resting on his chest.

He felt her swallow and heard the choke of held-back tears.

'Was my lovemaking so bad it's made you want to cry?' He strove for a lightness in tone but the fresh thuds of his heart made him fail.

It worked, though. She gave a tiny, shuddering laugh and groped for his hand. Entwining their fingers together, she squeezed.

'I didn't know it could be like that,' she whispered.

Making circular motions over her back with his free

hand, he rested his cheek on the top of her head. 'Are you saying it like a good thing or a bad thing?'

'Both.'

'How can it be both?'

'It just is.' She was silent for a moment before saying, 'I wasn't taught anything about sex when I was growing up. Johann and I were both virgins when we married. Neither of us really knew what we were doing. Johann knew the basics but I was clueless.' Her voice dropped even lower. 'I didn't know it could feel so good.'

She didn't have to say anything more. She'd already confessed that she'd never felt desire for the boy she'd married when she'd been only eighteen, a marriage he'd now formed a solid impression of that had been more of a friendly affection than that of true lovers.

He knew without her having to say that what they'd just shared had conjured up a wealth of mixed emotions in her. He guessed guilt played a part in it that she had found something with him that had been missing from the boy she'd had a genuine, if friendly, love for. It should make him preen but it didn't. All it did was make him feel sad for the young life that had been taken away too soon, which was actually quite disconcerting. Empathy had never been one of his traits.

'Eva…' He hesitated. He no longer felt sleepy. 'Eva, you're Dutch. Your country is famous for its adult approach to sex education. How could you have not been taught about it?'

'The word was forbidden in my house,' she said softly. 'I knew it was how babies were made but not how or why.'

'But what about school? Did you not learn it there?'

'My sisters and I were all withdrawn from those lessons.'

He hadn't heard her mention sisters before.

'Did your friends not tell you about it?' He thought of

his own school friends. As soon as any of them had discovered something to do with women and sex they would immediately relate it to the others like the revealing of some grand secret.

It was a long time before she answered. 'I didn't have any friends.'

His mind reeled. No friends?

All children had friends. They would roam in groups, like attracting like, the popular kids together, the trendy kids together, the cool kids together, the geeks together, the misfits who didn't fit into any particular group coming together like stray cats to form their own pack.

'The other children avoided us.'

'Children can be cruel.'

She nuzzled into his chest and squeezed harder on his hands. 'I look back and I understand why. Compared to them we were strange.'

'How?'

'Well... We had no television for a start, which immediately made us freaks. Our mother cut our hair, always in the same pudding basin style; she made our uniforms and our other clothes too and they were always plain and ugly clothes, which made *us* plain and ugly. I didn't know how to speak to people. I didn't know how to make friends. I had nothing to share or give to make the other children like me and could never have invited them home if I had made friends. Strangers were not welcome in our home. We lived a very controlled, very sparse life.'

Hearing her speak now, Daniele wondered how he could have thought her English. There was a true musical lilt to her voice that he would have heard before if he'd only opened his ears to listen. It was the most beautiful and seductive of voices.

'Did Johann go to your school?'

'We went to an all-girls school. He lived on the same

road as us. I thought he was strange because he always smiled at me.'

'How did you become friends?'

She was silent as she thought about it. 'I don't remember. It evolved over many years. Just secret smiles, you know? We didn't actually talk to each other until we went to high school. His finished before mine and he'd wait for me at my school gate and walk me home. Tessel covered for me so Angela and Kika didn't see. They would have told our parents and I would have been punished.'

'They're your sisters?' he asked, his brain hurting to hear the word 'punished' and not yet ready to ask what she meant by it, his heart thumping as if beating down the heavy hands of impending doom.

What had been the most fulfilling and, yes, he could admit it, emotional experience was turning on its head and dragging him to a place he didn't want to go.

No pillow talk. No confidences exchanged. That's what they'd agreed on.

'Yes. Angela was the oldest, then Kika, then Tessel, then me.'

'Was?' he queried, picking up on the past tense she'd used, his burning curiosity to uncover her secrets overriding the clanging sirens in his head to stop this conversation and go to sleep.

'Are. Is. I haven't seen them in ten years.'

'Since you ran away?'

'Yes. I reached out to Tessel a year after I left and she told me our parents had disowned me. They'd forced the truth out of her and then confronted Johann's parents— they knew my home situation and had given us a little money to help us—and learned we'd got married. Tessel said they burned all the pictures of me and cut me out of all family group photos.'

'So you're still in contact with her? With Tessel?'

'Not any more. I haven't spoken to her since before Johann died.' She raised her head and rested her chin on his chest. 'The last time we spoke she told me about this group she'd joined. When my emails to her started bouncing back I looked into it. It's a cult, a harmless one, I think, if there can be such a thing as a harmless cult, but one that insists on no contact with outsiders. So she ran away too. It just took her longer that me.'

Resting her cheek back on his chest, she sighed. 'It's strange how life turns out, isn't it? Tessel was always the rebellious one. Angela and Kika were very subservient and always obeyed our parents' rules. And there were a *lot* of rules. So damn many of them. It was so easy to break one and not know you were doing it, and Tessel seemed to break them all. You would think she'd have been the one to run away as soon as she could but she didn't, and when she finally did it was escaping one form of imprisonment for another.'

'You think of your parents as jailers?'

'We were their property. You have to understand, we were indoctrinated from birth to obey them. We were terrified of them and for good reason. We knew the consequences for disobedience.'

He swallowed and closed his eyes before asking, 'What were they?'

'It depended on the offence and their mood. If they were in a good mood you might just be forced to sleep in the garden shed for the night. If they were in a bad mood…well.'

'Well?'

'Tessel was once whipped across her back with a belt for bringing mud into the house.' Her fingers tightened on his. 'My mother once stamped on my fingers when I couldn't finish a meal and tried to sneak the scraps into a bin.'

Daniele swore quietly. His stomach was churning so

violently he feared he would be sick. 'How did people not know? Your neighbours?'

'My father was the local doctor. He fixed our injuries when they went too far. Adults thought him eccentric but they respected him. And I think adults tend to be blind. It was the children who knew something was wrong but they didn't know what they were seeing. They just saw a family of freaks.'

Nothing more was said for a long time. Daniele's mind was in a whirl.

He fingered the long strands of her hair. The vibrant colour that he'd always admired suddenly gained in significance. 'When did you start colouring your hair?'

'It was the first thing I did when we got to Amsterdam.' She gave the lightest of laughs but it warmed his blood that had slowly chilled to thick ice while he'd listened to her. 'You should have seen the bathroom when I'd finished. It looked like there'd been a murder.'

And then, before he could react to the quip that had lightened the heavy atmosphere that had enveloped them, she suddenly moved so her thighs straddled him and her face hovered above his.

Her nipples brushed against his chest and, despite everything she'd just revealed and despite having been replete such a short time before, his loins flickered back to life.

She stared intently into his eyes, loaded meaning firing from hers. 'Do you understand why I could never have agreed to this marriage if it had meant I was to be your possession? Us making love doesn't change anything, okay?'

His blood warmed a little more, relief pushing through his veins, yet, strangely, his heart tightened.

The rules they'd established from the outset were still in place.

Their pillow talk hadn't altered that.

But as her mouth closed around his, his last coherent thought before the desire reignited between them was to wonder if the colour she'd chosen to dye her hair had been a deliberate imitation of the colour of deadly creatures warning others that to come too close meant danger.

He wondered if it had been a subconscious signal to the world to keep its distance from her.

CHAPTER ELEVEN

THE NEXT WEEK passed in a flash. With all the work being done in their wing of the *castello*, they spent much of their time together exploring Florence and Pisa, visiting museums and eating long lunches, the nights spent making love with abandon.

They got to know more about each other, practical things, Daniele's architecture, his quest to create homes and buildings that were works of art, sympathetic to the location's heritage yet modern, the perfect blend of old and new. They discussed how Eva could start a not-for-profit consultancy business advising the rich and famous how best to help those in need. It was something they both agreed should be put on the back burner until the *castello* had been transferred into Daniele's name and they knew where they'd make their main home. They talked about so many things but never anything that could be construed as intimate.

It was safer that way.

Eva hadn't planned to tell him about her childhood but now it was done she didn't regret it. It wasn't something she had spoken about since Johann had died and in many ways it had been cathartic. Daniele was her husband. He *should* know about her past even if it was something he'd prefer not to know. It had also been a reminder to herself of her need to keep possession of herself. She would never belong to Daniele or anyone. She would not give him the tools to hurt her.

She was not a fool. Things were great between them at the moment but it was early days. Sooner or later Daniele would get bored and seek new adventures. She would learn when it happened if she was capable of turning a blind eye. If she couldn't she would pack her bags and leave.

She hoped he didn't stray too soon. She hoped he was capable of being faithful until their first anniversary so the charity could get its next huge injection of cash from him.

That's what she told herself. Only in the early hours when she'd wake in the safety of his arms did she hear the voice in her head telling her she was fooling herself if she believed any of that.

None of this stopped her wishing this wonderful honeymoon-like phase didn't have to end, but nothing lasted for ever and six days after they'd become lovers they returned from a matinee performance at the Teatro di Pisa to find Daniele's new office, created by knocking two bedrooms into one, finished.

'It's incredible they did it so quickly and so well,' Eva observed, staring at the teal-painted walls and rows of beautifully carved walnut cabinets and shelves. All that needed to be done was for it to be filled with his stuff.

'That's what you get when you pay your workforce triple time,' he said with the grin she'd come to adore. 'Most of them worked on the hospital in Caballeros and got used to the long hours and the extra cash at the end of the month.'

'It should be completed soon, shouldn't it?'

'The grand opening is in a month.' He pulled a face as he said this, making her laugh.

'Are we going?'

'If we don't, my sister will kill us.'

'What about your mother?'

'Nothing would keep her away from her favourite son's memorial.'

He spoke lightly but something made her think he wasn't jesting.

A swelling in Eva's chest erupted, propelling her to reach out a hand to gently stroke his face. 'I wouldn't know if he was her favourite or not, but I know she adores you.'

His jaw tightened but the smile stayed intact. 'I've never doubted my mother's love.'

Then he took the hand still resting on his cheek and kissed the palm. 'I need to check back into the real world. I need to check with my PA that my business is still in one piece, call my lawyer for progress on the deeds being transferred into my name, and call my accountant to make sure my fortune's still intact.'

'Anything I can do?'

He scrutinised her for a moment, a musing look crossing his face. 'Do you realise it's going to be Christmas in eight days?'

'That hadn't even occurred to me.' Christmas was something she'd only celebrated with Johann. It had been considered a worthless pagan festival by her parents, who had refused to even celebrate their children's birthdays. She and Johann had tried to create their own Christmases on their limited budget and she remembered how childlike their attitude had been towards it. Since he'd died there had been no one to celebrate it with so she'd learned to blank out the month of December, had perfected the art of walking without seeing, so the houses aglow with fairy lights and the stores gleaming with decorations didn't register in her consciousness. She'd even learned to tune out the Christmas songs that belted out of all the stores.

'I'm putting you in charge of decorating our quarters. We'll need a tree—something at least twelve feet tall— and whatever else you think is needed to make the place look festive.'

'I've not had much experience at that,' she warned, although Daniele detected a flash of excitement in the blue eyes he couldn't believe he'd once imagined were cold. Eva's eyes were as warm as her curvy body and her musical voice when she looked at him now.

'Serena can help if you need her.'

'Okay. That could be fun.' Then she asked in a more hesitant voice, 'What do you normally do on Christmas Day?'

'It's the one day of the year I'm nagged to spend with my family,' he said ruefully.

'Will I be coming this year?' There was the same hesitancy in her question.

Daniele look at her closely. He thought back to their talk the first night they'd made love. He would bet the *castello* that Eva had never celebrated Christmas in her childhood.

Who would she have celebrated it with since her first husband had died? He'd been forced to the conclusion that it hadn't been shame at their reasons for marrying that had stopped Eva from inviting anyone to it, but that there had been no one she'd felt close enough with to invite.

She'd had no friends growing up. There were no signs she'd had any since. Not real friends.

Enveloping her into his arms, he held her tightly. 'You're my wife. My mother and sister both adore you and would lynch me if you didn't join us. I'll make some calls and find out what's happening.'

There was more hesitancy in her voice as she asked, 'Do you want me to get presents for them?'

'Would you mind?'

'Not at all. It will be nice to buy them things. They've been very welcoming to me.'

Making a mental note to call his sister and tell her she didn't need to bother buying the family presents on his behalf this year—something she'd been doing for him since she was about thirteen—he wondered what he should buy his wife.

He'd pick Francesca's brain about it. But what he wouldn't do was allow his sister to buy it for him.

Eva deserved something special and she deserved to have her husband choose it for her.

He might not be able to eradicate her childhood memories but he could start creating new ones for her.

There was nothing sophisticated or muted in the way Eva had decorated their living quarters, Daniele mused a couple of days later. She'd taken him at his word and made the place look festive. So festive he could be forgiven for thinking he'd stepped into Santa's Grotto. The Christmas tree reached the high ceiling but he could see hardly any of the fragrant pine because she'd covered practically every inch of it with tinsel and shining baubles. Decorations hung everywhere, fake snow and stars sprayed artistically over all the windows, Christmas-themed throws and cushions on the sofas and their bed, Christmas ornaments filling every other available space. There was no great theme or underlying colour as his mother always ensured in her home, and nothing matched.

It was the gaudiest display ever and the complete opposite of what he'd imagined the usually serious and practical Eva would come up with. It was like someone had let a class of hyperactive toddlers loose on the place.

And he'd never seen a better display. He'd never walked into the *castello*'s living area before and instantly smiled with pleasure.

He'd never made love to a woman under a Christmas tree before either, but he had with Eva.

He kept waiting for her allure to fade but it wasn't happening. Not even walking into the bathroom to find her dyeing her hair had broken the spell she'd woven around him. He'd sat on the bathroom chair and watched, then, when the dye had been in for the allotted time, had rinsed it off for her. When he'd questioned why she didn't go to a hairdresser to do it and had been given the answer that she didn't trust them to get the colour right, he'd got on the phone to a contact to have a salon created for her in one of the spare rooms. When it was done in the New Year she could bring a hairdresser to the *castello* and give them the bottle of colourant.

Two days before Christmas and with Eva having disappeared in one of his cars on another shopping trip, Daniele took the opportunity to go through the brief of an underground house in the Swiss Alps he'd been recently commissioned to produce and construct. It would involve excavating tonnes of earth and…

His phone rang.

He picked it up, saw it was his PA, and turned down the music he had blaring.

'You're supposed to be on leave,' he scolded when he'd put it to his ear.

'Daniele… Have you seen the news?'

Something in her tone immediately put him on the alert. 'What news?'

'An exposé…'

He groaned. This was the last thing he needed, another of his ex-girlfriends cashing in on their brief time together, and immediately thought of Eva. He didn't want to think of her reaction if she should read it.

'Who's sold me out this time?'

His PA cleared her throat. 'It's not an exposé on you. It's your brother.'

'Pieta?' That was most unlikely. She must mean Matteo. His cousin had lived with them as a sibling for many years and people often mistook him for one of them.

'Yes. I'm sorry.'

'Sorry for what?' So his brother had been human after all? Well, so what? Who was he to judge? Who was anyone to judge? His brother was dead. He had no right to reply.

Just thinking that made his brain start to burn.

Who the hell did this woman think she was, selling out a dead man?

'Daniele… Please, just have a look.'

'Which paper's it in?'

'By now it's in all of them. It's everywhere.'

Disconnecting his phone, he reached for his tablet and turned it on.

Thirty seconds later he stared at it, numb with disbelief.

Eva got back to the *castello* much later than she'd anticipated. She'd gone to a specialist music shop in Florence and had ended up spending hours there.

Now all she had to do was hide her gifts with the rest of Daniele's presents in Francesca's room. It was the one room he wouldn't go into on his eternal *castello* modernisation quest. He seemed to earmark one room or another for a new purpose on a daily basis.

Once put away, she closed the door behind her then went to find him.

Their bedroom and his office were empty so she went to the living area.

The moment she stepped over the threshold she came to an abrupt stop.

All the happiness that had been glowing inside her drained away in an instant as she took in the devastation that had taken place.

The Christmas decorations had been ripped down, every single one of them, and all the ornaments smashed. Shards and chunks of porcelain lay strewn across the carpet. A chair lay on its side, two of its legs broken and splintered as if they'd been bashed against something, the bureau upended too, the drawers fallen open and the contents spilled out.

Her immediate thought was that there had been burglars, but then she saw the Christmas tree was still intact and the presents she'd spent so many hours wrapping were all whole under it.

'Daniele?' she whispered into the empty room, suddenly terrified.

As if he'd heard her call, the door that led to the *castello*'s kitchens burst open and Daniele came flying into the room, a quarter-full bottle of something that looked like Scotch in his hand. Or should that be three-quarters empty? For when he noticed her standing there and his eyes met hers, the wildness in them had her convinced that he was steaming drunk.

Staggering barefoot into the room, he said in Italian, 'Good trip?'

Did he not see the mess?

'Daniele, what's happened?'

'What?' He twisted round to inspect the room. 'Oh. Yes. This. Sorry. I lost my head a little. I'll get new decorations tomorrow. I didn't touch the tree,' he added, as if that was a good thing.

Eva couldn't have cared less about the tree. Right then she couldn't care about anything other than her husband who was clearly in some kind of shock. Since she'd left that morning he looked like he'd aged a decade.

'You did this?' she asked, making sure to keep her voice calm and non-threatening. 'Why? Has something happened?'

He nodded vigorously. 'You could say that. Yes. You could. Something. Has. Happened.'

'Do you want to tell me?'

'No.' He took a drink from the bottle and wiped his mouth with his sleeve. 'But you're going to hear about it anyway. You must be the only person in the world who doesn't know.'

'Know what?'

His face contorted into something ugly as he lurched towards her. 'That my perfect brother with the perfect life and perfect wife was gay. My perfect brother was a cheating *liar*.'

Utterly dumbstruck, Eva didn't know what to say or how to react.

That he was being deadly serious was not in doubt.

'Did you hear what I said?' he asked, taking another swig.

'I heard you,' she whispered.

'Do you know what it means?'

She shook her head, although she had a good idea.

'It *means*,' he stressed with venom, 'that my brother was a liar. Mr Perfect who everyone always said I should live up to, who everyone always said was better than me and could do no wrong, was a cheating *liar*.' And with that he swore violently and raised the bottle in the air as if preparing himself to throw it at something.

'Daniele, please, no.' Terrified he was going to hurt himself, Eva rushed to him and grabbed his arm. The muscles were all bunched as he prepared himself to release the bottle.

'Let me go,' he snarled.

'No. If you let go of that bottle now it will fall on me and hurt me. Is that what you want?'

His bloodshot eyes filled with confusion. 'I would never hurt you.'

'Then please, my love, put it down. Don't do any more damage.'

Whether it was her slip-of-the-tongue endearment or the pleading he must have read in her eyes, he relaxed his arm and allowed her to take the bottle from him.

As soon as she had hold of it she threw it onto the sofa, where it immediately spilled its little remaining contents onto the expensive fabric.

Then she took his hands and brought them together and waited until she had his wandering, drunken attention again. He swayed.

'Daniele, will you do me a favour?'

His brow furrowed in a question but he nodded.

'Come to the bedroom with me. I'm worried you're going to fall onto this mess and hurt yourself.'

'Oh.'

'You'll come with me?'

She caught a sudden flash of sobriety. 'Yes.'

He let her lead him out of the living area where she tried to create a pathway where the least amount of debris lay.

Her hopes that she could get him to the bedroom proved forlorn when halfway down the corridor he suddenly slumped against the wall and slid down to the floor.

He raised his knees and put his head in his hands, swearing out loud.

She lowered herself down on the floor to face him.

After a long pause he rested his head against the wall, stretched his legs out so his feet lay on her lap and gave a rueful smile. 'I'm drunk.'

'I know.'

'I'm sorry.'

'Don't be.'

She wrapped her hands around the handsome feet on her lap and gently rubbed them with her thumbs. It amazed her that he hadn't damaged them walking over all that debris.

He sighed and closed his eyes.

They sat like that for an age, pained silence enveloping them, Eva doing nothing more than massaging his feet in the hope it would calm some of the demons plaguing him. Her heart wanted to cry for him.

'Why did he lie?' he asked suddenly, opening his eyes and staring at her as if she could provide the answers he craved.

'Why does anyone lie?' she answered steadily. 'Normally it's because the liar thinks the consequences of the truth are too great.'

'What consequence would there have been for Pieta to tell the truth about who he was?'

'I don't know. The *castello*?'

'If he wanted it that much he could have still married.'

'He did marry,' she pointed out.

'He could have married honestly.' His face contorted again and his hands clenched into fists. 'He was in love with Alberto. They were together for over ten years.'

'Alberto? The man who ran his foundation with him?'

He nodded grimly. 'He's come out to the press. He's told them everything. He has handwritten letters and photos.'

'Why did he come out now?'

'To stop the media hounding Natasha.'

'Pieta's wife? The one who is having your cousin's baby?'

Daniele blinked. Even in the thudding fog of his drunk head it occurred to him that he had never discussed Matteo and Natasha with Eva.

Eva cast him that same gentle look again. 'Francesca told me about them when we went shopping together the first time.'

'You never said.'

She shrugged, her eyes full of compassion. 'I didn't think you wanted to talk about it.'

'I didn't.'

'There you are, then.'

'I called him.'

'Alberto?'

'He told me Natasha only found out about them after

she married. She'd been protecting his secret for his family's sake. For our sake. Do you think that's true?'

'How would I know? I've never met her.'

'Guess.'

'I can't. You know her. You tell me.'

He swallowed and tried to picture his sister-in-law. He'd known her all his life. Pieta had homed in on her the moment she'd turned eighteen then kept her waiting for six years before marrying her. He'd let it be known he'd put off the marriage so she could enjoy her young adulthood before taking the final step when all along it had been so he could continue his affair without the added danger of a nosy wife to catch him out. He'd only married in the weeks before their father died so he could then inherit the *castello* and the rest of the Pellegrini estate.

He took a deep breath in an attempt to quell the nausea roiling violently within him.

'She was protecting us. Not him. She'd waited for him to marry her for six years.'

And Eva, with her gentle touch on his feet, was protecting him now, using nothing more than her fingers and an understanding, non-judgmental calmness of voice.

It came to him that if she'd been there when he'd first discovered the truth he would never have gone on his furious rampage.

'I'm so sorry,' he said, guilt hitting him with force. 'All your decorations.'

She smiled. 'They're only decorations. We can get more.'

He gave a short nod. 'Yes. We can replace them. I can't replace my brother. I can't ask him why he lied.' He took a long breath. 'You know, all my life I've been compared to him. My father would always tell me to be like him. Nothing I did was ever good enough on its own, it always had to be compared to him and his achievements, even when my achievements were better.'

'You were rivals?'

'He was my rival.' He felt the bitterness well up in him. 'But I wasn't his. He had this way of speaking to me like I wasn't a worthy competitor. Without saying a word, he let me know that he could have much more than me if only his time and energy wasn't put into his oh-so-worthy foundation. I hated him.'

It was the first time he'd ever admitted that, not just to another person but to himself.

It felt good to admit the truth.

'I hated him. I hated his patronising attitude. I hated that my family thought the sun shone out of his arse.' Suddenly he looked at the calm face of his wife with fresh eyes. 'But not you. You saw through him.'

She didn't shy away from his stare. 'I thought he was a great man. I still do. But I think you're worth a hundred of him. A thousand of him.'

Her words were as soothing as the feel of her thumbs on his feet.

And just as suddenly as the bitterness had bitten him, a fresh wave of nausea sloshed into its place.

He gazed again at the only person in the world who he could ever talk so freely and openly to as he was at that moment. 'Tell me this, wife, if I hated him so much then why aren't I rejoicing that he's dead? Why do I feel so… bad?'

Her lips pulled together, a bleakness filling her eyes. She opened her mouth then closed it, then carefully moved his feet off her lap and shuffled forward to kneel at his side.

Putting her hands on his cheeks, she stared intently into his eyes and said, 'The reason you feel so bad is because you loved him. I'm afraid you have no choice over that. It's hardwired into you, the same as my love for my parents is hardwired into me. I hate them. I hate what they did to me and to my sisters, but if someone had asked me when I was a child if I wanted them reported to the police or social services I would have said no. I would have been terrified of being taken away from them. I have been free of them for ten years and have never reported their abuses and why? Because for all the damage they did to me I still love them.'

He wanted to laugh at her and tell her she was a fool to love people who had treated her worse than an animal. They didn't deserve her love.

But he thought there was something in what she said. He'd had no choice about loving his brother. Pieta being gone was a pain he had never imagined he could feel.

'I'm sorry for how I treated you that night when I tricked you into a date. I was in a bad place then.' This time he did laugh. 'I didn't know what a bad place I was in. No wonder you told me to get lost.'

She placed the lightest of kisses on his lips. 'Apology accepted. Now, shall we get you to bed before you fall asleep here?'

CHAPTER TWELVE

THREE HOURS LATER, Eva got into bed. She hadn't drawn the curtains around it. Daniele, who was fast asleep beside her, needed air. He'd thrown his clothes onto the floor, taken the painkillers with the glass of water she'd given him then fallen onto his back and gone straight to sleep. He hadn't moved a muscle since. She'd put a fresh glass of water on the bedside table for when he woke in the middle of the night with a raging thirst. Which he would. She had no doubt about that.

Facing him, she stared at his sleeping face and felt another wave of empathy. Those waves just kept coming.

She knew it wasn't the revelation about Pieta's sexuality that had been so hard for him to learn but all the lies his brother had taken to conceal it, all the deception. She could have understood it if the Pellegrinis were old-fashioned in their view of the world but she hadn't seen any evidence of that. Daniele had gay friends—one of them had joined them in Club Giroud and chatted happily about his own wedding plans. Francesca, who had called an hour ago to see how Daniele was and been unsurprised to hear he was passed out on the bed, had sounded completely bewildered by the revelations. Her primary emotion had been hurt that her eldest brother had felt unable to confide in her.

Stroking Daniele's stubbly jaw, Eva closed her eyes to another wave of emotion for her husband.

He hadn't wanted any of this. He'd never wanted to inherit the *castello* and the accompanying estate and had never wanted to marry. He'd done it for his family's sake and had never lied about it. The people he loved knew the truth. He'd never hidden anything from them. He'd never lied to her either. He hadn't fed her a pile of baloney to get her to marry him; he'd been completely open about his reasons. Even the priest who'd married them had known the truth but had been happy to officiate because he'd been content with their promises that they would take the vows they were making seriously.

Daniele had kept all his promises. He hadn't broken a single one.

Another huge pang hit her as she recalled his promise to never love her and she squeezed her eyes even tighter as the pang hit her heart and set it into a pounding boom.

She'd sworn to him she would never fall in love with him. It had been a promise made in the heat of anger when she had looked at him and wanted nothing more than to punch his arrogant, supercilious face. She'd hated him then. Everything about him. But she'd feared her sensory awareness of him, and she had been right to fear it. Making love to him had opened a whole new part of her that had been hidden away from her all her life, an earthy, pleasure-seeking side that was entirely centred round *him*.

She had to remind herself that overwhelming tenderness for the man she had amazing sex with did not mean she was falling in love. Daniele had chosen her specifically for her level head and her ability to contain her emotions and now she needed to use that level head and see things from a logical point of view rather than from an aching romantic viewpoint he would laugh at scornfully if he were to know of it.

The record Daniele was listening to came to a stop. He got up from his office chair and stood at the old-fashioned record player he had on display on a low cabinet, lifted the stylus and carefully placed the record that had been playing in its sleeve, then flipped through the dozens of twelve-inch vinyl albums stacked beside it. Eva had got it all for him. It had been his main Christmas present from her.

On a monetary level it was a drop in the ocean but the thought that had gone into it, and the time and effort she had taken getting it all together made his heart hurt to think about it. He remembered one very brief conversation where he'd told her how much better music sounded on vinyl records and she hadn't just committed it to memory but hunted one down for him *and* all his favourite albums to play on it. It had made his gift of a sports car that was all her own seem trifling in comparison.

Strange, he thought, how the simplest things could make a man feel so damned awful.

Christmas had come and gone with the joyousness of a wake. All the planning and preparation Eva had done for it had come to nothing. Daniele wished she had complained but, in her usual calm way, she had displayed only compassion and understanding, which made him feel even worse.

His mother had confined herself to her bedroom. Losing her beloved husband and favourite beloved son in a year of each other had knocked her badly but she'd forced herself to carry on in the way the Pellegrinis always carried on. Learning her favourite son had been a closet homosexual who had kept the love of his life a secret from her had knocked the last of her stuffing out. She couldn't stop crying.

Eva had said to him privately, gently, that she thought it was the grief of Pieta's death finally hitting her that had her acting like this because this was the first time his mother—all of them—had desperately needed to talk to him and confront him since his death but he wasn't there to either defend himself or ask for their forgiveness. He was dead.

Daniele had given a noncommittal grunt in answer and

bitten back from shouting at her that she didn't know what she was talking about. He'd been on edge around her since he'd woken on Christmas Eve with a thumping hangover and a throat as dry as the Gobi Desert. The glass of water on his bedside table had glimmered at him like a mirage, but it had been no illusion. Eva had thought to put it there for him. Of course she had.

At first memories of his drunken rampage had been hazy, little flickers that had taken their time to come together to create a whole scene. The drink had loosened his tongue. He'd revealed things to Eva that he'd never even admitted to himself and now there was a crater in his guts and a tightness in his chest that wouldn't ease. He'd revealed too much. That's if his memories could be relied upon. He could swear he remembered her addressing him as, 'my love'.

Neither of them had mentioned their talk. She'd enquired about his head and offered to get more painkillers for him but had said nothing about his confession.

His office door opened and the woman he'd been thinking of stepped hesitantly inside.

'Can I speak to you?' she asked, a hint of caution in her musical voice.

The easy closeness that had developed between them in the first three weeks of their marriage had gone. They were unfailingly polite to each other but now it was like they walked on invisible eggshells. He didn't know if this was Eva feeding off his own distance or if she too had realised at the same time as he that they had become too intimate too quickly and that it was time to take a step back and put their marriage on the footing that had originally been intended.

Or maybe his drunken rampage and cruel words about his brother had been the reminder she'd needed that despite the great sex between them and for all her words that he was worth a thousand of his brother, she saw much to dislike in him.

Whatever it was, the distance between them was good.

'Sure. Come in.' He went back to his desk and sat down.

She closed the door then stood with her back to it.

Tucking her hair behind her ear, she looked at him as if weighing up his mood—which she probably was—and said, 'Your sister just called me.'

He shrugged. Francesca and Eva had developed a close friendship. As far as he knew, they spoke every few days.

'She said you're refusing to go to the hospital opening next week.'

Eva saw his jaw clench and her heart sank.

'My sister knows my feelings about it.'

And so did she, although he hadn't said anything about it to her. Daniele no longer spoke to her, not about anything important.

Since he'd woken on Christmas Eve, he'd been a changed man. A distant man. The easy, sexy smile was gone. The witty quips and innuendoes were a thing of the past. Now he just got on with his work and spent hours with his lawyers, trying to get the transferral of the *castello* into his name speeded up. He'd mentioned over dinner the other night that it should be done within days. That had been right before he'd informed her he was going out. He hadn't said where he was going or asked her to join him.

Her pride had refused to let her question him and her pride had made her feign sleep when he'd got into bed hours past midnight.

The only thing they still did together was have sex and even that had taken a different hue. Only when they woke in the middle of the night already in each other's arms did the barriers they'd silently erected between themselves come down and they could make love with the emotional abandon she'd become dangerously used to.

It was as well Daniele had distanced himself from her, she thought, although it made her lungs cramp and her brain burn to think it. It made it easier for her to put her level head on and remind herself of what their marriage agreement was all about, which absolutely was not about emotions or feelings.

Instinct told her Daniele hadn't found another lover yet but she knew it wouldn't be long. A man like him thrilled in the chase. She'd been his prey, he'd caught her, and sooner or later he'd seek his next target.

And when he did…?

The cramp in her lungs extended to her stomach, twisting it with such violence it felt as if someone had put a vice in it.

'I understand why you don't want to go,' she said, choosing her words carefully. 'But you have to.'

This was something she couldn't keep her distance from any longer, not after Francesca had begged her to help. She seemed to be under the impression that Daniele listened to her and had been as cloth-eared as her brother when Eva had tried to correct this impression.

But she wasn't having this conversation for Francesca's sake. She was having it for Daniele's. If he didn't go to the opening he would regret it for the rest of his life. She knew better than to phrase it like that, though. These were waters she'd have to navigate cautiously.

His eyes narrowed dangerously. 'I don't have to do anything.'

'In this case you do. Do you want the world to think you're ashamed of your brother's sexuality?'

'That is *not* what this is about,' he said, a snarl forming on his lips and his hands curling into tight fists.

'I know that.' She refused to drop her stare from his. These were words he needed to hear. 'But that is how it will look.'

'I. Don't. Care. How. It. Looks.'

'This isn't about you.' Although it was to her. 'This is about your family. They need you—your mother needs you. If she's going to put on a brave face to the world's media, she needs your support.'

'She has never needed my support before,' he dismissed tightly.

'How do you know? Have you ever asked her?'

'What?'

'Have you ever asked her if she needs your support, or have you always assumed that because she had your brother and sister to hold her up that she didn't need you too? Because if that was what you thought, you were wrong.'

He half hovered off his chair and leaned forward, speaking as if she were an impertinent child. 'You don't know anything about it.'

'I know she loves you and I know she needs you. Did you know Matteo and Natasha are going?'

'They wouldn't dare.'

Eva breathed in deeply. 'They love each other. They never went behind Pieta's back, although in light of what's come out about your brother, I think they could have been forgiven for it. Your mother is desperate to make amends with them. She's desperate to bring her family back together. She loves you all. She wants to honour Pieta by attending the hospital opening but she needs you at her side.'

'If my mother wants all this then why hasn't she spoken to me about it?'

'Because you refuse to talk about it. Daniele... Your brother deserves this memorial. Whatever he did wrong it doesn't take away the good he did. If his own wife can forgive him and show that forgiveness publicly, then you can too.'

It was as if all the fight went out of him.

He closed his eyes and sank back down on his seat, then bowed his head and dug his fingers into his hair.

Unable to witness his pain—and she knew in her heart that Daniele was in terrible torment—Eva stepped over to him and placed a hand lightly on his shoulder. Swallowing to get moisture into her dry throat, she said, 'I told you when you were drunk that you're worth a thousand of your brother. Prove me right. Be the man I think you are, not the man I thought you were when I first met you.'

Silence filled the room before he answered with a coldness that chilled her. 'I haven't changed, Eva. Whatever you thought or think you know about me, I will never change.' Then he covered her hand resting on his shoulder and pushed it gently away. 'Please excuse me. I have work to do.'

Fighting with all her might to hide her hurt, she managed the smallest of smiles. 'Will you at least think about coming to the opening?'

He jerked a nod and opened a desk drawer. 'I will think about it.'

'Thank you.'

As she walked out of his office, she couldn't help but note that he'd only addressed her by her given name since the day the truth about his brother had come out.

Daniele was as good as his word. Two days later he told her over breakfast that he'd thought about it and would attend the opening of the hospital in Caballeros, which would be the permanent memorial to his brother.

And now here they were, five days after that decision, in a convoy of cars with the tightest of security driving over the potholed narrow Caballeron roads to the hospital itself.

It felt like a lifetime ago since Eva had been in this country but it had hardly been two months. She didn't see any material changes, not until their driver slowed for a security cordon and showed their pass, and they were directed to the hospital car park where she saw what Daniele and his family had created.

In the middle of a city where the electricity failed on a daily basis stood a huge gleaming white building that was obviously a hospital but which had been constructed with a sympathy to the country's Spanish-Caribbean heritage. Hundreds of people stood inside the cordon, the vast majority of them from the press. A little apart from them, heavily guarded by Felipe's men, were Daniele's mother, sister, aunt, cousin and sister-in-law, along with dozens of other faces she didn't recognise but guessed were friends or colleagues of Pieta Pellegrini. She saw the Governor of the city and his entourage too. They were all keeping a wary eye on Felipe, who hadn't let go of his fiancée's hand since their arrival.

On the other side of the cordon stood, literally, thousands of Caballerons, there to witness the opening of a hospital in their desolate country, a place they could give birth in, take their injured children to and be treated for all manner of diseases and ailments.

Daniele held her hand tightly as they joined his family. He embraced his mother and sister then looked at Matteo.

Eva held her breath. She thought she heard everyone else hold theirs too.

Matteo held his hand out to him.

The last time Daniele and Matteo had seen each other had been the fight that had brought Daniele to her refugee camp so she could patch him up.

Then, the flashlight of cameras going off all around them, Daniele ignored his cousin's hand and pulled him into a bear hug that made Eva's belly turn to mush. After this wonderful display of Italian affection, Daniele then stood before his sister-in-law and kissed and embraced her too.

With the Pellegrinis all back together, they stood by the main hospital entrance, beneath the plaque that bore Pieta's name.

A small podium with a microphone had been set up for the speeches that would follow.

To Eva's shock, Daniele stepped onto it first.

Silence fell.

He cleared his throat and darted a glance at her. Her hand at her throat, she gave the briefest of nods.

He spoke in English. 'Ladies and gentlemen, I thank you all for coming here today for the opening of the hospital my brother, Pieta, had planned to build before he was so cruelly taken away from us. My brother was a good, inspirational man who always used the privilege he was born with to help others.'

A murmur rippled through the crowd. Eva didn't need to guess what it was for.

'I'm sure many of you have read the stories about him in recent weeks. They are all true.'

Now the murmurs turned into muffled gasps. No one had expected him to tackle the issue head on.

'He made mistakes. He was human. He lied and he cheated and like every one of us here his blood ran red.'

Now hushed silence fell again.

'I wish—we, his family, we all wish—that he'd had the courage to be open with us about his sexuality. Nothing would have changed. We would have still loved him. We *do* still love him and we want nothing to detract from the good work my brother did or detract from the immense courage he showed in the rest of his life. Without him, without his vision, without his refusal to simply accept that some things could never be done, none of us would be here today and this ground we stand on would be the wasteland it once was. This hospital was Pieta's response to the hurricane that devastated this country and I know that if there's a heaven he'll be the happiest soul in it to see what's been accomplished in his memory.'

Then he nodded his thanks to his captive audience and stepped off the podium and went straight back to Eva's side, taking her hand and holding it tightly.

'That was amazing,' she whispered, so full of pride she struggled to get the words out.

He squeezed a response and then they both watched as the self-important corrupt Governor took his place on the podium.

Her heart was beating too loudly to hear anything else that was said.

It wasn't just Daniele's acceptance of his brother and the past that had her so choked, it was the way he held her hand.

Other than in the bedroom, there had been no affection between them since Christmas and only now that he was showing it again did she realise how badly his withdrawal had hurt her. She'd carried on as best she could, pretending to herself that it didn't matter, that this was the marriage she'd signed up to, but now, his fingers locked through hers, her pride for him as real and as filling as anything she'd ever known, the truth hit her like a cold slap.

She didn't want the marriage she'd signed up for. She wanted the real thing. She wanted to have a dozen of his babies and raise them with him. She wanted to watch his hair turn from dark to grey. She wanted to see the lines that had begun to etch his face deepen into grooves. She wanted to hold his hand for ever.

'Are you okay?'

She blinked out of the trance she'd fallen into.

The speeches were over and Daniele was staring at her with the creased brow that would one day turn into the groove she wanted to be there to see.

She needed to smile some reassurance at him but the muscles in her face didn't want to work.

'I'm fine. Just a little overwhelmed.' No, not a little overwhelmed. *Completely* overwhelmed, by her feelings and by the sheer terror making her skin chill and her blood feel like ice.

She'd been frightened before, many times, but never had she felt fear like this.

She'd done the worst thing she could have possibly done and fallen in love with him.

How could she be so *stupid* and make herself so vulnerable as to love someone who could never love her back?

And then she looked at the worry in his eyes. Even if he didn't love her, he did feel something for her. Didn't he…?

He cupped her cheek. 'Do you still want to go to the camp?'

She'd mentioned that she'd like to visit the children there and see how everyone was getting on. He'd suggested she go after the memorial as they'd be flying back to Italy in the morning. He'd then surprised her by asking if she wanted him to go with her. Thinking he should spend the time with his family, she'd reluctantly said no. The Pelligrinis would fly to the neighbouring island of Aguadilla and she would join them in a few hours. It was all arranged. Felipe had arranged for three of his men to go with her. She'd laughed at the idea of having bodyguards until Daniele had reminded her, with more force than he usually spoke with, that she would only go to the camp with armed protection at her side, that she needed to remember she was a wealthy woman married into a famous family and so would have a price on her head.

Remembering that insistence made her wonder again if it was possible his feelings for her had developed as hers had for him. Now that all the stress that had been hanging over him had gone, could they look at creating a proper future together, as a real husband and wife? Was there a chance for her, for them, to be happy?

Eva raised herself onto her toes and kissed him lightly on the mouth. 'I'm sure. Go be with your family. I'll only be a few hours behind you.'

His eyes bored intently into hers. 'Promise me you'll be careful.'

'I promise.'

Then he kissed her, his first real kiss in so long that she felt she could cry from the joy of it.

Tonight, she promised herself as she got into the waiting car that would take her to the camp. Tonight she would talk properly with him. She would tell him her feelings and see if they had a true future together.

CHAPTER THIRTEEN

'WHAT ARE YOU so worried about?'

Daniele turned his head to find his sister standing by his side.

'Eva's still not here.'

He was sitting at a table near the entrance in one of the Eden Hotel's bars, a huge glittering room with an open wall that led out to the moonlit beach.

Francesca took the seat beside him. He could sense her rolling her eyes. 'She messaged you an hour ago to say she would be late. A delay at the airport, wasn't it?'

He nodded. When they'd made their plans to leave Caballeros for Aguadilla, they hadn't factored in that scores of press would also be fleeing the country en masse. No one with any sense would stay in Caballeros any longer than necessary, not unless they were compassionate people like his wife, who would still be working in the refugee camp there if he hadn't paid her to marry him. The airport was backlogged with aeroplanes trying to take off.

'She'll be here soon enough.'

'Her phone's battery was going flat.' If Eva needed him she wouldn't be able to get in touch. Anything could happen to her and wouldn't know until it was too late.

He should have insisted on going to the camp with her but at the time it hadn't sounded at all unreasonable for her to go without him so long as she had adequate protection.

'So? Seb and a couple of his men are with her. Nothing's

going to happen to her so stop worrying.' Seb was Felipe's right-hand man and ex-British Special Forces.

Francesca pointed at their mother, who was having a tearful but animated conversation with a noticeably pregnant Natasha. Their aunt Rachele was chatting with Matteo, who was staring at her with barely concealed bemusement. From her wildly gesticulating arms and the frizzing of her hair, Aunt Rachele was already two sheets to the wind. 'I'm so glad we've all made amends. I still feel guilty about cutting them off.'

'Don't. You didn't know.'

She sighed. 'No. I didn't. I should have known, though.'

'What? That Pieta was gay?'

'No, silly. I meant that Matteo wouldn't have touched Natasha if he hadn't had such strong feelings for her, and Natasha would never have started an affair with Matteo if she were grieving for Pieta like a real wife.'

'What's a real wife supposed to mean?'

'One who loves her husband and is loved in return. The way Felipe and I feel for each other and the way you and Eva feel for each other.'

'Eva and I don't feel anything for each other, not in the way you mean.'

'Don't pretend, Daniele. I've seen the way you look at her. You can't tell me you're not developing feelings for her.'

His heart made a sudden thump against his ribs. 'We get along well,' he said stiffly. 'But that's the extent of it. We were very firm about what we wanted our marriage to be and it's not one like you're suggesting and nor will it ever be.'

'What's that smell?'

'What smell?' he asked, perplexed.

'Oh. I know what it is. It's bull.'

'Francesca…'

She ignored the warning tone in his voice. 'You're falling in love with her.'

'How much have you drunk? Love and romance are for fools. I know that and Eva knows that. We agreed on the rules when we agreed to marry.'

'Rules are made to be broken.'

'Not in this instance. I'm not in love with her and I never will be.'

'If you say so.'

'I do.'

'Shall I tell Felipe you think he's a fool? He's romantic. And he loves me.'

'Either we talk about something else or you can find someone else to annoy.'

'Am I getting under your skin?'

'Yes.'

She laughed. 'How's Eva getting on with the Maserati you got her for Christmas?'

'Francesca...'

'Drop the threatening tone, you big bully. I've changed the subject.'

He had to laugh. His sister was incorrigible. He had no idea how Felipe put up with her. Eva adored her too.

He sucked in a breath.

He didn't know how he would have got through that speech without Eva standing there with her silent but heartfelt support. Just that one small nod of her head and the glistening in her eyes had been enough for the words to pour out.

But for his sister to suggest he was falling in love with her was ridiculous.

There was a light tap on his shoulder.

Daniele whipped his head round and found Eva standing behind him. She must have come in through the side door.

She gave a smile that didn't meet her eyes. 'Sorry I'm late. The airport was in chaos.'

He got to his feet and looked closely at her. She was as white as a sheet, the starkness of her pallor contrasting strongly with the red of her hair and the black trouser suit she wore. 'Are you okay? You look like you've seen a ghost. Did Seb and his men look after you?'

'They were great, thank you, but I've got a really bad headache. Have you got our room key? I hope you don't mind but I'm going to go to bed.'

'I'll come with you.'

'*No.*' Her sharpness took him aback. She gave another smile and said in a softer tone, 'Sorry. Please, stay with your family. I just need some sleep. I'll be fine.'

With great reluctance he gave her the spare key. 'We're in the same suite as last time.'

'The suite you bribed me into marrying you in?' There was no malice in her tone but still he looked closely again at her. She really did look ill.

'I'll be up soon.'

'Okay.' Then she leaned over to Francesca and kissed her cheek. 'I'm sure I'll see you at breakfast.'

She walked away without giving Daniele a kiss.

He met Francesca's worried stare.

'She's had a long day,' he said, unsure if his explanation was for his sister's benefit or his own.

For once Francesca kept her mouth shut. 'I'll get us some more drinks.'

When Daniele made it to the suite only his bedside light was on. Eva was curled up under the covers on her side of the bed, her eyes closed, her breathing deep and even.

He made as little noise as he could so as not to disturb her but even as he climbed under the sheets with great care, he couldn't help but feel certain that she was wide awake.

* * *

Eva opened her eyes and stared at the dark wall before her. From the sound of his breathing, Daniele had fallen asleep. One of his hands rested on her hip and it was taking everything she had not to shove it away. It had taken everything she had not to flinch when he'd first put it there.

He didn't love her and he never would.

She'd heard it from his own mouth.

I'm not in love with her and I never will be.

You didn't get clearer than that.

How could she have been so careless? Daniele had chosen her because he'd believed she would never fall in love with him. He'd been so abundantly clear about his feelings he might as well have etched it in wood.

Staying with him was out of the question. Now that she knew the truth about her feelings, how could she sleep with him every night and listen to his intimate caresses that would always fall short of the words she burned to hear? Without love, there was nothing to glue them together. There would be nothing to stop his eye from wandering and nothing to stop her heart smashing into pieces to witness it.

She couldn't do it. She couldn't take the pain.

As soon as they got back to the *castello* she would pack her things and leave.

The flight back to Pisa airport felt like the longest flight Daniele had ever taken. His mother and aunt travelled with them in his jet but not even their presence could push out the feeling of impending doom that had lodged in his gut.

Eva had woken with the same headache that had seen her take herself to bed so early the night before. An hour into the flight she'd excused herself to get some more sleep in their bedroom.

She insisted it was only a headache but he was certain she was lying. He would have to wait until they got home and had some privacy before shaking whatever was troubling her out of her. Whatever it was, it spelt trouble. He could feel it in his marrow.

So while she slept, he passed the time playing cards with his mother and aunt. He only learned the two sprightly women were keen poker fiends after they'd cleared him out of all his cash.

He was coming to realise there was lots about his mother he didn't know and, despite his worry about Eva, he found himself enjoying this time with her.

He didn't know if Eva was right that his mother had always needed him but he knew that right then they were enjoying each other's company even while the guilt at all the neglect he'd shown her throughout his adult life pecked at him like an angry woodpecker.

So many thoughts were crowding in his head he was in danger of getting a headache of his own. About to make his excuses and crawl into bed with Eva, his mother dug into the giant handbag she carried everywhere and pulled out a travel-sized game of backgammon.

'Do you want to see if you can beat me at this?' she asked, her eyes gleaming with challenge.

His aunt Rachele cackled wickedly.

Never one to resist a challenge, even if it came from the sixty-six-year-old woman who'd given birth to him and her younger sister, Daniele cleared the table of the cards. And soon found himself thrashed at the game by both of them.

It was mid-afternoon when they landed back in Pisa. His driver was there to collect them. They dropped his mother and aunt home first and then, finally, he was alone with Eva.

'How are you feeling?' he asked her.

'I'm getting there.'

Before he could question her further, she suddenly asked, 'Has the *castello* been transferred into your name yet?'

'All done. I received official confirmation yesterday when you were at the camp.' His lawyer had emailed him. 'I've got a number of calls to make when we get in and then I'm going to take you out.'

She shrugged her shoulders.

'And while we're out you're going to tell me exactly what's wrong with you. And no more lies about a headache.'

'I haven't lied about a headache,' she answered listlessly.

'But there is something troubling you.'

She didn't answer but as they'd arrived home, he told himself it could wait for half an hour while he got his affairs in order. He could then give her his undivided attention without fear of interruption. He would take her out somewhere private and neutral, switch his phone off, insist she turn hers off too, and get her to open up.

It would also give him time to prepare himself...

Suddenly it occurred to him that she could be pregnant. They hadn't discussed having children since that meeting in his suite in Aguadilla when he'd bribed her into marrying him. She'd scorned at the idea of having his children then but everything had changed since then and they'd never used contraception...

He was no pregnancy expert but was sure, having heard from friends with offspring, that tiredness was a big thing in the early stages. It wasn't beyond the realms of possibility for loss of skin colour and headaches to also be factors, was it?

If she was pregnant, he'd have to learn fast.

Holed up in his office while Eva disappeared to their bedroom to shower and change, Daniele called his lawyer and then checked in with Talos Kalliakis to firm up the dates for the renovation of the concert hall Talos owned in Paris.

Him, a father. With Eva's brains and looks their child could be anything in the world. An astronaut. A brain surgeon. A Michelin-starred chef. Anything.

'Daniele, did you hear what I said?' came Talos's gruff tones down the line.

'Sorry. I was miles away. What did you say?'

'Amalie's next to me and is insisting I arrange a date for us to get together. She wants to meet Eva.'

'That sounds great. Let me get my diary.' He refused to trust modern technology when it came to his diary and put all his appointments and meetings in a thick leather-bound tome.

Now, where had he put it?

Spotting it on the sideboard by his record player, he got up from his seat. Just as he stretched his fingers out to grab it, something caught his eye from outside.

Abandoning the diary, he walked to the window, which overlooked the courtyard, and looked out.

Eva was putting a suitcase in the boot of the car he'd brought her.

All thoughts of his conversation forgotten, he dropped his phone and banged on the window.

'Eva!'

She looked around, clearly trying to see where the noise had come from.

He banged on it again. If he used any more force the glass would shatter.

Now she saw him.

Even with the distance between them he saw the panic in her eyes.

Never in his life had his fingers been as useless as they were right then as he tried to open the latch of the window.

She'd closed the boot shut and was rushing to the driver's side when he finally threw the window open and hollered out, 'Don't you dare go anywhere. Do you hear me? Stay right where you are.'

Then he ran, through the corridors, down the stairs, through more corridors, every step he took the certainty growing that by the time he reached the courtyard she'd be gone.

She wasn't gone. And neither had she moved.

'Where are you going?' he demanded, racing over to her and snatching the car keys from her hand.

But he already knew the answer.

The answer had been with him since she'd arrived at the hotel last night as white as a sheet and throughout the long night when she had slept like a statue beside him. He'd just refused to see it.

'Away.'

'Away where? For how long?'

He knew the answer to the latter question too.

She closed her eyes and rubbed a knuckle on her forehead. 'Daniele, I can't do this any more. The *castello*'s in your name. It can't be taken away from you. It's safe with your family. You don't need me any more. I'm free to leave.'

'Without saying goodbye? Without even a word of explanation? You were just going to leave?'

'I've left a note for you in our bedroom.'

His hand clenched around the keys, fury shooting through him and overriding the dread that had clutched at his throat when he'd looked out of his window and known exactly what she was doing. 'Well, that makes everything fine. You left me a note'

'Please, Daniele, don't make this any harder for me than it already is. Give me the keys and go back inside.'

'You want the keys? Come and get them. But you're

not going anywhere until you tell me why you're prepared to up and leave without a word to me, and don't you dare mention that bloody note. I've never thought you a coward before. Tell me to my face why you would treat me with such contempt.'

'Me treat *you* with contempt?' She rubbed her forehead again then raised her eyes to the sky. When she lowered them and fixed them on his, the panic and fear he'd seen in them had gone. Now they blazed. '*Me*? How you have the nerve to say that after the way you spoke about me to your sister...'

'What are you talking about?'

'I heard you,' she snarled. 'I heard everything you said. *Love and romance are for fools. I'm not in love with her and I never will be.* You said it. You said that about *me*.'

'So what? That's what we agreed on when we—'

'To hell with what we agreed!' she screamed, charging forward to thump his chest. 'This is why I wanted to escape without seeing you. I knew you'd be blasé about it, just as I knew I wouldn't be able to bear to hear you dismiss what we have to some stupid agreement we made.' She thumped at his chest again. 'You thought you'd married some emotionless bitch who would never be so stupid as to fall in love with you. *Love and romance are for fools. I know that and Eva knows that. We agreed on the rules when we agreed to marry.*'

Her mimicry over, she stepped back, visibly shaking, her face twisted with a strange combination of grief and fury that it hurt him to see. 'I've broken the rules. I've screwed up. I've fallen in love with you and I do not want to pretend happy marriages any more. I want a real happy marriage. I want you to love me. Can you love me? Can you?'

She threw her words at him as a challenge.

'Eva...'

'Of course you can't. I heard you say it. You're emotionally spineless.'

Her insult stoked his anger at what she was doing and his incomprehension. 'You call me emotionally spineless when you're the one running away?'

'I'm not running, I'm leaving.'

Like that made any difference whatsoever.

'You *always* run away. You ran away from your parents and then when you lost Johann you ran away from your life, and now you're running away from me, and you know why? Because you're too much of a coward to stay and fight.'

'How was I supposed to fight my parents? I was a *child*!'

'Running from them taught you the only way to cope is by running away.'

'Well, seeing as you're now a self-appointed shrink, maybe you could tell me what kind of life I was supposed to fight for after Johann. What life did I have? Who did I have? I'd cut myself off from my family. Johann's family had emigrated to Australia. I had no real friends. So you tell me what life it was I was fighting for.'

'*Your* life! Not a life hiding away in a Third World country shunning friendships and relationships.'

'Oh, so now you're an expert on relationships as well as a shrink? You're the one who's spent their entire life shunning relationships, not me, too busy trying to best your brother in everything you did and prove your worth to the family that has always loved you, living the playboy life, showing off in your fast cars and your jets and your yachts and hand-stitched clothes to want anything deeper or meaningful. Everything's disposable for you, including me!'

His fury coiled into such rage he shook with the violence of it. 'You've gone too far.'

'The truth hurts, doesn't it?' she spat. 'A nice, simple

marriage with a woman with the emotional capacity of a goldfish, that's all you can cope with, isn't it? Well, sorry to disappoint you but it turns out I'm a lot more emotional than you thought. Sorry I'm not level-headed, sensible Eva. Turns out I actually do have feelings and unless you can return them then there is nothing for me to fight for so I suggest you give me those car keys and let me go.'

'Eva…' He took what felt like the longest, deepest breath of his life. If he didn't get hold of his anger right now there was every chance he would throw her over his shoulder and march her back inside and lock her in the cellar.

'Unless you can tell me that you love me or that there's a chance you could one day love me, I don't want to hear another word.'

The pounding in his chest vibrated through every part of him, from the soles of his feet to the hair on his head, the noise so loud he could hardly think straight. 'How can I make a promise like that? I want you. I like and respect you. Isn't that enough?'

'Not for me it isn't. I want everything. I want your babies. I want to grow old with you.'

'I want, I want, I want,' he mimicked. 'Everything's about what you want, isn't it? Where does what I want come into it?'

'Well what do you want?'

'The marriage we agreed on!'

'Then that's too bad because that's not what I want. And seeing as you don't want to hear what I do want, I'll tell you what I don't want. I don't want to waste the best years of my life pining for you and wishing like a lovesick fool for you to feel things you're not capable of feeling. I might not have much but I do have my self-respect. Now, for the last time, give me the keys.'

'Fine.' He threw them as hard and as far as he could,

at the other side of the car from where she stood. 'You want the keys, then you go and get them. You want to leave then be my guest. I never wanted a needy wife in the first place.'

CHAPTER FOURTEEN

HATE AND FURY filling her so much she could vomit, Eva scrambled on the cold ground for the keys to her escape while Daniele shoved his hands in his pockets and strolled back into the *castello* without a backward glance. All that was missing was a cheery whistle.

Hands shaking so much she had to put one on top of the other to insert the key into the ignition, it took three attempts to turn the engine on.

The sound of the wheels screeching as she sped out of the courtyard was extremely satisfying.

She must have been mad to think she loved him. Must have been. How could anyone love a bastard like Daniele Pellegrini? He was cruel beyond belief.

Why couldn't he have just let her go without making a fuss? He was the one who wanted to stick to their original deal, and their original deal had been that she could leave without any issue, any time she wanted. Sure, he'd asked her to explain her decision if she ever did decide to leave, and she'd done that. She'd left him a letter.

How dared he accuse her of cowardice and of running away? He was the coward, not her, the selfish, egotistical…

Almost too late, she saw the tight hairpin bend mere yards ahead and slammed her foot on the brake. The car skidded and there was one long moment that seemed to last for ever, when she was certain the car was going to fly off the road with such force that not even the metal barrier would stop her hurtling down the steep olive grove on the other side of it.

The barrier did its job.

When she finally had the car under control and had brought it to a stop, both her knees were jerking manically. She caught a glimpse of her reflection in the rear-view mirror and saw her face was as white as her knuckles holding onto the steering wheel for dear life.

A little ahead of her was a passing place and somehow she managed to steer the car to it, crawling at a snail's pace in fits and spurts.

Then she turned the engine off and rested her head back, taking deep shuddering breaths into her petrified body.

The passenger door had buckled under the impact of the collision with the barrier.

But no matter how many breaths she took it wasn't enough for her to keep it together a minute longer. The first tear spilled out and landed on her jumper with a splash, the second and third falling in quick succession until she was crying so hard her eyes were blinded and her heart felt like it was ripping out of her.

Eva had left her note on the dressing table.

Daniele snatched it up, scrunched it into a tight ball, and threw it into the fire.

He didn't care what she'd written. She'd said everything she wanted to say. They'd both said everything that needed saying.

Good riddance to her.

It was just a shame she'd only had the time to pack one suitcase before running away like the yellow-bellied coward he'd never thought she could be. Her dressing room was still filled with the clothes he'd paid for.

He stared at them for a long time then slowly backed out

of the dressing room, his hands clenched in fists to stop himself from grabbing it all and shredding it into rags.

It felt like he had a living being inside him, twisting and biting into his guts, and it needed purging and killing *now*.

He'd hardly drunk a drop of alcohol since his drunken exploits when he'd learned the truth about his brother; even yesterday in the hotel after the memorial he'd limited himself to only a couple. Now seemed the perfect time to remedy that, and while he was remedying it, he could celebrate having his freedom back.

Yes, that's what he would do. He would celebrate his regained freedom. He'd get changed and go to Club Giroud...

Before he could take more than two paces back to his bedroom, his phone rang in his pocket.

He pulled it out and was disconcerted to find his hands were shaking.

His heart sank to his feet to see it wasn't Eva's name that flashed up.

Why would he want her to call? he asked himself bitterly. For someone who professed to be in love with him, she clearly didn't think he was worth enough to stay and fight for. She didn't think what they had was worth fighting for.

If it had been anyone but his mother, he would have ignored the call but he couldn't ignore her. He'd spent enough of his adult life avoiding her calls.

She wanted to know if Eva was feeling any better.

Opening his mouth to say, 'I don't know and I don't care. Eva's gone and she's never coming back,' he instead found himself saying, 'Yes, she's much better.'

Eva was so much better that she'd driven away with a parting screech of tyre for good measure.

'Good,' his mother said. 'I was worried about her.'

'You have nothing to worry about.' He quickly changed

the subject, swallowing back the monster in his guts that had reared up again.

The chatted for a couple more minutes before he said, 'I need to go now, Mamma.'

He couldn't remember the last time he'd addressed her so informally.

'Okay, my son. I'll see you soon. I love you.'

'I love you too,' he whispered.

Disconnecting the call, he closed his eyes.

When had he and his mother last verbalised their love for each other? He honestly could not remember.

For so many years he'd practically demonised her in his own head, just as he'd demonised his father.

He'd let his semi-estrangement from his father prevent him from being there for him when he'd died and it was something he regretted more and more as time passed. All those years when his father had been ill and still Daniele had kept his distance.

He slumped onto the floor, dimly aware this was almost the same spot he'd slumped down at before when he'd been drunk and Eva had been so compassionate and attentive in her care of him.

Eva was right. He *was* selfish.

The only member of his family he'd ever been close to was his sister and that was because she was impossible not to love and, he had to admit, a bit of a wayward rebel just as he'd been but with different things to rebel against.

What had his parents ever done for him to create such distance from them? Comparisons to his brother? Encouragement for him to be more like his brother? Chastisement for the times his exploits had brought shame on them?

The feeling that nothing he did would ever be good enough for them?

What about all the good times, and there had been many of those. His mother's face lighting up when he'd walked into her private hospital room as an eleven-year-old meeting his brand-new baby sister for the first time. His mother had made room on her bed for him to sit beside her so she could cuddle him tightly to her.

And what about the time his father had taken a teenage Daniele, and only Daniele, to the Monza track for a day driving at high speed, the pair of them racing each other like lunatics.

It had been too easy to push aside the good memories and embrace only the bad.

His father was dead. It was too late to make his peace, but it wasn't too late for him and his mother. She was a loving woman. She had her flaws but who didn't? Daniele had so many that Eva had spat them all at him just a short while ago.

He'd married Eva for the sake of his family's happiness and peace of mind. He'd never cared for the *castello* and would have been happy for it to be sold off.

Through Eva he'd learned to love the cold castle where they'd made their home and now he found himself wanting to be embraced back into the bosom of the family he'd neglected for so long.

Had the distance between him and his parents been a creation of his own making, driven by his jealousy and single-minded rivalry with his brother? Because surely it was his relationship with Pieta that had clouded every other relationship he'd ever had; that feeling of always being second best.

Eva never made him feel second best. When she looked at him she saw him whole. She knew him better and more intimately than anyone else had ever done and still she loved him.

Eva loved him.

Eva had driven out of the courtyard like a woman possessed…

A sudden image of her car lying in a crumpled heap struck pure terror into his veins, followed by an eruption of emotion so big the waves rippled out of him; the truth he'd refused to see flashing in colours so bright he could no longer deny them.

Eva loved him.

And he loved her.

Snatching his phone, he dialled her number—he'd learned it by heart—but found it went straight to voicemail. She'd either turned it off or hadn't bothered to recharge the battery.

He scrambled to his feet and raced around, looking for a set of car keys.

The first ones he located were for the Ferrari, and he ran to it with lungs fit to burst.

He had to find her. He couldn't let her go. He couldn't.

His clever, serious, compassionate, passionate, beautiful wife *loved* him.

What they hell had he been thinking, letting her drive away?

Which way had she gone? Left to Pisa or right to Florence?

Instinct told him she would have gone left to Pisa. She was familiar with its airport.

Yes, that's where she'd gone.

He blinked the image of her crumpled in her car from his mind. If he let it take that route he would go mad long before he found her.

Fighting the need to thrash the hell out of his Ferrari, he nevertheless raced through the winding roads, leaving a trail of dust behind him.

Ten minutes into his drive and he only just remembered to brake in time to steer round the tight hairpin bend everyone familiar with this stretch of road knew as the Death Bend, for obvious reasons.

Fresh tyre tracks lay on it, evidence that someone had had a near-miss here very recently...

His heart lodged fully in his throat, he steered round the straight and slowed even more.

Then his heart just stopped.

The barrier that was there to stop cars hurtling down the steep olive grove had a contortion in it that hadn't been there when they'd driven back from the airport earlier.

Someone had recently—very recently—crashed into it.

But where was the car?

Eva had run out of tissues with which to blow her nose.

She couldn't stop crying. Every time she thought she was all cried out and capable of driving, fresh tears would fall. All she had left to cry into was a napkin she'd scavenged from the bottom of her handbag.

But she couldn't stay here. The sun was starting to set and she needed to find her way to the airport on roads she still wasn't completely familiar with in a car she loved but still hadn't quite got to grips with.

She had the rest of her life to mourn.

Taking one more deep inhalation, she turned the engine back on and gritted her teeth.

Her heart might feel it had been ripped out of her but that didn't mean she was suicidal. On the contrary.

She wanted to live. And that meant driving without tears blinding her.

Her feelings for Daniele had crystallised during her few hours back at the camp in Caballeros. So many of the children and teenagers had come over to say hello and embrace her, Odney hunting her down specifically to show off his number three ranking in the colourful ball phone game. The few senior members of staff at the camp at the time had been thrilled to see her—a rich husband who'd donated three million dollars in recent months was bound to make her popular with *them*. But none of her regular colleagues, who knew nothing about Daniele's donation, had gone out of their way to say hello.

She'd never realised the distance she'd created between her colleagues and herself. She'd always thought they got along well, and they *had* but only in a professional sense. She'd turned down their social offers so many times that they'd stopped asking her. Her weekends off had always been spent alone in a cheap hotel room.

Daniele had brought the sunshine into her life without her even realising.

How had she lived without that sunshine? But, then, she hadn't been living, had she? Ever since Johann had died she'd been alone in the world and simply functioning.

Daniele had made her feel again, all the things she'd been so frightened of because having real emotions and feelings for people meant you could get hurt.

She was hurting now, hurting more than she'd ever hurt before in her life, yet, somehow, the sunshine he'd blessed her with felt like a gift and she knew if she drove the sunshine out of her again and slipped back into the darkness she would stay in that black hole for ever...

Slamming her foot on the brake, she brought her car back to a stop.

What did she mean, *if* she drove the sunshine out again?

She was driving this car. She was driving it away from Daniele and away from the sunshine. The sun would still beat down on her but it wouldn't beat as strongly. She would never feel it soak into her skin and into the very heart of her without him.

And she wasn't driving away, was she?

She was running away.

Daniele was right. She was a coward. She'd thrown her feelings at him and then thrown a tantrum because he hadn't returned them. She'd already told herself what response to expect from him, had overheard his talk with his sister and convinced herself that what he'd said was the truth and he would never love her.

But what about the truth in the loving, possessive way he made love to her? Or the truth in the way he looked at her and valued her as a person as well as his lover? Or the truth that he had kept every promise he'd ever made to her?

Wasn't all that worth fighting for?

A car hooted loudly as it swerved past her, jolting her out of her trance.

She needed to go back.

Spinning the car round, she sped back along the road she'd just travelled, having to control herself to keep only just above the legal limit.

Please be there, Daniele, she prayed. *Please be at home…*

She screeched the brakes again as she flew past the passing place she'd only recently steered the car away from.

She recognised the car that was parked exactly where she had so recently parked.

She recognised the man looking over the barrier, a distance ahead of the car.

Only just remembering to use her mirrors to make sure no one was approaching her from behind, she reversed sharply and slid her car into the tight space in front of his.

Throwing herself out, she saw his long legs were already marching towards her.

And then her own legs, which so desperately wanted to run to him, turned to jelly.

She couldn't take a step. She couldn't work her vocal cords to make a sound.

It didn't matter.

Daniele was before her in moments, his face grim and twisted. He didn't hesitate, simply grabbed hold of her and pulled her to him to crush her against his chest, holding her so tightly that she couldn't breathe.

'Don't you ever do that to me again,' he said into her hair, speaking in a voice she'd never heard before. 'Do you hear me? Don't you *ever* leave me.'

Managing to dislodge herself enough to look up at him, she realised with complete shock why his voice sounded so different.

Daniele was crying.

He took her face roughly in his hands and brought his down to hers, his salty tears falling onto her cheeks.

'I thought you were *dead*.' His voice broke completely. 'I saw the damage to the barrier and thought you'd gone over.'

And then he was kissing her, her mouth, her cheeks, her nose, her eyes; smothering her, the kisses born of desperation and relief. Then with an oath he crushed her to him again, one hand tight around her waist, the other wrapping itself in her hair.

'I have never been so scared in my life. I thought I'd lost you.'

'Never,' she whispered, her words muffled against his sweater. 'I'm sorry for—'

'Don't,' he cut her off. '*Dio*, Eva...'

For a long time, they just stood there clinging to each other, Daniele's heart thudding heavily against her ear, her heart thudding heavily against his abdomen, his mouth pressing into the top of her head.

'You're mine, Eva Pellegrini,' he whispered. 'You belong to me and I will never let you go again.'

She'd never thought she would want to hear those words but hearing them from Daniele's lips made her heart swell with such joy the tears started falling again.

'And I belong to you,' he continued in the same low voice. 'My heart is yours to do with as you will. You're my wife and I love you. I would do anything for you. Anything. I want you to have my babies and I want to wake up beside you every day and know you are mine and that we belong together. I want to wear your ring on my finger as you wear mine. I'm sorry for the cruel things—'

'Don't,' she said, this time the one to cut *him* off. No explanations were needed. They knew each other too well for that. 'We both said cruel things.' She raised herself to breathe into his neck. 'I love you.'

'Not as much as I love you.'

'More.'

'Not possible.'

He took her face in his hands again and their tears mingled as his lips found hers and he kissed her with such tender passion that it was as if the fading sun had given one last burst of energy to shine a spotlight on them.

When a car drove past them and honked loudly at their entwined figures, Daniele broke the kiss with a laugh.

'Let's go home, wife.'

'As long as I'm with you, I don't care where we go, husband.'

EPILOGUE

THE FAMILY WING of the *castello* was completely over-run with children. Everywhere Daniele went he seemed to tread on some toy or other and had grinned wickedly when he'd seen his cousin Matteo walk barefoot onto a tiny building block.

Daniele's three children were playing hide-and-seek with their cousins. After the game of War Against the Girls, this seemed safer. His sister's son Sergio, a sturdy six-year-old with his mother's bossy nature, had teamed up with Daniele's middle child, Pieta. The two imps had stalked then cornered the two older girls, Matteo and Natasha's shy daughter Lauren, and his and Eva's oldest daughter Tessel, and fired a round of rubber bullets at them. There had been lots of screams and name calling after that.

Those damn rubber bullets got everywhere. He wondered if his mother knew she had one stuck in her hair.

He dreaded to think what kind of state the place would be in tomorrow when all the Christmas presents had been opened.

Sneaking out of the living room, he dodged small children and threw himself into his bedroom with mock relief.

Eva was on the bed, reading, the look on her face serene.

'Escaping again?' she queried with a raised brow.

'It's all right for you,' he grumbled, getting onto the bed and snuggling up next to her. 'You've got a perfect excuse to escape the carnage.'

His beautiful wife was two weeks away from giving

birth to their fourth child. This meant she could legitimately hide herself away when the noise rose to the level of a rock concert on the pretext that she needed to rest.

'You can carry the next one if you want,' she teased.

'The next one? You want *five* children?'

'No.' She grinned. 'I was thinking of six.'

Completely unable to resist, he kissed her. 'I'm happy to keep going until you say stop.'

She hooked an arm around his neck. 'You might live to regret that.'

It amazed him that even now, after six years together and with Eva huge with child, he still desired her as much as he ever had.

But there was no chance to act on it when their bedroom door flew open and Pieta and Sergio charged in.

'Mamma, Papa, Father Christmas is here!' Pieta shouted, his little face alight with glee.

'Really? Are you sure?'

'He's really here,' Sergio confirmed, nodding his head vigorously. 'Mamma says you've got to stop playing alone with Aunty Eva and come!'

Exchanging a secret smile with his wife, Daniele helped her off the bed and they all went back into the living room, where Father Christmas was making bellows of 'Ho-ho-ho!' whilst drinking a large glass of red wine.

If any of the children cared to look beneath the bushy white beard they would see the less bushy black beard of his macho brother-in-law Felipe who, much to his disgust, had been coerced into playing Father Christmas a number of years ago, and now found himself stuck with the role every year. And every year Daniele's evil sister would cackle like a loon to watch him do it.

'Your sister is evil,' Eva whispered into his ear, her thoughts, as was so often the case, concurring perfectly with his.

'She certainly is,' he agreed, kissing her temple.

From the corner of his eye he saw Matteo and Natasha whispering together with giggles and felt quite sure they were saying the same thing. Or maybe they were laughing at Aunt Rachele, who'd fallen asleep with a glass of sherry still in her hand.

All his family. All here together. Just how he liked it.

And, best of all, his Eva was holding his hand and tonight he would go to bed and make very gentle love to her.

She was definitely his happy Eva after.

* * * * *

If you enjoyed
BUYING HIS BRIDE OF CONVENIENCE,
why not explore the first two parts of
Michelle Smart's
BOUND TO A BILLIONAIRE *trilogy?*

PROTECTING HIS DEFIANT INNOCENT
CLAIMING HIS ONE-NIGHT BABY

Available now!

MILLS & BOON®

MODERN™

POWER, PASSION AND IRRESISTIBLE TEMPTATION

1017/01

MILLS & BOON®

EXCLUSIVE EXTRACT

When chauffeur Keira Ryan drives into a snowdrift, she
and her devastatingly attractive passenger must find a
hotel…but there's only one bed! Luckily Matteo Valenti
knows how to make the best of a bad situation—with the
most sizzling experience of her life. It's nearly Christmas
again before Matteo uncovers Keira's secret. He's avoided
commitment his whole life, but now it's time to claim his
heir…

Read on for a sneak preview of Sharon Kendrick's book
THE ITALIAN'S CHRISTMAS SECRET
One Night With Consequences

'Santino?' Matteo repeated, wondering if he'd misheard her.
He stared at her, his brow creased in a frown. 'You gave him
an Italian name?'

'Yes.'

'Why?'

'Because when I looked at him…' Keira's voice faltered
as she scraped her fingers back through her hair and turned
those big sapphire eyes on him '…I knew I could call him
nothing else but an Italian name.'

'Even though you sought to deny him his heritage and
kept his birth hidden from me?'

She swallowed. 'You made it very clear that you never
wanted to see me again, Matteo.'

His voice grew hard. 'I haven't come here to argue the
rights and wrongs of your secrecy. I've come to see my son.'

It was a demand Keira couldn't ignore. She'd seen the
brief tightening of his face when she'd mentioned his child
and another wave of guilt had washed over her.

'Come with me,' she said huskily.

He followed her up the narrow staircase and Keira was

acutely aware of his presence behind her. She could detect the heat from his body and the subtle sandalwood which was all his and, stupidly, she remembered the way that scent had clung to her skin the morning after he'd made love to her. Her heart was thundering by the time they reached the box-room she shared with Santino and she held her breath as Matteo stood frozen for a moment before moving sound-lessly towards the crib.

'Matteo?' she said.

Matteo didn't answer. Not then. He wasn't sure he trusted himself to speak because his thoughts were in such disarray. He stared down at the dark fringe of eyelashes which curved on the infant's olive-hued cheeks and the shock of black hair. Tiny hands were curled into two tiny fists and he found himself leaning forward to count all the fingers, nodding his head with satisfaction as he registered each one.

He swallowed.

His *son*.

He opened his mouth to speak but Santino chose that moment to start to whimper and Keira bent over the crib to scoop him up. 'Would you...would you like to hold him?'

'Not now,' he said abruptly. 'There isn't time. You need to pack your things while I call ahead and prepare for your arrival in Italy.'

'What?'

'You heard me. You can't put out a call for help and then ignore help when it comes. You telephoned me and now you must accept the consequences,' he added grimly.

Don't miss
THE ITALIAN'S CHRISTMAS SECRET
By Sharon Kendrick

Available November 2017

www.millsandboon.co.uk

LONDON IN AN HOUR

Kate Hodges

Virgin BOOKS

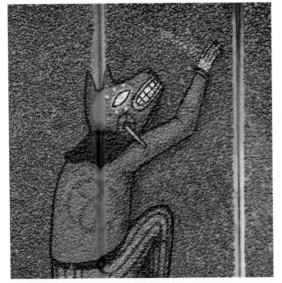

Frank's Cafe and Campari Bar

Bonnington Square

Londoners are busy people. We have lengthy commutes and working hours that stretch from espresso-o'clock to evening nightcap. Sometimes in the hustle of our working days and rushing from one place to another on the train, Tube or bus, we forget to stop and look at our extraordinary city and appreciate it. It's time to reclaim a few minutes for yourself, and use them to remind yourself that London is a city packed with exciting mini-adventures.

This book will inspire you to exploit your precious spare moments and pack them with fascinating trips and time outs. London is a city bursting with history, culture and fun things to do, all within a few square miles.

This book is a collection of cultural must-sees, new activities to try and places to explore that can all be done in an hour or less. Read on and discover how to drive a hard bargain at an antiques market before work, dive into cold, wild water in your lunch break, escape to the solitude of a twelfth-century church or drink a cocktail with friends watching the sun set over the city skyline. There are secret pleasures and treasures to find all over London; on every street, in every patch of green, and even underground. It's a city packed with potential micro-experiences; this is your roadmap to finding them.

I hope that this book will inspire you to grab your precious minutes of downtime and do something special with them. It's written for both Londoners in search of new sensations and visitors hoping to uncover some of the hidden joys of the city. Pack a lunch, leave your desk, turn off your phone and head outside. We've done the planning for you – now find that small window of spare time and fill it with something wonderful.

Photographers' Gallery

AN HOUR FOR CULTURE

London is the cultural heart of Britain, throbbing with music, art and theatre. Sometimes, though, it can be hard to find time to visit that latest exhibition, to see that site-specific dance performance, or even to hear the band playing in the bar at the end of your road. Life gets in the way. The solution? Be cunning.

Get your arts fixes in short bursts, as and when you can. Go to a free lunchtime concert, head for a mini night out at an hour-long show or go to a drop-in DJing session. Take in a small exhibition after work and still be home in time for dinner. There's so much happening in the city, you'll always find something small-but-perfectly-formed going on.

Wigmore Hall

Stand-up at the Soho Theatre
Comedy taster sessions and sneak previews

———

The Soho Theatre offers very funny shows that are just 60 minutes long, featuring a single stand-up comedian rather than a huge line-up with MC. They are perfect for a quick after-work dash of fun, no matter how late you work (start times can be anything from 7pm–10.30pm). During the summer, you'll catch pre-Edinburgh Festival works-in-progress from upcoming comics and established stars alike. The venue also has an excellent bar (great for comedy industry people-watching).

sohotheatre.com
21 Dean Street, W1D 3NE
Tube Tottenham Court Road

Wind-down at the Wigmore Hall
Home of the BBC Radio 3 Monday lunchtime concert

———

Held weekly in this beautifully gilded and painted theatre, the BBC's series of classical concerts is a relaxing way to spend a lunch hour. Featuring well-known international artists and groups, as well as up-and-coming performers from the New Generations scheme, these recitals last an hour, with no break. It's a pure shot of culture that will restore your mind after a hard morning's work. Book in advance to secure your seat – and get yourself away from your desk. If you can't get down to the Wigmore in person you can listen in live on BBC Radio 3 or online.

wigmore-hall.org.uk
36 Wigmore Street, W1U 2BP
Tube Bond Street

Eclectic arts at the Ace Hotel
Dip into a hub of cutting-edge culture
—

The Ace Hotel in Shoreditch isn't just a place for sophisticated travellers to lay their heads; there's always something going on that you can get involved in. Most evenings, the lobby hosts music-spinning sessions, with DJs and creatives picking their favourite tunes of the moment. It's free – anyone is welcome to wander in and out. Check out the venue's website for bigger evening events held in their downstairs room, plus craft and cooking workshops, guided running sessions around local sights, yoga classes and storytelling. There's even a black-and-white photo booth you can visit to immortalise your micro night out.

acehotel.com
100 Shoreditch High Street, E1 6JQ
Overground Shoreditch High Street

A world of music at the Royal Festival Hall
Free music every Friday
—

If you can't make Mondays at the Wigmore, try Friday lunchtimes at the Central Bar at the Royal Festival Hall. Every week the bar reverberates to the sound of live music and the buzz of the people listening. You might hear classical, jazz, folk or world music. The show's free, so buy a cup of coffee or a glass of wine, pull up a chair, and ease yourself into the weekend. If you really can't switch off from work – even for an hour – there's free Wi-Fi so you can catch up on emails while you listen.

southbankcentre.co.uk
Belvedere Road, SE1 8XX
Tube Waterloo

Ace Hotel

Royal Festival Hall

Satire and songs at the News Revue

A funny, lightning-fast charge through the week's events

———

Running since 1979, this topical, constantly changing show is held at the picturesque Canal Café, right in the middle of Little Venice, and runs Thursday to Sunday. The line-up changes on a regular basis, but the format stays the same – a funny series of skits, song parodies, impressions and sketches performed by two women and two men, hooked around breaking news stories. Although only an hour long, each show is so jam-packed with gags and songs it feels like a full evening's entertainment. A fun way to catch up on the week's current affairs.

canalcafetheatre.com
Delamere Terrace, Little Venice, W2 6ND
Tube Warwick Avenue

Get the lowdown on new London architecture

Showcasing the city's construction projects

———

London is constantly evolving; a hub of change and a leading light in all that is new and cutting edge, and the buildings in the city reflect this innovation. If you are interested in the look of our capital city, take a quick spin around the NLA exhibition to stay on top of the latest plans for the city's skyline (it's do-able in less than half an hour). You can't miss the huge, shiny, 3D map that dominates the ultra-modern gallery, highlighting new and proposed buildings and giving you a picture of how familiar streets might look in a few years. Let your fingers glide over high-tech screens and display tables to highlight what's new for your neighbourhood.

newlondonarchitecture.org
The Building Centre, 26 Store St, WC1E 7BT
Tube Goodge Street

TOP TEN
Exhibition spaces

Photographers' Gallery, *Soho*
Breathtaking snaps, often with a political edge.

Estorick Collection, *Highbury & Islington*
Italian modern art with a pretty garden café.

Whitechapel Gallery
An egalitarian, contemporary collection of art. Don't miss the video installations.

Stolen Space Gallery, *Brick Lane*
Browse the art and perhaps make a wise investment in works by contemporary, underground artists.

House of Illustration, *King's Cross*
Their whirlwind, illustrator-led, 20-minute tour (times vary) of their current exhibition is brilliant and helps you get the most from the show.

South London Gallery, *Camberwell*
Thoughtful shows from contemporary artists and a wonderful café.

Hayward Gallery, *Southbank*
Exhibitions by major artists. An hour of world-class innovation that will inspire and delight.

St Paul's Cathedral
Indulge in their two sumptuous Bill Viola videos.

The Serpentine Gallery, *Hyde Park*
Major exhibitions from the likes of Marina Abramović and Yoko Ono.

Lazarides Rathbone, *Fitzrovia*
Cutting-edge urban art.

TOP TEN
Talks and lectures

The Hunterian, *Holborn*
Tuesday lunchtime lecture with gruesome-yet-fascinating stories from medical history.

Wellcome Collection, *Bloomsbury*
Scientists discuss their latest experiments and research at the Packed Lunch talks.

Open Data Institute, *Hoxton*
20-minute tech and online communication lectures on a Friday.

Guildhall Library, *City*
Afternoon talks about the absorbing history of London – around eight free events per month.

The National Gallery, *Trafalgar Square*
Free lunchtime talks of 30–45 minutes on Mondays and Tuesdays that uncover the history of their paintings.

The National Army Museum, *Battersea*
Head to the formal surroundings of the Army and Navy Club for free, fortnightly military history lunchtime talks.

Royal Academy of Arts, *Piccadilly*
Monthly, free, Monday lunchtime lecture that offers a deeper insight into their exhibitions.

The British Museum, *Bloomsbury*
Learn more about ancient objects at the Tuesday–Saturday, 45-minute, lunchtime gallery talk.

National Portrait Gallery, *Trafalgar Square*
Fascinating, funny and insightful, try the daily Portrait of the Day chats.

Wallace Collection, *Marylebone*
Wednesdays mean Brief Encounter talks; a 20-minute lecture focused on one of the gallery's objects.

Get comfy at the BFI Mediatheque
A free, filmic jukebox

——

The BFI Mediatheque is a cosy place to while away an hour on a winter's day. You'll be given a pair of headphones and shown to a booth, then left to pick a film, TV programme or documentary to watch from their huge archive. You can choose an episode of *Sherlock* or *Absolutely Fabulous*, but why not embrace the moment and choose something more esoteric? Perhaps watch a three-minute short of music hall performer Billy Merson skipping around with a lyre, Princess Diana presenting the 1989 British Fashion Awards, home hints from 1926 (including how to turn your dog into a burglar alarm), or Kenneth Williams declaiming and showing us around his London.

whatson.bfi.org.uk
Belvedere Road, South Bank, SE1 8XT
Tube Waterloo

Discover late-night art at First Thursdays
Celebrate East London's bleeding-edge art

——

East London is home to swathes of emerging artists and raw talent, and on the first Thursday of every month, many of those artists open their studios and spaces to the public, with over 150 venues holding shows, talks and workshops. You've only got an hour? Fine, take in a selection of smaller shows that are within stepping distance of each other, or spend the whole hour at one larger exhibition. The galleries are open late, so you might even squeeze in a quick post-work drink before you set off on your cultural tour of East London.

whitechapelgallery.org/first-thursdays
Tube Aldgate

Celebrate music, words and pictures at Rough Trade East

Huge emporium of music, film and books

———

Rough Trade East is a vast, airy, high-ceilinged warehouse packed with music, words and pictures in every format imaginable. Brand new vinyl imports and old classics sit in racks waiting to be flicked through; track down something on your wants list, or browse for new sounds. Elsewhere there are obscure CDs and artfully curated books to browse. Take a look at the staff selections for quick tips as to what will be the next big thing, or sip a cup of Monmouth coffee in the café at the front.

roughtrade.com
Dray Walk, Old Truman Brewery,
91 Brick Lane, E1 6QL
Overground Shoreditch High Street

Pack in a show at the Lunchbox Theatre

Bite-sized morsels of drama, dance and comedy

———

The St Bride Foundation is tucked away behind the St Bride's Church on Fleet Street. It's primarily an arts space and educational centre, but at lunchtimes it hosts Lunchbox Theatre, a 45-minute play or musical – anything from political satire to (abridged) Shakespeare classics. Indulge in some non-work-related drama with your sandwiches on your lap and be back at your desk, refreshed and inspired, within the hour.

sbf.org.uk
Bride Lane, Fleet Street, EC4Y 8EQ
Tube Blackfriars

TOTAL CONTROL

EW WAVE/POST PUNK

WAVE/POST PUNK

UK DECAY/ARISING FROM THE DREAM

WIRE

Rough Trade East

Rivington Street

Chance Street

Southbank

Brick Lane

Lunch-hour lectures at UCL
Learn something new in your break
—

Want to get your neurons connecting and your grey matter moving? UCL's experts serve up years of research in 40-minute, easy-to-understand talks. The University's Lunch Hour Lecture programme takes place in the Darwin Theatre and covers a hugely diverse range of subjects; the taboo history of the toilet, the science of fireworks, the theory of attention spans. Open to everyone, the talks are informal, entertaining and thought-provoking. If you can't get away from the office, you can watch the live webcast, or dig them up from YouTube archives and learn in your own time.

events.ucl.ac.uk/calendar/tab:lunch_hour_lectures
Darwin Theatre, UCL, Malet Place, WC1E 6BT
Tube Euston Square

Hunt out a Street Art Safari
Track down the city's finest spray-can masterpieces
—

There are more organised street art tours than Banksy postcards in Camden Market, and some longer walks (like shoreditchstreetarttours.com) are truly brilliant, but what can you see in just one hour? Spraycan pickings are richest around Shoreditch and Brick Lane; visit streetartlocator.com beforehand to create an itinerary. Don't be disappointed if some of the listed art has disappeared – the form's ephemeral nature is part of its appeal. Alternatively, take a speculative wander around the neighbourhood and see what's on the walls. There are usually some good pieces on Fashion Street, Grimsby Street and Sclater Street. If you're desperate to spot a genuine Banksy, head to Cargo's beer garden, where his *His Master's Voice* painting is preserved behind a Perspex screen.

Tube Aldgate

Golden Union

AN HOUR TO EAT AND DRINK

Lunching at your desk? Boring. Microwave dinner after a long day's graft? Predictable. Take a break from the norm and embrace the gastronomic delights of the capital city; London makes it easy to turn your mealtimes into fun and sociable adventures.

The city's restaurants are starting to double up; you don't just go out to eat or drink, you play board games, talk with the food's producers, find out how things are made, do some work in an inspiring place, or even draw while you nibble. Dining is not just about dinner, it's an immersive, fun experience.

No time to linger over a long hour's lunchbreak? No problem. London is an incubator for new food trends, and increasing numbers of street food vans and pop-up bars and cafés are making exciting flavour combinations more and more accessible for those in a rush.

Remember, a mini cuisine adventure takes only a lunchtime or an hour after work – and you should always have time to eat. So make it special, it's the perfect excuse to seek out another side to the city. All the inspiration you'll need for your foodie (and drinkie) forays is right here.

Gin o'clock at the City of London Distillery
Find out the secrets of spirit-making

——

Gin and London go together like, um, gin and tonic. The City of London Distillery, opened in 2012, is packed with shiny pipes and copper stills, all overlooked by a speakeasy-style bar. Find out about the art of combining botanics on a 45-minute lunchtime tour, taking in the history of the drink, a trip to see the stills (named Clarissa and Jennifer), and watch them bottling up the fragrant liquor. You'll even get a sample to take back to the office to brighten up the afternoon. If you go really gin crazy, go back for one of their longer tasting or making events when you've got more time.

cityoflondondistillery.com
22–24 Bride Lane, EC4Y 8DT
Tube Blackfriars

Kick-start the weekend at the craft beer mile
A place to talk beer with brewers

——

Home to some of London's greatest independent breweries, on Saturday mornings the Bermondsey 'Beer Mile' is packed with real ale fans. There are no fancy trimmings at the tasting rooms and breweries here; it's all about the flavour. We suggest starting at Fourpure's Tap Room, with beers on draught and ping-pong tables, then perhaps a drink at Partizan, whose gorgeously designed labels clash wonderfully with the brewery's rough-and-ready pallet seating. Stop off at Bottleshop, with its expertly curated selection of obscure and wonderful beers from around the world. Many of the breweries and shops' staff help brew the beer and are happy to answer the geekiest of questions. Grab some food from nearby Maltby Street Market (we love Monty's Deli's super-stacked, salt-beef sandwiches) and treat yourself to a super-quick, boozy lunch.

Tube Bermondsey

Twinings

Mix it up at The Bar With No Name

The place to drink one perfect, experimental cocktail

———

If you've only got time for one or two drinks, better make them outstanding. Overseen by cocktail alchemist Tony Conigliaro, who concocts the unique drinks in his Heston-style 'laboratory', the Drink Factory, The Bar With No Name (otherwise known as 69 Colebrook Row) is a tiny gem of a venue (really tiny, so book in advance to be sure of a seat). The intimate, 1950s Italian-style bar serves up a seasonal menu of cocktails that feature unexpected ingredients such as smoked frankincense, lichen and colloidal silver combined with more familiar spirits. If you enjoy your taster, you can return for one of their superb cocktail masterclasses.

69colebrookerow.com
69 Colebrooke Row, N1 8AA
Tube Angel

Time for tea at Twinings on the Strand

Sip and sample exotic and obscure brews

———

The shelves that stretch along the walls of this long, narrow shop groan with hundreds of varieties of teas and coffees, the air thick with intoxicating fragrances that'll have you yearning for a cuppa. Some with exotic names: osmanthus pearls, jade pillars, grey dragon oolong; others with rainbow flavours: salted caramel, orange and lotus flower, camomile and maple. Give in to temptation and try a few at the sampler bar at the back, where a smiling lady brews small cups to whisk your tastebuds around the world – all free. Stay for a ten-minute sip, or half an hour if you're really enjoying your drinks. Take a packet back to the office to perk up your tea break.

twinings.co.uk/about-twinings/216-strand
216 Strand, WC2R 1AP
Tube Temple

Ziferblat – join the community
Pay by the minute to work, eat and drink

———

Welcome to a new way of social networking. Rather than paying for food and drink at this friendly Old Street café/workspace, you fork out for the time you spend here. It costs 5p a minute (3p for members) to sit down and use the Wi-Fi, make or be served a cup of coffee, browse the book selection, enjoy a performance, or grab a complimentary snack. If you prefer not to watch the clock tick, you can pay 50p for a smash-and-grab raid on the coffee maker or snacks trolley, £3 for an hour's leisurely web surfing, or a tinkle on the in-house piano. If you want to meet new people or simply have a chat with a different crowd, head down to one of Ziferblat's 'Talking Socials' events.

london.ziferblat.net
388 Old Street, EC1V 9LT
Tube Old Street

Cutting-edge food at Kerb
Experience lip-smacking new food trends

———

Lewis Cubitt Square, near King's Cross, is an unexpectedly pleasant spot to while away an hour or wait for a train or the Eurostar. Each lunchtime a selection of brightly coloured street-food vans park up, offering sensational new tastes at take-away speed. This is the place to try new food crazes before they hit bricks-and-mortar establishments; there's usually something spicy, something veggie, and something laden with caffeine on offer. If it's sunny pull up a deck chair, or recline on grassy areas watching the dancing fountains and have a relaxed-but-fast, outdoor lunch.

kerbfood.com
Granary Square, N1C
Tube King's Cross

Kerb

ASIAN SLAW
MINT, CORIANDER, LIME
+ SWEET CHILLI VINAIGRETTE

AWESOME SIDES

Fine dining at Fortnum's
Eat a grand picnic

——

The finest way to dine al fresco in London? First pick up one of stately department store Fortnum and Mason's magnificently indulgent hampers. The Festival is packed in one of the company's iconic initialled hampers, and contains Glenarm beef carpaccio, a tarte tatin and a bottle of Minervois, while the simpler Bunhill includes a bottle of ale, a stick of Cheddar and a fresh apple. Click and collect from their Piccadilly store, then stroll to St James's Park and eat your fine feast on the grass. On a sunny day, with charming company and a blanket, this is the grandest way to dine – no queues, no snooty waiters and wonderful, pelican-enhanced views. Plus you get to keep the stylish cool bag or hamper, too!

fortnumandmason.com
181 Piccadilly, W1A 1ER
Tube Green Park

Hurwundeki
Grab a haircut and a tasty lunch

——

This Korean café and hairdressers compromises on neither style nor taste. Owner Ki Lee does a speedy dry cut for under £20 for ladies and £15 for men, and the great value lunches are tasty and healthy. Try their spicy kimchi stew or sizzling bibimbap, or just grab a locally roasted Workshop coffee and fresh Yeast Bakery pastry. Show off your new trim while sitting outside among old carousel horses or nestle inside and listen to the rumble of passing trains.

hurwundeki.com
Arch 299, Cambridge Heath Rd, E2 9HA
Rail Cambridge Heath

TOP TEN
Happy hours

Señor Ceviche, *Soho*
Sip pisco cocktails and snack on ceviche at this Peruvian casa.

Slim Jim's Liquor Store, *Islington*
Settle into a red-leather booth under neon lights in Slim's American-style whisky bar.

Fifty Five, *Camden*
Loud, brash and with happy hours every night, an unashamed party bar.

The Loft, *Clapham*
Look out over the High Street while enjoying a sharer cocktail with up to 19 close friends!

London Cocktail Club (*branches across central London*)
Try a Heisenberg – served with blue salt.

Barrio (*branches across central London*)
Every night seems to get raucous at these Brazilian-inspired bars, whichever one you're in.

Bar Story, *Peckham*
Rough-and-ready, but wonderful. Try to bag an outdoor seat (there's a fire lit in winter to keep you warm).

The Mayor of Scaredy Cat Town, *Spitalfields*
Enter this speakeasy-style bar through a secret door (behind a Smeg fridge) for well-made, carefully considered cocktails.

The Social, *Fitzrovia*
Catch super-cool live bands while sipping on a £5 cocktail (or two-for-one beer) at this indie pop institution.

Zilouf's, *Islington*
TVs-turned-fish-tanks line the walls, and avant-garde cocktails are the order of the day.

TOP TEN
Take-away fish & chips

Poppies, *Camden, Spitalfields*
The full retro café experience with take-away orders wrapped up in newsprint. Stick a coin in the jukebox, or visit the Camden branch for free live music in the evenings.

Golden Union, *Soho*
Fish and chips with a home-cooked flavour served up in diner-style surroundings with a modern twist.

The Fish and Chip Shop, *Islington*
A posh, modern-day chippy which offers traditional favourites and upmarket specials, such as oysters and sea bass, or shrimp burgers.

Seashell, *Marylebone*
Rub shoulders with celebrities trying the delicious, home-made tartare sauce.

The Dining Plaice, *Soho*
Proper, old-fashioned fish and chips in the centre of town.

Fryer's Delight, *Holborn*
A no-frills experience and a perfect place to grab a bag of hot chips to eat on the way home from after-work drinks.

Golden Hind, *Marylebone*
Delicious traditional food and a BYO licence. The bright, airy restaurant is worth a visit just to see the classic, art deco, cream and pale green shop fittings.

Toff's, *Muswell Hill*
Super-fresh fish and chips using fish bought from UK docks. Beautifully blended batter (or they'll do your cod in matzo) and deep-fried in groundnut oil.

Kerbisher and Malt (*branches across London*)
Try their fireworks-in-mouth, no-preservatives-guaranteed, twice-cooked chips and delicate, hand-prepared battered fish. Traditional décor with a modern twist.

Masters Super Fish, *Waterloo*
Unfussy, long-established, traditional chippy. Go for the crunchy, super-fresh whitebait.

Snacks and ladders at Draughts

The place to try new board games

——

Avant garde ice creams at Chin-Chin Laboratorists

Haute-cuisine ice cream

——

Sandwiches are more interesting with a side order of Boggle. Draughts Café in Haggerston not only serves excellent meatball paninis, bruschetta and delicious fresh salads, but it has an enormous library of board games to play, try retro kids' games such as Connect Four or Guess Who?, or the more complicated Carcassone or Settlers of Catan. Warning: playing Hungry Hippos when drinking some of their local craft beers may lead to rowdiness and ball spillage.

draughtslondon.com
337 Acton Mews, E8 4EA
Overground Haggerston

You'll know when this Wonka-ish experimental gelato store is open thanks to the clouds of liquid nitrogen billowing onto the street, luring you inside to discover its secrets. Once through the doors, you can stick to the old favourites vanilla or chocolate, or experiment with guest flavours that might include green grass, beetroot or tobacco. Great for a summery speed date; take your ice creams down to the lock to watch the world go by and see if you can spot an Oompa-Loompa.

chinchinlabs.com
49–50 Camden Lock Place, NW1 8AF
Tube Camden Town

Scan the horizon at the Sky Garden
High times at London's most vertiginous public park

——

Boasting some of the most spectacular views in London, the public garden space at the top of 20 Fenchurch Street (or the Walkie Talkie as it's better known) is a breathtaking place to eat or have a drink. It's green, lush, with an open-air terrace, and sits 35 floors above the financial district. Head to the Sky Pod Bar for a drink and a light snack – sip a seasonal cocktail, sit on a chair with a cosy blanket or on a deckchair in the summer. Tickets to the garden are free (although you must book in advance).

skygarden.london
20 Fenchurch Street, EC3M 3BY
Tube Monument

Score a goal at Café Kick
London's home of table football

——

Café Kick feels like the kind of bar you dream of finding when you're hitchhiking around Europe. It's relaxed, artily scruffy, stuffed with soccer memorabilia, and filled with 'babyfoot' tables. On a blue-skied afternoon, with the sun streaming down Exmouth Market, grab a bottle of cheap house beer and a couple of plates of tapas, commandeer a table, and show off your twiddling skills.

cafekick.co.uk
43 Exmouth Market EC1R 4QL
Tube Angel
127 Shoreditch High Street, London E1 6JE
Overground Shoreditch High Street

Café Kick

KICK BABY FOOT ASSO

Bonnington Square

AN HOUR OF INNER PEACE

London is huge, crowded, and can be overwhelming, but she also has a peaceful, contemplative side. Find one of her quiet corners to tuck into where you can gather your thoughts. Use the silence to meditate, make plans, or just think of nothing for a while.

An hour in a quiet sunny park or a cosy library with only the odd rustle or scrape around you can be as restorative as a week's holiday. Seek out secret oases and surprisingly peaceful nooks amongst the city hubbub and spend a few quiet minutes, undisturbed. You'll emerge refreshed and ready to take on anything.

Discover everyday heroes at Postman's Park
Fifty-four melodramas, and tranquillity for contemplation

———

Nestled at the bottom of one of the city's urban canyons, Postman's Park is a sliver of shady, green cool, even in summer. Under a wooden awning you'll find 54 Victorian ceramic plaques, each dedicated to everyday heroes who lost their lives saving others. Their stories are dramatic and engrossing; a railway inspector who 'saved a lunatic woman from suicide at Woolwich Arsenal Station, but was himself run over by the train' or the 'pantomime artiste who died of terrible injuries received when attempting in her inflammable dress to extinguish the flames which had enveloped her companion'. It's easy to while away an hour gazing at the haiku-like tales of extraordinary self-sacrifice. Download the Everyday Heroes of Postman's Park app.

cityoflondon.gov.uk
St Martin's Le Grand, London EC1A
Tube Barbican

Have a quiet, thoughtful moment at the Saison Poetry Library
A small room filled with powerful words

———

Nestled unassumingly at the top of the Southbank Centre, the Saison Poetry Library contains the most comprehensive collection of post-1912 poetry in the UK. Browse the shelves and you might stumble across an independently published, letterpressed anthology, or rediscover a beloved, classic verse. The library is open until 8pm – perfect for a post-work browse, or to read a poem to restore your soul before an event at the centre or the commute home. Take the glorious, glass-walled, singing lift to get there and feel your spirits soar before you even open the library's door.

poetrylibrary.org.uk
Level 5, Royal Festival Hall, SE1 8XX
Tube Waterloo

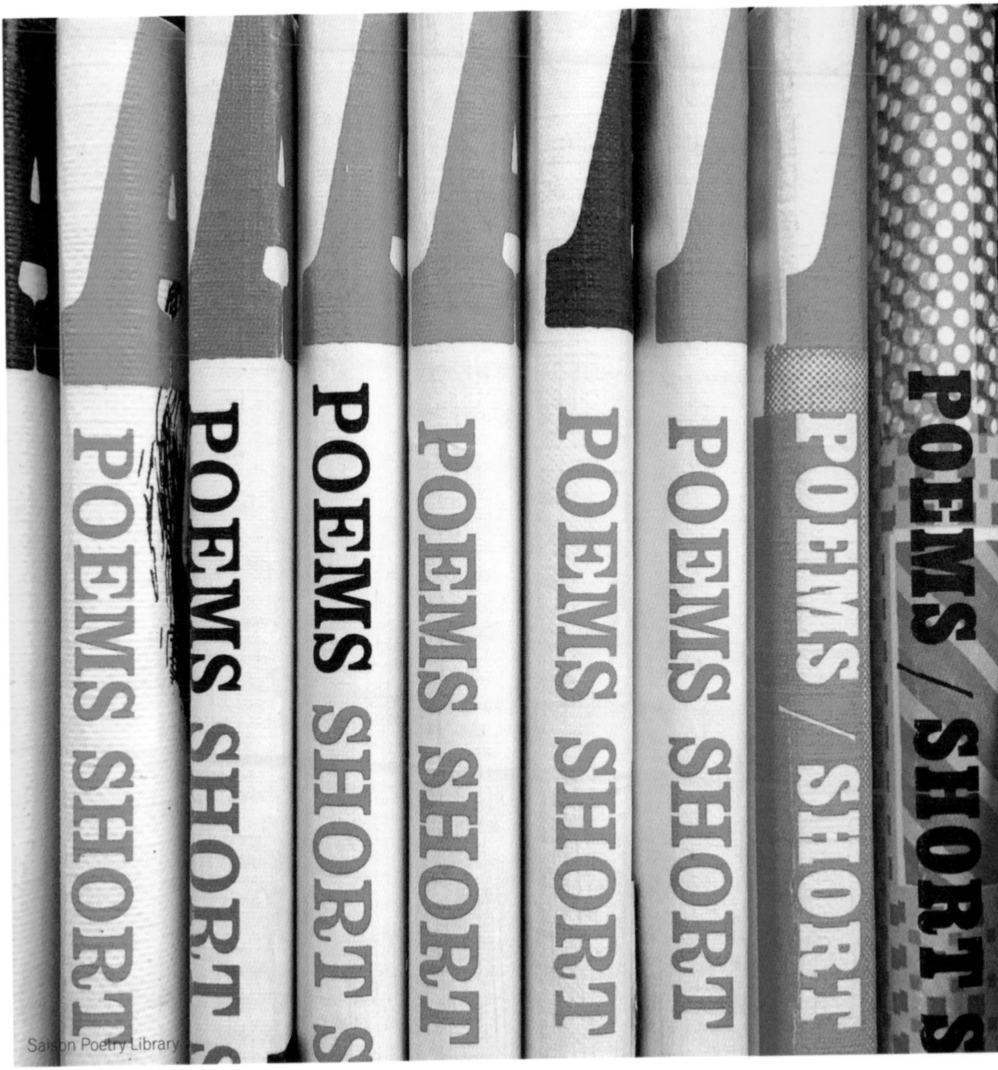

Saison Poetry Library

St Dunstan in the East

Find peace at St Dunstan in the East

A refuge for the mind in the centre of the city

——

Hemmed in on all sides by traffic, concrete, tourists and noise, the existence of this tiny, tranquil place feels like a miracle, having survived the Great Fire of London and being bombed into a ruin during WWII. It's now a public garden; the ornate window arches hang heavy with vines, creepers and ivy, while palms and tall trees provide welcome shade on a hot summer's day. Sit at one of the benches that surround a bubbling fountain and allow the noise of the city to recede for an hour.

cityoflondon.gov.uk
St Dunstan's Hill, off Lower Thames Street, EC3R 5DD
Tube Tower Hill

Drift off at Floatworks

Soak away your cares

——

Something very curious happens when you lie in a flotation tank; you find a real sense of peace as you relax and allow the strong salt solution to help you blur into body-temperature water. Be brave and turn off the lights in the tank for the ultimate serene experience. The total relaxation and retreat into your own mind can be almost disconcerting, but it's a super-efficient, wonderfully intensive way to regain a sense of your soul and self amidst the chaos; a brief but effective escape for the totally frazzled and city-burned.

floatworks.com
32 Skylines Village, Limeharbour, E14 9TS
DLR South Quay

Bunhill Fields

Break with convention at Bunhill Fields
An unconventional place of contemplation

—

Traffic noise fades as you step through the gates of this ten-acre graveyard, which sits like an oasis of calm at the edge of the bustling financial district. The non-conformist burial ground is home to the graves of John Bunyan, Daniel Defoe and William Blake, wander through the graveyard to find them, or sit and look up and see if you can spot the resident jays that soar from one memorial to another. Students come to hang out, eat their lunches and smoke dope; the sweet smell of cannabis wafting between the tombs is a little whiff of counterculture still floating around the land of conformity.

cityoflondon.gov.uk
38 City Rd, EC1Y 1AU
Tube Old Street

Uncover historic treasures at the British Library

A quiet retreat stuffed with fascinating papers

—

A vast, cool atrium houses temporary exhibitions, a gift shop, stamp collection and plenty of quiet space to sit and take advantage of the free Wi-Fi. Hustle along to the Sir John Ritblat gallery for a whistle-stop browse of the library's greatest treasures. This dark, atmospheric room houses precious Shakespeare first editions, Leonardo Da Vinci sketches, Jane Austen's writing desk, the hand-written version of *Alice in Wonderland*, and scrawled Beatles' lyrics. A wonderful retreat for contemplation and literary inspiration. Don't miss the wafer-fragile pages from the Magna Carta, too. To experience the library at its most peaceful, head there early in the morning, or later in the evening.

bl.uk
96 Euston Rd, NW1 2DB
Tube King's Cross

Barbican Highwalks

A modernist, bold trip across the top of the city

—

Opened in 1982, the Barbican is a utopian, urban neighbourhood; residents can access a library, school, church, pub, shops and museum without ever stepping foot outside the estate. The series of high walkways keeps pedestrians separate from traffic and noise, which makes it an often deserted, peaceful place. Follow the walking tour that's downloadable from the Barbican website, or get deliciously lost for an hour, deep in idealistic dreams of communal living. In summer, the balconies are hung with red and pink geraniums; in winter it's beautifully, brutally bleak. Go on a Sunday to explore the huge conservatory, full of ferns, palms, tinkling water and terrapins (11am–5pm).

barbican.org.uk
Silk St, EC2Y 8DS
Tube Barbican

Barbican Highwalks

Clear your mind at the West London Buddhist Centre
Learn old-school mindfulness

———

Buddhism is a religion that has no God, but also a philosophy. Buddhists were super-early mindfulness pioneers, establishing hugely positive tenets of practicality, kindness and interconnection. The centre offers classes in yoga, mindfulness and meditation, so if you're looking for an easy introduction to taking stress-breaks, their weekday lunchtime drop-in classes are a fine place to start. Learn one of two meditation practices in a supportive environment, or just sit with others, clearing and refreshing your minds together.

westlondonbuddhistcentre.com
Royal Oak House, 45A Porchester Road, W2 5DP
Tube Royal Oak

Take a power nap at Virgin Active Broadgate
Boost your energy levels

———

It may sound counter-intuitive, but research shows that a 20-minute nap can boost your energy levels, improve your memory, alertness and creativity. It's not really the done thing to pop under your desk for 40 winks at lunchtime, so instead head to Virgin Active's super-modern Broadgate branch and their Metronap pods. These large, Pacman-shaped havens of peace and tranquillity are designed to help stressed workers drift off. Dream sweetly and happily, then, if you have time, follow up your nap with a quick spot of anti-gravity yoga or a swim in their gorgeous pool and a sauna, steam or 'sensation shower'. You'll either need to be a member, or search online for one of Virgin's regular, one-day, free pass offers.

virginactive.co.uk/clubs/broadgate
1 Exchange Place, EC2M 2QT
Tube Liverpool Street

Phoenix Garden, *West End*
Spot dragonflies, frogs and bees in this tiny sliver of green sandwiched between the busiest streets in London.

Kyoto Garden, *Holland Park*
Stroll around the Japanese garden and gaze at the koi carp to soothe your soul.

Regents Park
Search for the 'secret' St John's Lodge flower garden.

SOAS Japanese Roof Garden, *Bloomsbury*
Relax and meditate, Zen-style.

Eastern Curve Garden, *Dalston*
Snuggle up in the wooden pavilion with Stanley the cat.

The Geffrye Museum, *Dalston*
Wander the well-tended domestic gardens, each one designed as a snapshot of a period in time in the last 400 years.

Tower Hamlets Cemetery Park
Spot rare and endangered wildlife species in this urban nature reserve.

Bonnington Square Gardens, *Vauxhall*
A stunning, community-run oasis with a vegetarian and vegan restaurant at its heart.

Lincoln's Inn Fields, *Holborn*
Take in the history that surrounds London's biggest public square.

Westminster Cathedral Bell Tower
Find peace high above the city (except when the bells sound, of course).

TOP TEN
Bookshops

Gosh! Comics, *Soho*
Fresh-off-the-press graphic novels, dazzling kids books and cult author events.

Magma, *Clerkenwell, Covent Garden*
Slick art, fashion and design tomes, plus posters and cards.

Waterloo Bridge, *Southbank*
Head under the bridge and rummage through piles of second-hand books.

Bookmarks, *Bloomsbury*
Radical tracts and political biographies at Britain's largest socialist bookshop.

Daunt Books, *Marylebone*
Inspiring travel reads line this grand-dame of a bookstore.

New Beacon Books, *Finsbury Park*
An independent bookshop and press specialising in books covering Caribbean, African, Middle Eastern and Asian British issues.

Books for Cooks, *Ladbroke Grove*
Serves up a mouthwatering selection of foodie tomes, plus a café that cooks recipes from their pages.

Assouline, *Piccadilly*
The most luxuriously bound books line the walls of a Lutyens-designed building, to create the most opulent, elegant bookshop in the world.

Gay's the Word, *Bloomsbury*
Queer-positive fiction, life-affirming non-fiction.

Persephone Books, *Bloomsbury*
Quietly beautiful editions of books by overlooked, twentieth-century women writers.

The School of Life Secular Sermons

Find the meaning of life (and cake)

——

Emotional intelligence pioneers The School of Life run secular, ad hoc, welcoming gatherings of minds where non-conformist experts discuss the meaning of life. The morning sessions consist of lively debate, a few pop song 'hymns', and even some buns and biscuits. They take place at the Conway Hall and are a fine way to exercise your brain on a Sunday morning (hangover permitting). Start-to-finish, they clock in at over an hour, but the talk and discussion rarely goes over 60 minutes.

theschooloflife.com
25 Red Lion Square, WC1R 4RL
Tube Holborn

Music and silence in the Temple Church

Lose yourself in magnificent organ music

——

Built over 800 years ago by the secretive, strange Knights Templar, Britain's first gothic building is steeped in history. It's a little tucked away; head for where Chancery Lane hits Fleet Street and look for an ancient, half-timbered house, then duck through the arch beneath it. You can sit and ponder in this hushed, historic building (Shakespeare's *Twelfth Night* was premiered here), or be swept up in the elaborate and dramatic music of the regular organ recitals that are held here. Hearing the sounds of the notes swirling around the echoing spaces of the building is a fine way to clear the mind ready for a hard afternoon working (or shopping).

templechurch.com
Temple, EC4Y 7BB
Tube Temple

Neal's Yard Dairy

AN HOUR TO BUY A GIFT

Don't panic! Buying a perfect present is easy if you know where to shop. If you're not entirely sure exactly what you want to buy, head to one of these stores and you'll pick an appropriate gift with time to spare. Whether you're slipping out for an hour at lunchtime or in a last-minute frenzy after work, these are the places where you're guaranteed to find something that will make the lucky recipient smile with joy.

London is rammed with unique and inspirational shops – a choice so dazzling it can be daunting, so we've narrowed down the selection for you. From palm-printed shower caps to Flying V-shaped ukuleles, strange drinks to nerdy toys, there really is a store for everyone's tastes here. Be warned, you'll probably end up purchasing something for yourself, too.

Unique jewellery at Tatty Devine
Fun, personalised necklaces made while you wait

———

Wander into Tatty Devine's Monmouth Street store and lust over their signature Perspex necklaces, witty, willow-pattern earrings and cat-shaped rings. Towards the back of the small, white-walled shop is a laser-cutting machine, which staff use to make one-off, personalised necklaces. Choose a colour, font and charm shape, and watch as your friend's name is neatly cut out. The process takes about 20 minutes to half an hour. A perfect present for teenagers or anyone with a quirky sense of style.

tattydevine.com
44 Monmouth Street, WC2H 9EP
Tube Covent Garden

A touch of the exotic at House of Hackney
The home of elegant living

———

This design duo's extravagant and subversive prints are inspired by animal skins, lush jungle plants and wildlife; their sloths-smoking-hookah-pipes Hackney Empire design is to die for (very, very slowly, of course). Their flagship store sits just within Hackney on Shoreditch High Street. Like a modern Biba or Liberty, it's a shrine to all that is sophisticated and desirable. Buy pineapple-shaped candle holders, palm-printed shower caps, or bee-strewn silk pillowcases. A gift from here will win you a friend for life.

houseofhackney.com
131–132 Shoreditch High Street, E1 6JE
Overground Shoreditch High Street

House of Hackney

Forbidden Planet – gifts that are out of this world
Film, TV and comic nerd-vana

——

Wherever your friends sit on the sci-fi and fantasy spectrum, you'll find something to tickle their geek bones at the capital's biggest retailer of film- and TV-related ephemera. Flick through piles of popular and obscure comics, cute Japanese toys and brilliantly niche presents (think TIE Fighter bottle openers, *Breaking Bad* burned pink teddy bears and *Adventure Time* pillows). If you need extra inspiration, or are super-short on time, the staff are friendly and really know their stuff. Be sure to check their website to find out about one-off signings.

forbiddenplanet.com
179 Shaftesbury Avenue, WC2H 8JR
Tube Tottenham Court Road

The Vintage Magazine Company
Page upon page of style inspiration

——

Head straight down to the basement of this unprepossessing-looking shop and you'll find it piled high with old magazines; *Vogue*s, crackly music weeklies, ancient *Picture Post*s and 80s style rags. Some are filed in date order, and make perfect personalised birthday presents for style mavens or music fans. Expect to rub shoulders with fashionistas and photographers browsing and stealing ideas for their next shoots.

vinmag.com
39–43 Brewer St, W1F 9UD
Tube Leicester Square

Obscure instruments at Hobgoblin Music
Strings and things for the musical to master

—

In recent times, folk music has had an enormous resurgence. Once rare creatures, beards, ukuleles and banjos are now commonplace. Hobgoblin Music has been established since the 1970s and sells all kinds of traditional instruments, from harmoniums to harps – many of them incredibly affordable. The assistants are friendly, with ready advice for present buying – they'll help you find something for the most inexperienced of musicians. Even a complete novice can blow on a melodica (a reeded instrument with a keyboard), tinkle on a glockenspiel, or bang a drum, while the more musical minded will be delighted to receive an instrument that they can add to their repertoire.

hobgoblin.com
24 Rathbone Place, W1T 1JA
Tube Goodge Street

Gifts for the classy type
Communicate in super-retro style with a vintage typewriter

—

Buried in an unprepossessing block in Bethnal Green, Type is a secret haven of elegant and stylish desirables. Have a cup of coffee, then browse vintage pulp fiction, customised furniture, and carefully curated gifts by emerging crafts people (we love their stainless-steel, etched models of London landmarks). Best of all is the selection of vintage typewriters – great presents for analogue-loving friends, or a delicious indulgence for yourself (you can justify your purchase by the fact that you're going to create some beautiful, hand-typed missives). If you can't stretch to (or haven't got room for) a typewriter, get a special letter inked to order.

Typeeast.com
66 Sclater Street, E1 6HR
Overground Shoreditch High Street

TOP TEN
Dinner party presents

JJ Fox, *St James's*
Ultra-establishment purveyor of the finest, most aromatic – and decadent – Cuban cigars.

Scarlet & Violet,
Kensal Green
Where chic flower bouquets come charmingly wrapped or beautifully arranged in a quirky vase.

Neal's Yard Dairy,
Covent Garden
Choose a nutty Stichelton or classic Cheddar from their mouth-watering selection.

Choccywoccydoodah, *Soho*
Feeling generous? Their giant, hand-painted chocolate skull is a show-stopping gift.

Berry Brothers and Rudd, *St James's*
Britain's oldest wine merchant will help you pick out a great vintage.

Urban Outfitters
(branches across London)
Snap up a refurbished Polaroid camera (or a much cheaper disposable camera) to capture memories of a special evening.

Print Club, *Dalston*
Choose from a carefully selected range of limited-edition screenprints to brighten up your hosts' walls.

Divertimenti, *Knightsbridge*
Pick an obscure food utensil – perfect for a foodie host.

Selfridges Food Hall,
Oxford Street
Pick from a mouthwatering array of goodies, such as chocolate cigars, jellybeans or elderflower marshmallows.

Ladurée, *Harrods,*
Burlington Arcade
Delicate, multi-coloured macarons that the fashion pack swoon over. The salted caramel-flavoured creations are a mouthful of heaven.

TOP TEN
Museum and gallery shops

The Geffrye Museum,
Shoreditch
Impeccably stylish and
practical homewares, plus
retro books and toys.

The Science Museum,
South Kensington
Engineering kits, space ice
cream, and telescopes.

Tate Modern, *Southbank*
Art prints, bold homewares
and beautiful grand art books.

The British Library,
Bloomsbury
Stacked with fabulous books
(of course), and quirky gifts
themed around exhibitions.

V&A, *South Kensington*
Bold contemporary
jewellery and luscious
wall-candy prints.

The Museum of Childhood,
Bethnal Green
Colourful, tasteful toys, fun
games and glorious books.

The Wellcome Collection,
Bloomsbury
An eccentric and
idiosyncratic collection of
medical history-themed gifts.

Museum of London, *City*
Stylish London-themed
memorabilia, a far cry from
touristy bits and bobs.

London Transport
Museum, *Covent Garden*
Imaginative and stylish
gifts for travel fans or those
who love the iconic designs
of the Tube, bus and trains
through the ages.

Design Museum,
Southbank
Contemporary prints,
beautiful books and clever
homeware and gifts,
perfect for the discerning
design lover.

Coco De Mer – for the special woman in your life
Sexy gifts for the boudoir
—

Strange brews at Gerry's Wines and Spirits
Track down an obscure drink in minutes
—

This high-end sex shop sells feminine, lovingly crafted erotic wares. Their ethically made products are of the highest quality; gleaming wooden spanking paddles, handcuffs made from soft leather and suede, and Stella McCartney knickers hang alongside Atsuko Kudo latex dresses. Masks are scattered with Swarovski crystals, there are rolls of decadently rude wallpapers and 'strumpet' teacups. The atmosphere is inclusive and non-intimidating. Find the classiest hen-night presents in the city, or a sexy gift for someone very close to you.

Gerry's has an enormous range of strange and rare bottles of spirits, wines and beers, all crammed onto wooden shelves, jostling for your attention. Find Day of the Dead-style, skull-shaped bottles filled with tequila, deep jade-coloured bottles of absinthe, old English cordials, obscure saki and beers. Pick up dusty bottles of syrup – banana, cucumber, hibiscus and lavender – to inspire creative, experimental cocktails. Ask to see their bottles of classic rock-themed wines, which make great gifts for dads.

coco-de-mer.com
23 Monmouth Street, WC2H 9DD
Tube Covent Garden

gerrys.uk.com
74 Old Compton Street, W1D 4UW
Tube Leicester Square

Chinatown

Delicious treats from Chinatown
Hard-to-find, exotic presents for foodies

—

Chinatown, at the south end of Soho, is a colourful place to wander for an hour; you'll feel as if you've stepped out into another world as you amble down Gerrard Street. Here you'll find ugli, lychees and durian fruits piled high outside grocers' shops and displays of frozen, soft-shell crabs, dried jellyfish, bags of exotic spices and Chinese teas within. Other stores stock shiny lucky waving cats, Hello Kitty stationery, satin-covered boxes and brightly-coloured Asian sweets. Pack a cutesy rucksack full of goodies for a teenager's birthday gift, or pick out exotic ingredients for a foodie friend.

Tube Leicester Square

Browse through curios at Alfie's Antique Market
Search for vintage treasures

—

Find a gift for anyone in love with the past in the enormous Alfie's Antique Market; from a gleaming cigarette lighter, delicate glass ornament or mid-century light fitting, to a piece of Victorian costume jewellery. It's good for vintage clothes and accessories; pick up beaded purses, satin gloves and cocktail frocks, or silk scarves and felt hats for chaps. This curious building is a winding labyrinth of passages, tiny rooms stacked high with wonders, a fish pond, and, on the rooftop of the building, a café. The perfect place to find one-of-a-kind presents.

alfiesantiques.com
13–25 Church Street, NW8 8DT
Tube Marylebone

Bag something old and beautiful at Blitz
The cream of the vintage crop
—

A huge, vintage department store, Blitz is housed in an old furniture factory in the East End. All the stock is sorted, cleaned and steamed fresh, uncover acres of stone-washed denim, vintage, jewel-coloured kimonos, walls bedecked with knotted silk scarves, plus neon rucksacks to pack it all into. Pick over glittery shoes with a few more dances left in them, glam handbags, and round off your quick trip with a cup of coffee served from the shop's own, chromed machine. Be sure to pick up a flyer before you enter for extra money off.

blitzlondon.co.uk
55–59 Hanbury Street, E1 5JP
Overground Shoreditch High Street

Liberty – a touch of luxury
The gift-for-everyone shop
—

Buying a gift from Liberty feels like a treat. The iconic building is piled elegantly high with desirable and quirky objects. There really is a present for everyone here; from delicate Fornasetti teapots to lamps shaped like baby's heads or money boxes that look like guinea pigs. The softest leather handbags and beautiful textiles bring colour to the dark wood-panelled rooms, the fragrance of the hall of scents lingers as you browse beautiful stationery and elegant gifts for the home. And, no visit to Liberty is complete without a look through the infinite numbers of gifts made in the store's distinctive, flowery prints.

liberty.co.uk
Regent Street, W1B 5AH
Tube Oxford Circus

Liberty

Tooting Bec Lido

AN HOUR FOR YOURSELF

Got a few minutes before your big date? Want to wind down after an important meeting? You can feel a little guilty about spending your precious time on yourself, and it can seem hard to justify, but there are places you can go where even a little time can make a difference to your body and mind.

Exercise can be fun and effective and done in short, concentrated bursts. Beauty treatments can be indulgent yet speedy. The city is packed with places dedicated to making you more glamorous, fitter and happier in minutes. Here's our guide to the most efficient yet luxurious treats for you.

De-stress at the Aveda Institute
*Luxurious, unpretentious beauty
and body treatments*

—

Aveda specialise in beauty and body treatments
that manage to be indulgent without any fuss
or time-wasting. They use environmentally and
socially responsible products that will put your
mind at rest as your body is pampered. Their
London Salon and Spa in Covent Garden is
chic and calming; book a Lava Shells massage
or unwind with a Stress-Fix session that will
pummel away your cares. All treatments are
available in 30-minute or 60-minute blocks;
you'll relax safe in the knowledge your session
won't over run, and emerge rejuvenated and
ready to take on the toughest of afternoons.

avedainstitute.co.uk
174–177 High Holborn, WC1V 7AA
Tube Covent Garden

Watch your scent being created at Le Labo
Bespoke artisan perfumes

—

Housed in a stripped-down, New York-style
concession in Liberty, and in its own stores
in Shoreditch and Marylebone, Le Labo create
hand-poured, artisan perfumes that are blended
by technicians in front of your eyes. Each is
named for the primary ingredient, individually
labelled with a message or name, plus the date
and place made, and smells divine. Sample the
Poivre 23 – it's exclusive to the London stores.

lelabofragrances.com
61 Redchurch Street, E2 7DJ
Overground Shoreditch High Street
28a Devonshire Street, W1E 6PS
Tube Baker Street

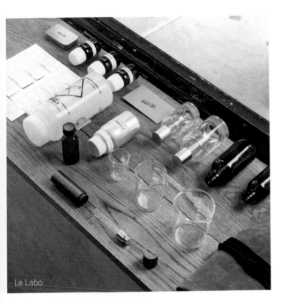

Le Labo

Get into the saddle at Hyde Park Stables

Feel the wind in your hair on a horseback ride through London

———

Cantering through Hyde Park on the back of a pony is an utterly joyful way to take in central London. Horses have been trotting down Rotten Row in Hyde Park since the 17th century, and it is still a bridleway today. Hyde Park Stables' lessons take place in the park under careful supervision; if you've never ridden before you can start from scratch, or hardened horse riders can brush up their jockeying skills. The joy of these stables is their location; because they are so central, it's a quick and easy hit of both fresh air and exercise, and a wholesome way to clear your mind after a day at work.

hydeparkstables.com
63 Bathurst Mews, W2 2SB
Tube Lancaster Gate

Hair-raising drama at
It's Something Hell's
Ultra-retro, flick-knife-wielding hairdressers

———

French power-cutting couple Mr Ducktail and Miss Betty run this retro hair-styling palace just off Carnaby Street. Decked out in leopard print, red leather and chrome, with a rockabilly-stacked jukebox belting out classic hits, this is hairdressing as immersive theatre. Miss Betty and her rock-a-hula team create curls, set styles and whip out the bleach for perfect, pin-up locks for the ladies. Meanwhile, rockabilly (and non-rockabilly) chaps can brave the quicker flick-knife hair cut. Demon barber Mr Ducktail creates quiffs like no other, shaving close to your neck with his trusty, sharp blade, but never nicking. Rock and roll.

itssomethinghells.com
2nd Floor, Kingly Court, W1F 9PT
Tube Oxford Circus

Get on board at Skates
and Ladders
One-on-one skateboard lessons for
wannabe sidewalk surfers

———

You're never too old to whip along the pavement on four wheels, but you may not feel like jumping straight on a board and surfing concrete if you've never done it before. Skates and Ladders teach skateboarding, longboarding and Pennyboarding in central London locations (skate parks, royal parks or commons) to complete beginners (they'll even provide rides and safety equipment). Head to a park near your work at lunchtime to master a skill that makes running around town fun, while keeping you fit and healthy and out in the open air.

skatesandladders.com
Across London

Top-to-toe makeover at Murdock Barbershop
Luxurious beard trims, shaves and shoe-shines
——

Super-sophisticated, and with one foot in the past and one in the stylish present, London's chain of Murdock barbershops cater for the dapper man about town. All haircuts come in at under 60 minutes, while a wet shave with a cut-throat razor takes only 45. More rugged chaps will be grateful for the beard trim or reshape service. It's also a great place for well-groomed men to slip in a beauty treatment; a facial takes only half an hour, or a manicure even less. Add on a quick shoe-shine at the end, and you will emerge buffed and filled with extra confidence for that hot date or important brainstorm.

murdocklondon.com
Branches across London

R&R at Cucumba
Regain your cool with a beauty pit-stop
——

Cucumba's beauty treatments come by the minute; tell them how long you've got, and they will suggest treatments that will fit your schedule. You can spend a relaxing hour having a luxury, full-body massage, 30 minutes on a full manicure, or ten on a no-nonsense, quick-fix back-and-shoulder rub. They've got tiny micro-treatments that are even quicker; have a mini facial or get your lips glittered in just a few minutes. It's all about taking a little break for yourself, no matter how short, and feeling happier at the end of it.

cucumba.co.uk
12 Poland Street, W1F 8QB
Tube Oxford Circus

TOP TEN
Swimming pools

Ironmonger Row Baths, *Clerkenwell*
Long lanes, high ceilings, this renovated 1930s building also houses a great Turkish baths complex.

Golden Lane Leisure Centre, *Barbican*
Light and bright, this covered pool is perched on a rooftop in the city.

Shoreditch House
A super-glamorous rooftop outdoor pool. You will need to be a member (or know one) to get in.

Oasis, *Covent Garden*
A public, outdoor pool in the heart of the West End.

Parliament Hill Lido
Open every day of the year, this huge, unheated outdoor pool is perfect for a cool-down on the hottest of days, but probably best suited for hardier swimmers in colder temperatures.

The Lido, *Hyde Park*
Do laps of the very central Hyde Park Lido (or bring a baby and splash around in the children's pool).

Of Soil and Water, *King's Cross*
The UK's first public, man-made, 'naturally' cleaned swimming pond is chemical-free, and surrounded by grasslands and flowers.

Porchester Spa, *Bayswater*
Elegant, beautiful art deco baths and steam rooms make you feel as if you're swimming through a Hollywood film set.

Tooting Bec Lido
It's enormous. It's picturesque. It's a South London summer institution.

The Serpentine, *Hyde Park*
Take a plunge into the cool, clear waters to revive and invigorate you, and let the hubbub of London drift away for a few minutes.

TOP TEN
Nail bars

MWnails, *Spitalfields*
Join the file-high club as you step aboard this salon crafted from the interior of a Boeing 737 aeroplane.

Hari's, *Chelsea*
Get a fashion-forward manicure or a swift Essie Spa pedi.

Sophie Gass, *Holland Park*
Super-chic, light and immaculate, this beauty destination is the last word in nail luxury.

Decadent Digits, *Islington*
Experiment with eye-popping nail art and cutting edge trends courtesy of Sheena, in her ultimate home studio.

The Paint Shop, *Selfridges, Oxford Street*
There's a huge selection of colours and finishes at the magnificent department store's in-house nail bar.

Wah Nails, *Dalston*
The hip East London salon that kickstarted the high-octane nail art trend hosts classes and takes private bookings.

Hula Nails, *Old Street*
Fabulously retro beauty parlour that uses super-modern gel and acrylic techniques to create talons tough enough to rock and roll.

Bliss Nails, *South Kensington*
If your hands are in need of some serious TLC as well as colour, go for Bliss' indulgent Hot Cream Manicure.

Blo Bar, *Chiswick*
This Chiswick salon has an on-site crèche; perfect for stressed parents in need of a buff and polish.

Milk Beauty (*branches across London*)
Don't even have time to leave the office? Book a polish change or manicure in your own home or at work.

Speedy workouts at Zip Fit
Minimum time, maximum burn;
keep-fit for busy bodies

———

Research shows that high intensity training (HIT) is incredibly efficient at burning fat, stimulating the body into consuming calories after sessions. Which is great news for time-poor Londoners. Zip Fit are the masters of outdoor HIT; their sessions are aimed at workers in London and take place in public spaces across the city, including Hyde Park, Lincoln's Inn Fields and Russell Square. A session starts with a five-minute warm-up, followed by 20 minutes of incredibly vigorous exercise, then a five-minute cool-down. It's full on, but the knowledge that it's only going to last for a short period helps you endure the burn.

zipfitclub.co.uk
Across London

Beauty in moments at the Blow Bar
A stress-free, time-efficient makeover

———

The Blow Bar's ethos is simple: make it quick, make it stylish. Their French Connection Regent Street styling bar offers blow-dry, make-up and nail services which all clock in at under 30 minutes each. You can even order a 'Hollywood'; two stylists – one hairdresser, plus a nail technician – double up so you can have both treatments simultaneously. If you then go for the Bar's Lord and Berry Make-Up session, which gives a fresh, super-modern look in another 30 minutes, you can get a full makeover in less than an hour. Squeeze your session in after work, pre-date for a seductive new look.

theblowbar.com
249–251 Regent Street, W1B 2EP
Tube Oxford Circus

Banish tension at Triyoga
Align your body and mind in harmony

——

Yoga is the perfect way to stretch tense muscles after you've been sitting hunched over a computer. Triyoga have a holistic approach to exercise and are passionate about their classes being accessible to everyone. Their welcoming, inclusive centres offer a comprehensive series of classes for all abilities at branches in Camden, Chelsea, Covent Garden and Soho. Their lunchtime sessions are the perfect excuse to get away from your desk; choose from a 55-minute Yoga Open, Hot Open or Vinyasa Open class, or try a 30-minute Meditation and Breath Open lesson. The perfect way to take a break on a stressful day.

triyoga.co.uk
Branches across London

Get down at Pineapple Dance Studios
Learn burlesque moves and keep fit

——

'Please bring high heels and clothes you can move in.' What glorious instructions for a dance class. Pineapple Dance Studios are famous for their professional drop-in workshops and expert instructors, but they also offer fabulous, lower-impact, shimmy sessions for beginners or less expert dancers. Burlesque is just one of the fun keep fit classes on offer, you can also try tap, ballet, jazz, street dance or belly dancing. Go alone to meet new people or take a gaggle of friends for after-work fun.

pineapple.uk.com
7 Langley Street, WC2H 9JA
Tube Covent Garden

Pineapple Dance Studios

Red Cross Garden

AN HOUR OUTDOORS

An hour outside, whatever the weather, is wonderfully restorative, provides the perfect escape from air-conditioning or central heating and is a chance to blow away the cobwebs after a morning in the office. London is one of the greenest cities in the world; there's a lot of wild space to explore. An aimless walk works wonders for the mind, but you'll find you have more motivation to get outside if you plan to go somewhere or do something. Use the time outdoors to try a new, fun exercise class, solve puzzles, volunteer in local parks, or seek somewhere to have your lunch while taking in a great view.

All the ideas here make perfect dawn excursions, lunchtime adventures or post-work wind-downs. Don't stay chained to your desk, get outside and snatch a slice of outdoor life in London; there's a whole raft of possibilities and adventures.

Step into another world at the Kensington Roof Gardens
Wander among bluebells and crocuses high above West London
——

Take a short lift ride up through a wonderful, 1930s, art deco building (formerly Derry and Tom's department store), step out of the doors and you'll be greeted with the spectacular sight of the Kensington Roof Gardens. In spring, the earthy floor is carpeted with narcissi, crocuses and beautiful bluebells. Head up with a book and your lunch, find a quiet spot and kick back in beautiful surroundings. Choose from the Spanish, Tudor or English Woodland gardens, depending on your mood, and be transported from central London. Be sure to call ahead to check opening times.

virginlimitededition.com/en/the-roof-gardens
99 Kensington High Street, W8 5SA
Tube High Street Kensington

Pitch up to King's Cross Outdoor Sports Pitch
Play team sports with friends for free
——

Part of the radical King's Cross revamp, this free-to-book, floodlit, all-weather sports pitch is suitable for five-a-side football or basketball. Round up a bunch of workmates, chip in for a ball, and have a weekly 45-minute game. It'll raise team spirits, get you fired up for the afternoon, and is a fun way to keep fit. There's even a little hatch café, run by Global Generation, the people from the adjoining Skip Garden, for half-time refuelling.

kingscross.co.uk/outdoor-sports-area
York Way, N1 0AZ
Tube King's Cross

Try a different route with London's self-service bikes
Take a low-stress cycle ride purely for pleasure

London's bike-sharing scheme cycles are ideal for a leisurely hour's pedal around the capital; avoid busy streets for maximum enjoyment. Pick up a bike at Hyde Park Corner, and do a lap of the green space; you'll have plenty of time to stop and take in views, lick an ice cream and dip your feet in the Serpentine. Or try riding for half an hour and back along a canal towpath or riverside; the Grand Union west of the junction with the Harrow Road is a good bet, as is the River Lea in the east. Be sure to swot up in advance on the routes to take where the waterways dip underground. Guaranteed happiness.

tfl.gov.uk/modes/cycling
Across London

London Cycle Hire Scheme

A little slice of greenery at Camley Street Natural Park
Commune with nature to restore your balance

——

A two-acre canal-side nature reserve in the concreted heart of London, Camley Street is home to shelter-seeking birds (including beautiful kingfishers), brightly coloured butterflies, pond-life and bats. Stroll through this leafy oasis to the Viewpoint – a floating platform on the canal modelled on the rocky islets of the Scandinavian coast – or wander around the ponds, marshland and meadow and feel at one with nature in an urban setting.

wildlondon.org.uk/reserves/camley-street-natural-park
12 Camley Street, N1C 4PW
Tube King's Cross

Tramp through Queen's Wood
Create your own leafy retreat in an ancient forest

——

London is one of the most verdant big cities in the world; you don't have to travel far to find cool, green copses or towering trees. Queen's Wood in Highgate is ancient woodland, full of twisted boughs and deserted enough in which to lose yourself. Wander into the middle of the wood on a sticky day, and let the sound of the city recede. You may spot jays, foxes, and the occasional dog walker.

Muswell Hill Road, N10
Tube Highgate

TOP TEN
Podcasts, radio and more

Londonist Out Loud
Take in the city's history or listen in on conversations between its fascinating residents (londonist.com/podcasts).

Guardian's London Walks podcast archive
Download a map and accompanying audio guide and take an informed stroll around the city (theguardian.com/travel/series/cityguides).

The Barbican podcast
Covering contemporary and classical music, film and events held at the cultural hub and beyond (barbican.org.uk/about-barbican/podcasts).

Resonance FM
London's quirky, avant-garde radio station (104.4 FM or resonancefm.com).

The London Sound Survey
Records evocative sounds of the city from street traders to Salvation Army bands (soundsurvey.org.uk).

Spark London
Storytellers from across the city relate their true tales, live (sparklondon.com).

Headspace
A free app that provides ten-minute mindfulness sessions to help beat stress and aid focus (headspace.com).

Talking Statues Trail
Scores of London monuments now have swipeable tags to listen to a phone call from whoever is immortalised in the sculpture (talkingstatues.co.uk).

Fabric podcasts
Download the super-club's guest-compiled-and-presented podcasts for a taste of the city's dance scene (fabriclondon.com/podcast).

Robert Elms on BBC London
A daily show that's steeped in the history and culture of London. Catch up on missed programmes via iPlayer.

TOP TEN
Beer gardens

The Canonbury,
Highbury & Islington
A huge, modern garden
with acres of seats and an
outside bar.

Edinboro Castle, *Camden*
Lots of space in which to
sprawl, the pub where
Camden's pale rock and roll
crowd come to get sunburned.

The Angel, *Soho*
Extremely central, this pub's
tiny courtyard is a secret
haven for real ale drinkers.

The Windmill, *Brixton*
Head here in the summer
for one of their live music
festivals with free barbecue.

The Faltering Fallback,
Finsbury Park
This cleverly designed space
uses high decking, steps and
roofs to create nooks and
crannies in which to hole up.

The Magic Garden,
Battersea
Well named, this bar is all
about the beautiful outside
space; twinkly lights, huge
canopies and heavily-scented
flowers abound.

The Stag, *Hampstead*
An enormous garden that
hosts live music in the
summer. Book a private
cabana for up to 14 of your
friends to be sure of a seat.

The Ship, *Wandsworth*
Right on the river, this is
a mellow spot from which
to watch boats and swans
glide by.

The People's Park Tavern,
Hackney
Covered and heated in
winter, this picture-perfect,
Astroturfed sanctuary on
the edge of Victoria Park is a
great place to sip on the pub's
microbrewed People's Pints.

The Gipsy Moth, *Greenwich*
In the shade of the Cutty
Sark, it's all too easy to while
away a whole afternoon on
this sunny patio.

The Thames foreshore
Find ancient treasures on the banks of the river

———

Poor Londoners once scratched a living mudlarking, or scrabbling around for finds on the shore of the Thames. Now, beachcombing is a great way to find out about the city's past, while inhaling lungfuls of fresh(ish) air. Check the tide-tables, pull on some substantial shoes and disposable gloves and go for a poke about. Good sites include the 'beach' near St Paul's Cathedral, Gabriel's Wharf and the areas around Southwark and Blackfriars Bridges. You'll need a permit to dig, so stick to peering hard at the surface. You're likely to find 16th-century clay pipes, pieces of ceramics and interesting old glass, or even flint arrowheads. It's a direct, real connection with ancient London, which can be emotionally intense, incredibly interesting and addictive.

pla.co.uk/Environment/Metal-Detecting-and-Digging-on-the-Thames-Foreshore

Get out on the water at Docklands Sailing and Watersports Centre
Sail a boat at dusk through the docks

———

Now clean and sparkling after years of industrial abuse, the River Thames provides a natural escape from the stresses and bustle of the city's packed pavements. Head to the Docklands Sailing and Watersports Centre and get onto the water for a short burst of sailing, windsurfing or kayaking. Their open evening sessions are great for those who have previous experience; glide gently around the dock in a dinghy as the sun sets, listening to the waves lap at the bow. On Wednesdays in the summer there's usually a barbecue on the go, with beer on offer to heighten the fun.

dswc.org
235a Westferry Road, Docklands, E14 3QS
DLR Mudchute

Release your inner child on Primrose Hill

Kite flying with a killer vista

——

A climb up Primrose Hill will reward you with magnificent views of the city, from Canary Wharf's towers to the mast at Crystal Palace, and offer fresh wisps of wind on even the most still day. Banish stress and indulge your inner child by flying a kite. It's a cheap, quick-to-master hobby; inexpensive kites fly just as well as pricey ones. Feel your spirits soar as the kite rises, dips and bobs.

NW1
Tube Chalk Farm

Pinot and petanque at the Prince of Wales pub

Play petanque in the glow of the evening sun

——

Bowl over to Cleaver Square in Kennington on a sunny evening for a leisurely throw at sunset and it's as if you've been transported to a dusty town square in the French countryside. You don't need all the kit; you can borrow a set of balls from the excellent Prince of Wales pub for a small deposit and unwind with a game in a group, drinks in hand.

shepherdneame.co.uk/pubs/kennington/ prince-wales
Cleaver Square, SE11 4EA
Tube Kennington

Red Cross Garden

Get your hands dirty at the Red Cross Garden
Volunteer in Southwark's 'open air sitting room'

——

'Nature breathes in darkest Southwark' exclaimed social reformer Octavia Hill triumphantly, as she created the Red Cross Garden. Built in 1887, this space was part of a Victorian community improvement scheme that included cottages, a reading room, library and hall. Almost lost to development in the 1940s, the garden is now being restored and maintained as an urban oasis and community asset. Philanthropy is an excellent motivator. Volunteer to help maintain and plant the garden and you'll be guaranteed an active hour outside each week, plus the satisfaction of having given something to the community. There's a regular, scheduled lunch-hour session on Wednesdays at 12.45, or drop them a line to agree a time that works for you.

bost.org.uk/open-places/red-cross-garden/
50 Redcross Way, SE1 1HA
Tube Borough

Where online and real worlds collide – geocaching
Follow clues and find hidden treasures

———

A digital-to-real-world treasure hunt, geocachers hide trinkets or sign-in sheets around the world, mark the spot on an online map, then wait for others to discover them. Hunting down the caches is a novel way to explore a city and surprisingly rewarding. Some geocaches are simply boxes of goodies to discover (always leave an equivalent in return), others are more complex; a multi-cache might lead you on a walk guided by clues through Marylebone. Many caches in London are virtual, requiring you to email answers or proof of location to claim them. Plan your caching online – from your desk perhaps – then go out on a puzzling adventure in your lunch hour.

geocaching.com

Score a hole in one at Hyde Park Putting Green
London's most central golf 'course'

———

Playing a tiny round of golf on a putting green is huge fun, and when it's within striking distance of your office and do-able in your lunch hour, there's no excuse for not pitching up with a club and some balls. This miniature course near the south side of Hyde Park is beautifully kept; neat lawns and well-stocked flowering borders encircle the winding holes, and the course is decorated with over-sized concrete pineapples and acorns. The course is open long hours in summer; from 7am–9pm on weekdays, or 8am–9pm at weekends, which means there's even time for a quick round before work or before you head home.

willtowin.co.uk/hyde-park-putting-bowls/
South Carriage Drive, W2 2UH
Tube Knightsbridge

London Coliseum

AN HOUR TO SEE THE SIGHTS

In London, you're never more than five minutes from a museum, gallery or historic landmark. There's something of interest on each corner and down every narrow alley. If you've got an hour to spare, spend it wisely – visit somewhere you've never been before, drop into a tiny exhibition in your lunch break, or, if you've got half an hour to kill before your train departs, take in a little slice of London's past before you run to the platform.

Even over a lifetime in London you'll struggle to see all it has to offer. So get started on your mini adventures now and rediscover your city.

Aldwych Tube Station

London's hidden gem – Sir John Soane's Museum
An eccentric, charming jumble of treasures

——

The eclectic treasures of architect Sir John Soane are displayed in three knocked-through townhouses. A notorious hoarder, Soane collected furiously throughout his lifetime, cramming antiquities, statues, paintings and furniture into the tiny, dark, higgledy-piggledy rooms of his home. You'll squeeze past busts, be confronted by a giant sarcophagus and get up close to Hogarth's series of paintings, *The Rake's Progress*. Stepping into the museum is a real sensory overload; the darkness, dust and strange juxtaposition of objects make for a jolting, spooky ride. Emerge into the sunlight with a different perspective on London.

soane.org
13 Lincoln's Inn Fields, WC2A 3BP
Tube Holborn

Take a trip into London's Underground past
Explore the disused Aldwych station

——

A few times a year, Aldwych Tube station – closed since 1994 – opens up for one-hour tours. It's very difficult to get a ticket, but if you're keen and willing to keep an eye on on-sale dates, it's possible. Visitors get to descend into a time capsule: the place where *Sherlock*, *Paddington* and the Prodigy's 'Firestarter' video were filmed. The station also provided shelter to Londoners in the Blitz – prepare for a real glimpse into the hidden city.

ltmuseum.co.uk/whats-on/events-calendar
The Strand, WC2R
Tube Temple

Step back in time at Pollock's Toy Museum
A place to feed a fevered imagination

⸻

Narrow, rickety stairs in this quirky, infamous toy museum lead to tiny rooms with cases stuffed to bursting with tin cars, robots and building bricks, paper theatres and stereoscopes, and dusty cabinets with hundreds of dolls staring out, blankly. If dolls give you the creeps, this is not the place for you, but if you love old-fashioned toys, it's a real treasure trove. You may well be the only person creaking around the higgledy-piggledy, toy-filled house, and an hour is plenty of time to linger. If the gently mouldering playthings start to overwhelm you, hurry down to the toyshop below, grab a few cheap-and-cheerful, modern stocking fillers, then get out.

pollockstoys.com
1 Scala St, W1T 2HL
Tube Goodge Street

Peek backstage at the London Coliseum
A short-but-perfectly-formed tour; the story of London in microcosm

⸻

Home of the English National Opera, the London Coliseum preens and winks just up from Trafalgar Square, topped with a gigantic, light-studded ball. A 60-minute tour is a fascinating, focused glimpse into a building with an astonishing history; it's been a variety theatre, a cinema, a canteen for war workers, and a West End theatre. Nose into the goings-on behind the scenes (and under the revolving stage!), the grandest of smoking rooms, staircases that curl up to gilded, painted ceilings and the maze of shabby, backstage corridors. This tour of 'The People's Palace' feels like a real peep behind the curtain. Book well in advance.

eno.org/guidedtours
St Martin's Lane, WC2N 4ES
Tube Leicester Square

Royal Courts of Justice

Watch the law in action at the Royal Courts of Justice
The centre of gossipy cases and legal intrigue

The Royal Courts are extraordinary, anyone can wander in and look around; there's a self-guided tour (pick up a leaflet from the information desk), which takes you up and around the vast, spectacular building, including through an exhibition of legal costumes, and into the 'bear garden' (a spectacularly decorated robing room). But the real thrill comes from the intrigue; rub shoulders with crusty legal eagles, and, best of all, sit in the public gallery. The cases heard at the Royal Courts are all civil, so think big, bitter celebrity divorces, high-profile contract disputes, libel and retrials (head to the Old Bailey down the road if you want to sit in on bloodthirsty murder trials). A juicy, totally unique way to spend an hour.

justice.gov.uk
The Strand, WC2A 2LL
Tube Blackfriars

Ascend the Monument
The windy view at the top makes every step of the climb worthwhile

———

Immerse yourself in Wilton's Music Hall
A picturesque shrine to faded glories

———

Standing 62m tall, the Monument commemorates the Great Fire of London. A trip to the top is a perfect, clear-day, lunchtime adventure; climb 311 steps to reach the outdoor viewing platform, brace your wobbly legs, and stare out across the city with the wind on your face. It's the perfect place from which to mull over the huge changes London has seen; spot graceful Wren churches and cathedrals, now dwarfed by shiny, optimistic financial towers. Peer into the distance to glimpse the iconic chimneys of Battersea Power Station, the Thames snaking off to the sea, and, closer by, the tops of lunching workers' heads.

themonument.info
Fish Street Hill, EC3R 8AH
Tube Monument

Wilton's Music Hall is one of the most gloriously atmospheric places in London. The dilapidated (but still functioning) theatre is set deep in the East End. The living embodiment of faded grandeur, it's a real joy to hang out in the picturesque bar and sip a cocktail, before watching a film or a show. Most Mondays, there's an hour-long tour of the venue, which tells the story of the venue's colourful past; from sailors' pub, to music hall, Methodist Mission, and finally arts venue. It is a romantic building, saved from demolition by a long campaign by the community and celebrities such as Spike Milligan; restored, it is a glimpse of living, breathing, old London.

wiltons.org.uk
1 Graces Alley, London E1 8JB
Tube Aldgate East

Wilton's Music Hall

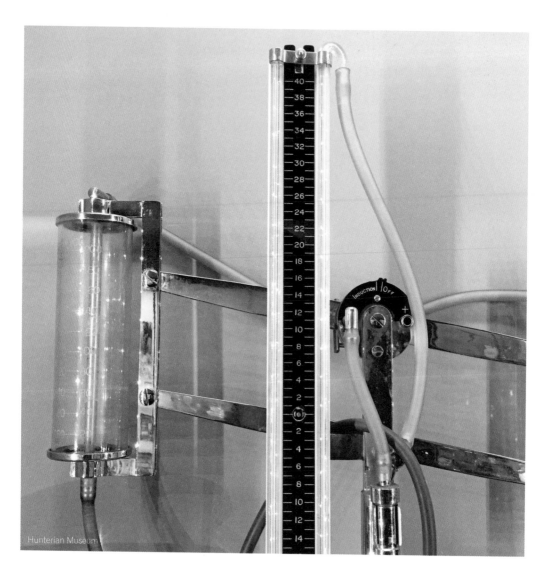

Be charmed by the Rolling Bridge
Elegant street architecture that unfurls weekly

——

Every week, on Friday at noon, a little ceremony occurs in Paddington. Heatherwick Studio's Rolling Bridge, which spends the week curled into a ball, creaks into life as two workers unfurl it across the Grand Union Canal. Anyone who is interested is allowed to walk across the bridge, after which the structure is refolded back for another week. It's a beautiful little performance that will brighten your day. Get there early to be sure not to miss it (timings can vary slightly). If you get the folding water crossing bug, the Edward Scissorhands-style Fan Bridge is just around the corner, and springs into action every Wednesday and Friday at noon.

merchantsquare.co.uk/about_paddington/
canal-crossings/
Paddington Basin, Grand Union Canal
(near N Wharf Rd), W2
Tube Paddington

Hunterian Museum – for the hardened constitution
Curiosities from medical history

——

The Hunterian is not for the squeamish. The old, dramatic building in which it's housed contrasts with the sharp, contemporarily lit displays. See the skeleton of Charles Byrne, the 'Irish Giant', surgical instruments belonging to Lister, wax anatomical models, and jars full of body parts distorted through disease. There are spectacles with silver noses attached to replace those that have dropped off due to syphilis, and an exhibition of early facial reconstruction surgery. It's easy to spend just an hour in this riveting place, even easier to linger longer.

hunterianmuseum.org
35–43 Lincoln's Inn Fields, WC2A 3PE
Tube Holborn

Look into the hallowed Freemasons' Hall
The art deco temple of an ancient secret society

——

For a supposedly covert group, the Freemasons aren't that shy. Their headquarters sits proudly on Great Queen Street like a curvy ocean liner and is dotted with masonic symbols. You don't even need a secret handshake to get past the friendly doorstaff. There's a museum packed with masonic paraphernalia (the bejeweled, rams-horn snuff box is particularly delicious) that's worth a look, but try to catch one of the 45-minute guided tours of the main hall. It's a beautiful, gilded, white marble cathedral, with signs and symbols everywhere; Egyptian hieroglyphics, Greek characters and scenes from the Bible. Join the dots to create your own, outlandish conspiracy theory. One of London's most magnificent gems.

ugle.org.uk/freemasons-hall
60 Great Queen Street, WC2B 5AZ
Tube Holborn

The bizarre world of Viktor Wynd's Museum of Curiosities
A higgledy-piggledy collection of everything weird

——

Viktor Wynd collects. And collects. Like a modern-day John Soane, his Museum of Curiosities tumbles with wonders such as walls of glass jars filled with innards, specimens and browning animals, gruesome taxidermy, and Amy Winehouse's poo in a jar sits alongside hunched skeletons, Chinese dildos and African masks. There is no order, or attempt to categorise, and the place is all the more glorious for it. Housed on (night) Mare Street inHackney, the museum is also home to the Last Tuesday Society, who hold lectures on subjects as diverse as fish keeping and fairy tales.

thelasttuesdaysociety.org/museum-curiosities
11 Mare Street, E8 4RP
Tube Bethnal Green

Freemason's Hall

Get familiar with the Museum of Brands, Packaging and Advertising
A temple of everyday nostalgia

—

When you enter this museum though a 'time tunnel', the examples of twentieth-century crisp packets, washing powder boxes and chocolate wrappers will jog memories and evoke surprisingly strong nostalgic emotions. You can wistfully recall your childhood days over a cup of tea or an old-fashioned ice lolly in the tea room afterwards, while you watch old adverts on the TV screens.

museumofbrands.com
111–117 Lancaster Road, W11 1QT
Tube Ladbroke Grove

Wesley's Chapel Toilets – water closets with a difference
The most stylish, elegant public bathrooms in London

—

On the bustling City Road, Wesley's Chapel and house is an 18th-century, ornate shrine to the Methodist movement, formed from burnished wood, boiled sweet-coloured stained glass and glossy marble imported from every country where the religion was practised. Downstairs, however, is something more prosaic, but still as inspiring, and extremely quick to tour. The men's toilets were designed by Thomas Crapper (no laughing at the back, please), and the extravagant stalls by George Jennings. Ladies are allowed to visit the immaculately kept bathroom (ask a member of staff) to admire the shining tiles, mosaic floors and chain pulls that come with the instructions: 'pull and let go'.

wesleyschapel.org.uk
49 City Road, EC1Y 1AU
Tube Barbican

The British Museum,
Bloomsbury
Take one of the Eye Opener tours that last 30–40 minutes and run throughout the day.

Science Museum,
South Kensington
Head to their monthly Lates night for talks, silent discos, performances, drinks and more.

Petrie Museum, *Bloomsbury*
This tiny, quirky museum contains Egyptian artefacts, including a sexy beaded dancer's dress from 2400BC.

V&A, *South Kensington*
Do the Theatre and Performance galleries on level 3 for amazing showbiz-related artefacts, and stage costumes that dazzle.

Royal London Hospital Museum, *Whitechapel*
See the Elephant Man's hat and models he made, as well as some Jack the Ripper-related material.

The Brunel Museum,
Canary Wharf
If you don't have time for a descent into the gigantic Thames Tunnel Shaft chamber (you'll need to take a guided tour), head to the wonderful Apothecary bar in the rooftop garden.

The Fashion and Textile Museum, *Bermondsey*
Small but perfectly chic, a vibrant walk through the history of fashion from 1950 to the present day.

The Foundling Museum,
Bloomsbury
The art gallery is packed with paintings donated by celebrated artists to support the children's charity, Coram.

The Horniman, *Dulwich*
Piled with eccentric curios; an over-stuffed walrus, a merman sculpture made from dead fish and tribal masks.

The Grant Museum of Zoology, *Bloomsbury*
Preserved remains of animals include a jar of moles, gorgeous glass models of invertebrates, and a cleverly presented celebration of tiny flora and fauna, The Micrarium.

TOP TEN
Houses of style

Dr Johnson's House, *City*
A peaceful, atmospheric place to wander and imagine witty writer Samuel Johnson hard at work.

Sutton House, *Hackney*
A Tudor survivor in the heart of the East End. Walk around the art-filled Breakers Yard for a trip into Wonderland.

2 Willow Road, *Hampstead*
Fans of mid-century architecture and interiors will lust over Ernö Goldfinger's home.

Carlyle's House, *Vauxhall*
Once the place for Victorian writers to be seen in Chelsea, its wonderful interiors are perfectly preserved.

Keats House, *Hampstead*
Full of paintings and letters, this gloriously romantic building also holds regular poetry performances. You can imagine a consumptive Keats wandering pensively through the rooms.

575 Wandsworth Road, *Battersea*
An ordinary 19th-century terraced house on the outside, but with an interior covered in hand-carved fretwork, created by one, very dedicated, man.

7 Hammersmith Terrace
Home to the last Arts and Crafts interior in Britain, this was the house of Doves Press owner and friend of William Morris, Emery Walker.

John Wesley's House, *Hoxton*
A place of pilgrimage for Methodists. Look out for his depression-treating Electrical Machine.

The Isokon Gallery, *Hampstead*
Tells the story of the stunning, modernist Hampstead building saved from demolition in the 1990s.

Benjamin Franklin's House, *Embankment*
Theatrical Historical Experience tours bring the home of the founding father of the United States to life.

Fly the Emirates Airline Cable Car
Swing across the Thames

———

London has so many modes of travel; aim to try out more of them on your way in to work this year. A ride across the Thames on the cable car is one of the most fun and dramatic. Use your Oyster card to pay for your trip and get a discount, take the Discovery experience – a non-stop round trip with an on-board video tour, or, if you're feeling flush, hire out an entire cabin for a little under £100. On weekdays, the cars start running at 7am (early enough to catch the sunrise in winter), and soar up to 90m over the Thames, looking out at Docklands and the O2. Journeys in the morning are speedier than at any other time of the day – five minutes as opposed to ten – so you'll have to be quick with your camera.

emiratesairline.co.uk
27 Wester Gateway, E16 1BW
Tube North Greenwich

March down to the Roman Amphitheatre
History hidden under the City's feet

———

The Square Mile is packed with history, but this is one of the oldest, most bloodthirsty sites you'll find: a 2000-year-old Roman amphitheatre, where thousands gathered to watch animal fights, executions and gladiators. Discovered in 1988, the ruins are now exposed below the Guildhall Art Gallery, and the original lines of the building are traced out in black across the yard above. The display provides plenty of wonderfully executed context (there's actually more context than bricks), and takes less than half an hour to look around; if you've got more time, head up to the art gallery above.

cityoflondon.gov.uk
Guildhall Yard, EC2V 5AE
Tube Bank

AN HOUR TO GET CREATIVE

Make the capital your muse. Having a creative outlet is a release; even if your 9–5 is something imaginative and arty, it feels good to have a project that is all your own. Whether you collaborate with others – learning to play instruments, mastering a new language, even hitting the high notes together at karaoke, or go solo, setting up a street-style photo blog, or scribbling poetry – expressing yourself is good for the soul.

Wandering around any part of London is inspirational; the legacies of artists, writers and musicians are dyed fast into the fabric of the city. It's also throbbing with the imaginative people of today and the future, all seeking to collaborate, or to pass on their skills. Get involved and make the most of their talent and knowledge, then go and get productive!

Learn a craft at Drink, Shop & Do
Socialise, eat snacks, make giant, papier-mâché robots

———

Having a drink is more interesting when it is accompanied by a creative activity, and creative activities are more interesting when accompanied by a drink. Drink, Shop & Do is an airy, colourful, café-by-day bar-by-night that holds regular workshops in screenprinting, embroidery, sewing, papier-mâché, and much more. If you're pushed for time, head to one of their drop-in nights and have a glass of wine while you attempt to create a Lego robot, a David Bowie album cover, or a clay model of Lionel Ritchie's head (accompanied by the soundtrack of his greatest hits). Enormous fun and all that silliness makes for great ice-breaking material with neighbouring tables full of sexy, single people.

drinkshopdo.com
9 Caledonian Road, N1 9DX
Tube King's Cross

Strum a ukulele at Learn to Uke
Master the four-stringed instrument in less than 60 minutes

———

The ukulele is a democratic instrument. Even the most unmusical person can learn to play a couple of songs quickly. The most sociable way to master a few chords is in a group. Learn to Uke run classes in the back rooms of London pubs, and they make them really fun. There's an hour-long evening taster class, which includes the loan of an instrument, and takes place at a centrally situated venue. If you like it, sign up for a full course. Next stop, the Pyramid Stage at Glastonbury.

learntouke.co.uk
Courses across London

Drink, Shop & Do

Poetry Café

Take the stand at the Poetry Café

Write, then perform a poem in public

———

Writing poetry is a way to make sense of your city experiences, to reflect and refract them, and to create something from nothing. Head to the veggie-friendly Poetry Café in Covent Garden for an hour of inspiration and self-expression at one of their open mic nights. Perhaps you'll even be tempted to take to the stage. If time really is at a premium, or you're a sparse writer, Poetry@3 limits poems to four minutes.

poetrysociety.org.uk/content/cafe/
Covent Garden Market, 22 Betterton Street, WC2H 9BX
Tube Covent Garden

Get up and improvise

Gain confidence and improve speaking skills through entertainment

———

Improvisation isn't just about making people laugh – although that's a great by-product – it's a means to gain confidence, improve public speaking and hone pitching skills. Improv drama classes are becoming more and more popular with nightly events springing up across the capital. Join a group to explore your imagination and reflexes and learn how to work as a real creative team. City Academy run regular, hour-long taster classes that introduce you gently to the skill. It's an addictive thrill; you will return.

city-academy.com
Courses across London

Lunch with a difference at L'atelier des Chefs
Learn a single dish in half an hour

——

There's something deeply satisfying about adding a new favourite recipe to your repertoire. Once it's there, you can wheel it out at will; another arrow to your culinary bow. L'atelier des Chefs has two branches – one near Oxford Circus, one near St Paul's Cathedral – and run single-recipe 'Cook, Eat & Run' lunchtime courses that take only half an hour. They're hands-on; you do the cooking and the eating – you can either sit and enjoy your meal in the dining area once it's finished, or pack it up to take with you. Recipes are wide-ranging, from Moroccan spiced chicken to steak with Caesar-dressed potatoes. Knives out!

atelierdeschefs.co.uk
19 Wigmore Street, W1U 1PH
Tube Oxford Circus
10 Foster Lane, EC2V 6HR
Tube St Paul's

Dabble in the magical arts at Davenports
Learn a trick in ten minutes

——

Hidden away at the back of an unprepossessing mall under Charing Cross station is a shop of magical tricks. The window is full of old David Copperfield posters, books promising to reveal Houdini's secrets and women dressed as butterflies. Inside are DVDs, trick dice and dozens of different packs of cards. If you play your cards right, a staff member might show you a basic illusion. If you have a deeper knowledge of magic, it's an even more wonderful palace of delights.

davenportsmagic.co.uk
7 Charing Cross Underground Arcade,
The Strand, WC2N 4HZ
Tube Charing Cross

Craft and create at the Machines Room
Kickstart your Etsy business in double-quick time

————

Maker spaces (open-access, communal workshops fitted with machines, printers, software and workbenches) are springing up across the capital. They're perfect for space-short Londoners who need expensive or bulky equipment on a short-term or infrequent basis. You pay to use the spaces by the hour; perfect for craft projects, making prototypes, or playing at being a mad inventor. Jump on a laser cutter for half an hour to cut acrylic charms, build a guitar effects pedal at their electronic bench, or make a dress with their sewing machines. If you need a little help or inspiration, they also run craft events and demonstrations. Machines Room is the perfect incubator for your fledgling creative business.

machinesroom.org
Ground Floor, 45 Vyner Street, E2 9DQ
Tube Bethnal Green

Discover the art of museum sketching
Draw for pleasure and observe objects in more detail

————

You don't have to be a great artist to enjoy sketching. It's relaxing, creative, and a great way to spend a rainy lunch-hour. A good pad of cartridge paper, a 2B pencil and soft rubber will act as cheerleaders in your endeavours. Head to your nearest gallery or museum (the Victoria and Albert is just perfect for this), find something that inspires you, sit down and start drawing. Check out the V&A's excellent sketching guide before you go, for some top tips from the experts on how to capture particular moods and styles.

vam.ac.uk/content/articles/t/drawing-in-museums/

TOP TEN
Perfect sunset watching spots

The **Sky Garden,** *City* at the top of the Walkie Talkie.

The penthouse suite of the **Corinthia Hotel,** *Whitehall.*

The top of **Primrose Hill.**

A **waterbus** on the Thames.

Across the **Serpentine,** *Hyde Park.*

Over a beer at **Frank's Café and Campari Bar,** *Peckham* situated on top of a car park.

The **Queen Elizabeth Hall Roof Garden,** *Southbank* on top of the Southbank Centre.

From **Henry VIII's mound,** *Richmond Park.*

Out of a hot tub at the **Hot Tub cinema,** *Shoreditch.*

The **Radio Rooftop bar,** *Strand* on the tenth floor of the ME London hotel.

TOP TEN
Creative suppliers

I Knit, *Waterloo*
Pop in to buy yarns or linger longer in the cosy and club-like shop – it offers a sociable place to sit and stitch with likeminded people.

London Graphic Centre (*branches across London*)
Gorgeous inks, pens, paint and papers for arty motivation.

MacCulloch & Wallis, *Soho*
For the serious home-sewer; run your hands over pretty fabrics, ribbons and jewel-like buttons.

Beadworks, *Covent Garden*
Piled high with enough crystals, pearls, pendants and chains to fill your jewellery box.

G Baldwin, *Elephant & Castle*
A wonderfully atmospheric place to stock up on essential oils as well as soap-making and candle-making kits.

Clifton Nurseries, *Maida Vale*
A wonderful, fragrant gardeners' paradise; a visit will fire you up to spruce up your plot, balcony or windowsill.

Penfriend, *Picadilly, City*
Poets, writers or just note-takers will find words flow more easily with a vintage writing implement purchased from here.

Slanchogled, *Camden*
A truly inspirational range of craft supplies, from dried flowers and interesting pieces of wood to clay, papers and cutters.

Macari's, *Soho*
A friendly, jam-packed cavern of instruments, with plenty of sound-proofed areas in which to try out your new Colorsound pedal.

The Lomography Gallery Store, *Soho*
The creative's choice of Lomo Cameras, film and accessories, and exhibitions to inspire your snapping.

Step up to the mic at Karaoke Box
Sing your heart out by the hour

———

Karaoke Box have bars in Soho, Mayfair and Smithfield, and rent out rooms – you pay per person, per hour. So gather a group of friends (it's five minimum), and warm up those vocal cords. The bars open at midday; if you're feeling really bold, head there at lunch time for a raucous, sweaty, 60-minute break before brushing yourself down, clearing your throat, and returning to your quiet office.

karaokebox.co.uk
14 Maddox Street, W1S 1PQ
Tube Oxford Circus
12 Smithfield Street, EC1A 9LA
Tube Farringdon
18 Frith Street, W1D 4RQ
Tube Tottenham Court Road

Broaden your horizons with King's College's Language Courses
Little and often is the key to learning a new language

———

Learning to speak a foreign tongue is satisfying, and looks great on your CV (not to mention its usefulness on holiday). Drip-feeding lessons via podcast or downloads on your morning commute or lunchtime stroll is a great way to begin (there's a good list at openculture.com), but to really give yourself a jump start, enrol in a class or take regular lessons. King's College offers bespoke tuition in a huge range of languages; their 1-to-2 sessions are good value and can be taken at the college or even at your place of work.

kcl.ac.uk
Strand, WC2R 2LS
Tube Temple

Get snappy with street fashion photography
Document the city's most stylish citizens
—

Love fashion? Want to record a passer-by's outfit that makes your style radar ping? Getting up the nerve to photograph people on the street isn't always easy, but a lunchtime course will give you the confidence and technical skills to start snapping. City Academy's hour-long sessions in street photography take you out onto Brick Lane to capture passing fashionistas during the hectic lunch-hour.

city-academy.com
Courses across London

Be at one with the music at Schott Music Shop
Practise your piano skills
—

One of the most common regrets as an adult is having given up on music lessons as a child. If you gave up learning to play piano when you were younger or, due to London-sized homes, have had to ditch your instrument, the Schott Music Shop is a great place to lose yourself in minims and crotchets for an hour. Hire one of their practice rooms (which include a wonderful Steinway baby grand), take in some sheet music (or a *Play in a Day* book) and let those fingers fly. If you start to feel really confident, the shop even has a performance space with 50 seats that you can hire.

schott-music.co.uk/shopnav/practice
48 Great Marlborough Street, W1F 7BB
Tube Oxford Circus

Schott Music Shop

Battersea Park

AN HOUR IN THE MORNING

London is truly special in the early hours. The crowds have not yet built up and even a walk around the most touristy of spots feels gloriously alien, the streets naked and wide. You might see the odd street cleaner, night bus, or nightclub straggler, but you'll have the run of the place. It's a great time to snap some pictures or sketch undisturbed.

There are some adventures that you can only have in London in the morning: markets that are closed by sunrise, clubs that wind down as the working day begins, deserted swimming ponds that are illuminated orange in the dawn. Build an extra hour into your day and have an adventure before the rest of the world has even rubbed its eyes.

Nab a bargain at Bermondsey Antiques Market
Pick over treasures at dawn

———

Haul yourself out of bed (or stay out late enough) to get to Southwark for a pre-work bargain hunt. Bermondsey opens early; traders arrive at 4am, the junk hawks soon after. Half-flea market, half-high-end antiques exchange, old furniture, china, jewellery, silverware and bric-a-brac is piled high in teetering heaps. Be prepared to haggle; there are bargains to be had, but the traders really know their stuff. Bring a torch to illuminate dusty surfaces and discover hairline cracks before the sun emerges. It's atmospheric, exciting, and, who knows, you might even go home with something really special.

bermondseysquare.net/bermondsey-antiques-market
Bermondsey Square, Southwark, SE13
Tube Borough

Join the club at Morning Gloryville
Rave yourself awake

———

Going to a club first thing in the morning, stone-cold sober, and with a day of work ahead of you might seem odd. However, Morning Gloryville's brand of 'conscious clubbing' sends worker bees off to their offices with a natural buzz. There's no alcohol, and the only chemical stimulants are caffeine and smoothies. Held at venues across London, expect massage stations, motivational dance teams and a dancefloor heaving with bright-eyed ravers. The event lasts for a good four hours, but you're welcome to drop in and out if you're counting minutes. If you want to save even more time, you can even go there in your pyjamas.

morninggloryville.com
Across London

Mouthwatering nibbles at St John Bakery
The early bird gets the doughnut

——

Some food experiences are worth getting up early on a Saturday morning for. Or staying out very late on a Friday night for. Just behind Maltby Street Market, St John Bakery opens at 9am every Saturday morning, selling the freshest, crispiest, sourdough doughnuts, stuffed with seasonal fillings (we can't resist the custard ones). They sell out quickly, so get there early and grab a box to take round to a friend's for an indulgent breakfast that will earn you a gold star.

stjohngroup.uk.com
72 Druid Street, SE1 2HQ
Tube Bermondsey

A floral fanfare at Columbia Road Flower Market
Find perfect blooms at the most photogenic Sunday morning in town

——

You'll need to get here early for the pick of the bunch (stalls open around 8am). Flowers spill out of buckets; spot velvety roses, ruffled peonies and picture-perfect tulips. Gardeners jostle to get to the bedding plants and bulbs, and, at Christmas, there's holly and ivy, wreaths and Christmas trees. As the area has become more gentrified, numerous interesting little shops have sprung up; hunt for antiques, or pore over desirable homewares in the stores that line the road. Your time is limited, so grab a coffee to go, a currant bun from Jones Dairy, and eat your breakfast as you buy your stems.

columbiaroad.info
Columbia Road, London E2 7RG
Tube Bethnal Green

St John Bakery

Columbia Road Flower Market

Catch of the day –
Billingsgate Fish Market
Eat a scallop and bacon sandwich for breakfast

Packed with glossy, silvery sardines, clear-eyed mullet and inky-blue lobsters. Billingsgate Fish Market, in the depths of Poplar, is seafood nirvana. Sail over early at 4am to get the best catch. The stallholders generally sell to the trade, but are happy to accommodate greedy kitchen cooks who eagerly splash through the melted ice-water on the ground to get to the great value, super-fresh fish. True cockneys head to Mick's Eel Supply, with his drawers full of live wrigglers, thick and shiny, while elsewhere there are spiny urchins, whole, slobbery octopi and rainbow tins of anchovies. If you have time, grab a take-away bacon and melt-in-the-mouth scallop roll from the small café.

billingsgatefishmarket.org
Trafalgar Way, Poplar, E14 5ST
Tube Canary Wharf

Take a gamble at the
Hippodrome Casino
Avoid the queues at the temple of Mammon

Entering a casino at dawn feels subversive, whether it's at the end of a long night on the tiles, or at the start of a working day. The Hippodrome Casino is a slice of Vegas crash-landed on Leicester Square. Retreat from the cold-fingered early morning into a warm hall of flashing lights, gilded balconies and acres of gaming tables. Join the hardcore at the poker table, invoke Lady Luck on the roulette wheel, or chug coins into the slots. Like an elderly, wintering seaside town, it's the kind of super-touristy experience that takes on a different, deliciously seedy aspect when you're there off-peak.

thecasinolsq.com
5–6 Leicester Square, WC2H 7JH
Tube Leicester Square

Hippodrome Casino

Sing out with the Dawn Chorus
Start your day with a song
—

Hear icy tales on the HMS *Belfast*
Watch the sun rise from the deck of a battleship
—

Start your day as the birds do – by making some joyful noise. The Dawn Chorus meet at 8.30am at the Phoenix pub just off Oxford Street for an hour-long session of harmonies and rousing choruses from your favourite rock and pop tunes. The hosts are welcoming, regardless of your ability, and you'll trip into work with a song in your heart and several earworms in your brain.

starlingarts.com/dawn-chorus/
37 Cavendish Square, W1G 0PP
Tube Oxford Street

The hulking, grey form of the battleship HMS *Belfast* dominates the strip of the Thames between Tower and London Bridges. It's a great place to take the family for an afternoon, but a private dawn tour is a more intimate, special way to see this historic ship. Take a group of friends for a reveille visit, led by a yeoman or a senior member of staff. In the depths of winter, you'll be able to watch the sun rise while standing on the deck, before disappearing below to hear tales of sailors surviving freezing conditions in Arctic convoys, and stories of derring WW2 dos.

iwm.org.uk/events/hms-belfast/hms-belfast-private-tours
The Queen's Walk, SE1 2JH
Tube London Bridge

TOP TEN

Places to have breakfast

The Fox & Anchor,
Smithfield
It's next to the meat market, so breakfasts at this traditional Victorian gin-palace are flesh heavy (have yours with a pint of stout).

Banners, *Crouch End*
This music-loving locals' Jamaican breakfasts include ackee, bacon, boiled eggs, spicy beans and a warm roti.

Hamilton Hall,
Liverpool Street
London's most beautiful Wetherspoon pub, the chain that always provides great-value, hearty and satisfying cooked breakfasts.

The Wolseley, *Piccadilly*
People-watch over your newspaper in the grandest of surroundings.

Caravan, *King's Cross*
Serves enticingly exotic treats to start the day from coconut bread to courgette and corn fritters.

Inn on the Park,
St James' Park
Eat elderflower pancakes or fried pork hash while gazing at geese in this glass-walled building.

Dishoom, *Shoreditch*
Sit on the verandah and enjoy a breakfast lassi.

Cereal Killer Café,
Brick Lane
Serves obscure sugary stuff in a variety of forms, from cereal to milkshakes to simply cereal-flavoured milk. Beware of beards.

Brick Lane Beigel Bake
Open 24 hours a day; you'll never be too early (or too late) to grab a salt-beef or smoked salmon snack.

Koya Bar, *Soho*
Try their very Japanese take on the full English; dashi soup with bacon, egg, shiitake mushrooms and udon noodles. Instant hangover cure.

TOP TEN
At night

Bar Italia, *Soho*
A London institution – for good reason. Refuel with an authentic Italian espresso at any time (it's open 24 hours a day) before your journey home.

HK Diner, *Chinatown*
Eat roast duck, noodles and seafood and drink bubble tea until 4am at this superior diner.

Neil Cornelius, *Bond Street*
Get an expert blow-dry at any time of the evening, right up until midnight.

Southbank
Taking a stroll along the Southbank at night shows off the iconic London skyline.

Late-night shopping, *Oxford Circus*
Avoid the hurly burly and get instant access to the changing rooms every Thursday evening. Topshop is open until 10pm.

V&A Friday Late, *South Kensington*
Evening party on the last Friday of every month; performances, film, installations, DJs, bars and food. Until 10pm.

Hampstead Observatory
Drop in for a spot of romantic star gazing through their huge telescope on clear Friday and Saturday nights in the winter.

The Dolphin, *Hackney*
Want to keep the party going late into the night? At weekends you can hop on the karaoke machine or choose a song on the free jukebox until 4am.

The View from the Shard, *London Bridge*
Open until 10pm Thursday–Saturday, see the glittering lights of the city from way up high.

Tate Modern, *Southbank*
Hit this hugely-popular art destination up until 10pm on a Friday or Saturday for a clearer view of some of the finest modern art.

Go foraging
Find park-fresh food for free

———

Wild mushrooms, herbs and edible flowers are now on the menu in even the most grand of restaurants. The best time to pick your own is first thing in the morning, when the mushrooms are freshly risen, the wild garlic is still covered in dew, and sloes are still chilled from the night. You'll have a surprising amount of competition; much of the good stuff will be gone by the time the sun has risen. Make sure you know what you're picking (foragelondon.co.uk run some fantastic wild food walks to get you started), then go for a rummage in the undergrowth (Alexandra Palace Park, Burgess Park and Richmond Park are great places to hunt). Breakfast doesn't get tastier than freshly picked, butter-fried mushrooms on toast.

Across London

Watch a monk greet the sun in Battersea Park
Get spiritual perspective at the start of the new day

———

Walking through London at sunrise is a powerful, otherworldly experience. In summer particularly, when there are few people around, it feels like you have the city to yourself. Primrose Hill is the classic place from which to watch the sun burn the deep blue sky into purple and orange as it rises above the wide-ranging cityscape; carry a flask of coffee and some croissants to the top to make the climb more bearable or head to the peace pagoda in Battersea Park to watch its saffron-robed, Buddhist caretaker walk slowly from his temple to the tall building, gently beating a drum. You may be his only witness.

batterseapark.org
SW11 4NJ
Overground Battersea Park

St Paul's Cathedral

Breakfast with a view at the Duck and Waffle

The most perfect sunrise in London

———

Perched on the 40th floor of the Heron Tower, the Duck and Waffle serves fantastic food 24 hours a day. Floor-to-ceiling windows make for spectacular views; order the 'Full Elvis' waffle with PBJ, bananas brulée and cream, or ox cheek Benedict and watch the rosy tones of the rising sun illuminate the financial district. It's flashy, indulgent, and off limits to anyone with even the slightest fear of heights.

duckandwaffle.com
Heron Tower, 110 Bishopsgate, EC2N 4AY
Tube Liverpool Street

Start the day with a service at St Paul's Cathedral

Avoid the crowds at an early morning service

———

Everyone is welcome at St Paul's Morning Prayers, which run from 7.30am–7.50am, Monday–Saturday. They take place in one of the Cathedral's side chapels, usually the Middlesex, whose *Light of the World* painting provides a spectacular centrepiece. Expect to rub shoulders with City workers on their way into their offices, grabbing a sliver of reflection and peace before they launch into a heavy working day. You don't have to be a practising Christian to enjoy the spoken service, it's a perfect chance to enjoy a look at the cathedral before the space fills with tourists and clamour.

stpauls.co.uk
St. Paul's Churchyard, EC4M 8AD
Tube St Pauls

London Eye

AN HOUR FOR SOMETHING SPECIAL

There are some experiences that are
exceptional. Things that are so good for the
soul, or just such fun, that you just have to
make the time to do them. These are our
top picks; if you need to make an hour truly
spectacular, choose one of these and you'll
be smiling about it for weeks.

Dark drama at Dennis Severs' House

Take an atmospheric, candle-lit tour around this piece of living theatre

———

Dennis Severs created his 'still-life drama' during the 1980s and 90s. Step through the arched door and you'll step back in time to the 19th century, when the fictional Jervis family, a group of Huguenot weavers, lived there. There's a hushed atmosphere as you walk through the darkened house; bread lies broken on the table, smells drift into your nostrils, creaks and miaows echo. It's a truly immersive, fascinating experience. A tour of the house takes around 45 minutes; go on a dark winter evening and allow the full, candle-lit atmosphere to envelop you.

dennissevershouse.co.uk
18 Folgate Street, Spitalfields, E1 6BX
Tube Liverpool Street

Feeding time at London Zoo

Hop over the fence and in with the animals

———

Make a trip to the zoo extra special by opting for one of ZSL's Meet the Animals experiences. You get to pass into the enclosures and come face-to-snout with some of the most popular animals in the park. Take the ultimate selfie with a giraffe, help feed an aardvark, or hang loose with the colony of penguins. It's a remarkable opportunity, and the kind of magical experience that will have you reverting straight back to your childhood.

zsl.org
Regent's Park, NW1 4RY
Tube Camden Town

Get a tattoo at the Family Business
Get permanently inked in style

———

Light years away from back-alley scratchers, the Family Business tattoo shop in Exmouth Market is stylishly old-school, light, scrupulously clean, and full of the most talented artists from around the world. Our favourite tattooist? The tiny, smiley Inma; she specialises in gorgeous work inspired by nature; cats in ruffs drinking cups of tea, crows sitting proudly on arms, and snake skulls swathed in flowers. In an hour you can get a small, relatively simple tattoo, but bear in mind that walk-in appointments are rare; it's best to book months in advance.

thefamilybusinesstattoo.com
58 Exmouth Market, EC1R 4QE
Tube Angel

Family Business

The O2

The O2 – feeling on top of the world
Climb across the roof for a new view of the city

———

Indulge your daredevil side and clamber up and over one of the city's iconic landmarks: the dome of the O2 arena. The ascent isn't too demanding; you don't need to have previous experience and you get all the kit you need, and when you get to the wind-buffeted viewing platform, the vista is stunning. You'll be laughing in delight – if a little nervously. Take a trip as the sun sinks over the city for rose-tinted views and a whole different take on London. The climb itself is 60 minutes, but you do have to arrive earlier for a briefing and to get into your adventure gear. Worth it, though.

theo2.co.uk
Peninsula Square, SE10 0DX
Tube North Greenwich

Stand behind the most famous clock face in London
Climb Big Ben and hear the famous chimes mark the hour

———

Could this be London's best-kept secret? Free tours of Elizabeth Tower – the official name of the building that houses Big Ben – run through the year, bookable in advance (you may have to wait up to six months to get a place). Security is tight – you'll have to leave your camera at home, but the red tape is worth navigating. A guide will take you up the 334 stone spiral steps (there's a small room to rest in half-way), to behind the famous clock face, where you'll see the shadows of the hands moving around the clock, and hear the familiar bells ring out bone-shakingly loud. It's the epicentre of London, a truly special place. You'll never be able to see the clock in the same way again.

**parliament.uk/visiting/visiting-and-tours/
tours-of-parliament/bigben/**
Houses of Parliament, Westminster, SW1 0AA
Tube Westminster

Get locked in at the Tower of London
Be part of history at the Ceremony of the Keys
——

The locking up ceremony at the Tower of London has taken place every night, without fail, for 700 years. A small group (40–50 nightly) of visitors are admitted to the Tower, under escort at 9.30pm promptly. At eight minutes to 10pm, Beefeaters carrying candlelit lanterns bring the Queen's Keys to lock the outer gates, then begins the famous exchange: 'Halt, who comes there?' 'The Keys!' It's high drama, spine-tingling stuff which concertinas the ghostly past into the present. It's an experience every Londoner should have. You need to apply months in advance, but it's worth the wait.

hrp.org.uk/TowerOfLondon/WhatsOn/ theceremonyofthekeys
Tower Hill, EC3N 4AB
Tube Tower Hill

Bag all the seats at the Electric Cinema
Have a private screening at one of London's most beautiful cinemas
——

The Portobello Road's Electric Cinema is looking tremendously dashing for a 100-year-old. There are leather armchairs with footstools and side tables, two-seater sofas, and even double beds in the front row. It's available to hire by the hour, too, so round up 80 of your closest friends, pick something you'd like to watch on the big screen – a short film, series of classic cartoons, or even something you've made yourself, perhaps – and spend a fun-packed 60 minutes accompanied by popcorn and champagne. Indulgent? Totally.

electriccinema.co.uk
191 Portobello Rd, Notting Hill, W11 2ED
Tube Ladbroke Grove

Drink in the history of the Beaufort Bar
Drama-filled cocktails and champagne

—

The Savoy has one of London's most handsome interiors, all dark wood, gold and shine. Adjourn to the Beaufort Bar for a drink; it's decadent – black with gold leaf, a backlit, Lalique bar. There's history embedded in the gilded walls; Gershwin once performed on the stage and some of the most famous people in the world have asked for a martini at the bar. Order a Coco (dedicated to Ms Chanel), which includes champagne and red wine, or the Impressionist, which arrives at your table garnished with a smoking rose. Many of the cocktails are served in glassware appropriate to the era in which they were created. Elegant and sophisticated.

fairmont.com/savoy-london/
The Savoy Hotel, The Strand, WC2R 0EU
Tube Covent Garden

Beaufort Bar

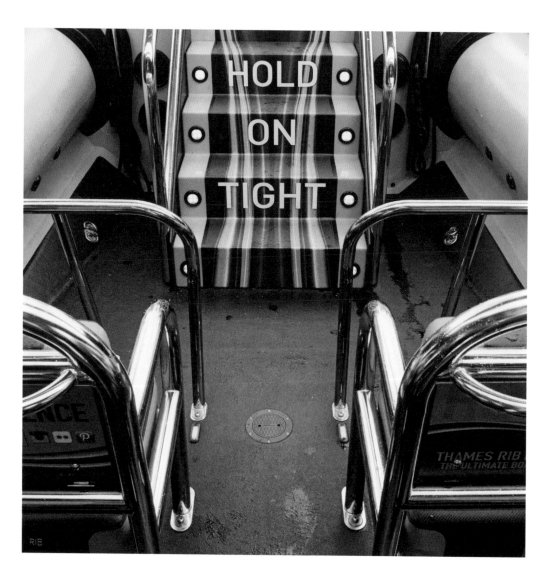

Take a trip on the Thames with the RIB
Ride a speedboat down the wind-whipped river

——

Even the most street-hardened Londoner will discover something new about their city from a RIB boat ride. You zoom up the Thames from the London Eye, spotting sights that look surreally different from the water, passing under bridges along the way. Once the boat gets to Canary Wharf, the engine opens up to a sprightly 30 knots and you sprint through the water. It's an experience that will stay with you for months; every time you cross the Thames you will smile at the memory.

londonribvoyages.com
The London Eye Millennium Pier, Westminster Bridge Road, SE1 7PB
Tube Waterloo

Scan the city from the sky
Take a thrill-packed helicopter tour

——

Live out your James Bond fantasies with a fast-paced helicopter soar around the city. As well as a shaken-not-stirred adrenalin hit, you'll get a fresh, giddy perspective on familiar sights, including Battersea Power Station, the London Eye and Tower Bridge. For the ultimate indulgence, £1000 will get you the airborne vehicle all to yourself – take up to six friends for an intimate whirl, or treat someone special to an impressively flash date.

thelondonhelicopter.com
The London Heliport, Bridges Court, SW11 3BE
Overground Clapham Junction

See the highlights at the Tate Modern

Get a very private view of one of London's best modern art galleries

—

One of the most inspiring buildings in London, the cavernous Tate Modern is even more impressive when it isn't swamped with visitors. Their private guided tours at breakfast time are a serene chance for small groups to view artworks without waiting for the crowds to disperse, allowing calm study and contemplation with a knowledgeable guide on hand to answer any questions. Choose a highlights tour, or pick a specific artist or movement to focus on. Go alone for the ultimate cultural indulgence.

tate.org.uk/visit/tate-modern/group-visits/ private-tours-groups
Bankside, SE1 9TG
Tube Southwark

360° view of the city from the London Eye

Hire your own pod for the best views in London

—

A trip on the London Eye is a shortcut way of seeing the sights; depending on the weather, one rotation provides views across the city and beyond. For a truly special treat, hire out an entire capsule all to yourself. Perhaps you'll spend the 30 minutes it takes to complete a rotation watching the sun set, indulging in a Vinopolis wine tasting, having a mini-rave above the Thames, or watching fireworks light up the sky (be cunning and book 5 November or the date of the Lord Mayor's Show in advance). If you've a spare £5000, you'll get a three-course meal for eight, a champagne reception and bespoke wines, and three rotations on the Eye. The gigantic wheel will also pause for ten minutes at the top so you can take photographs.

londoneye.com
Jubilee Gardens, SE1 7PB
Tube Waterloo

Tate Modern

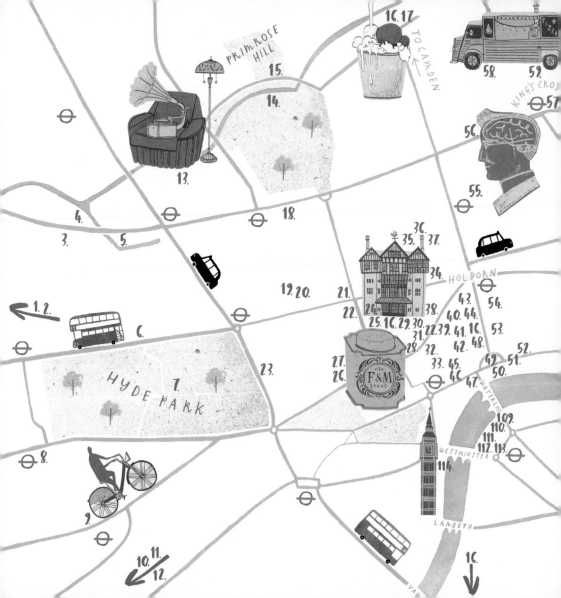

KEY

INDEX

Huge thanks to Gareth, Arthur and Dusty for their hugs and jokes, to my mum and dad for their support, and to Esther, Tom, Guri, Sarah, Sarra, Denise, Alix, Victoria, Nadia and Hege for their love, ideas and help. A big high five to Dr Martens and their Airwair soles that took me around the city without too many blisters. Extra special thanks to the dream team of Juliet Pickering at Blake Friedmann, Elen Jones at Virgin Books, Helena Caldon, Linda Lundin at Park Studio, Lucy Panes and Peter Williams.

1 3 5 7 9 10 8 6 4 2

Virgin Books, an imprint of Ebury Publishing, 20 Vauxhall Bridge Road, London SW1V 2SA

Virgin Books is part of the Penguin Random House group of companies whose addresses can be found at global.penguinrandomhouse.com

 Penguin
Random House
UK

Copyright © Kate Hodges 2016

Kate Hodges has asserted her right to be identified as the author of this Work in accordance with the Copyright, Designs and Patents Act 1988

First published by Virgin Books in 2016

www.eburypublishing.co.uk

A CIP catalogue record for this book is available from the British Library

ISBN 9780753556399

Design by Park Studio
Photography © Peter Williams
Map illustration by Lucy Panes
Printed and bound in China by C&C Offset Printing Co., Ltd

Penguin Random House is committed to a sustainable future for our business, our readers and our planet. This book is made from Forest Stewardship Council® certified paper.